AN IMBAL...

Ariadne had heard ... tenths of the law— ... Peverell most decid... ...sed almost all of her now.

Not only was she his lawfully wedded wife, she also was his prisoner on a yacht that was carrying her under full sail ever further away from the one man who could save her from the fate that Sir Iden's ardent interest and iron determination clearly intended.

All that she had to protect her was Sir Iden's promise to respect her refusal to totally give herself to him.

But how long could that promise withstand the strength of Sir Iden's desires, and her own growing weakness. . . ?

Rogue's Bride

ROGUE'S BRIDE

by
Ellen Fitzgerald

A SIGNET BOOK
NEW AMERICAN LIBRARY

SIGNET, SIGNET CLASSIC, MENTOR, PLUME, MERIDIAN and NAL BOOKS
are published by New American Library,
1633 Broadway, New York, New York 10019

First Printing, January, 1986

1 2 3 4 5 6 7 8 9

PRINTED IN THE UNITED STATES OF AMERICA

PART I

Chapter One

Ariadne Caswell-Drake, her face turned up to a wind heavily scented with sea salt, tar, and other less definable odors, stood at the railing of *The Argonaut* watching the Cornish coast recede. A sniff beside her reminded her of Miss Gore's unwelcome presence. Her chaperone was still waving in the general direction of the quay with its blur of people. Among the small group that had gathered to see them off was Mr. Huntley Gore, Miss Gore's clergyman brother. Ariadne was sure he was still there, a thin, pale, cross-looking man who might have been his sister's twin. He had acted as if she were a missionary going among heathens rather than one bound for the fabled isles of Greece. His chief concern appeared to be the number of barbarous Turks they might encounter. He had frightened Minnie, Ariadne's young abigail, by suggesting that all three of them were in danger of being kidnapped and taken off to a seraglio. In spite of her far from happy mood, Ariadne could not restrain a smile at the idea of herself and Miss Gore as odalisques. Minnie, slim and pretty, might pass muster. She and Miss Gore would probably be tossed overboard.

Glancing at the ever-diminishing quay, she wondered if Lady Lovett, whom she called Aunt Isabel, had lingered to watch the yacht cast off. She doubted it. Her ladyship, belatedly doing her so-called duty as a near relation, had not weathered the long journey from London to Falmouth well. Furthermore, she was deeply incensed about a voyage which would take at least two months.

" 'Tis the height of folly," she had said more than once. "If I had had any say in the matter you'd not have been going off to Greece at the beginning of the London Season. You are seventeen years of age and ought to be presented at court and would be had you been placed in my guardianship!'' She had also had a great deal to say about Mr. Iden Peverell, the owner of the yacht.

Unlike her brother-in-law Sir Arthur Caswell-Drake, who was thanking Apollo and other gods that Mr. Peverell, who had been in India for the past three years, was traveling to Athens to see his father, Sir Marcus Peverell, and could offer both passage and escort to Ariadne, Aunt Isabel could only decry the fact that he had actually trusted his daughter to so notorious an adventurer. That Mr. Peverell was being officially received once more into the family fold by the said Sir Marcus carried no weight with her ladyship.

In common with a great many older members of the ton, she could not forget that Iden Peverell had committed the crowning indiscretion of taking the beautiful daughter of an Indian potentate to wife! Fortunately, the bride had died after a mere six months of marriage, but that could not wipe out the stain on his character or the blot on his escutcheon! Aunt Isabel had made Miss Gore promise that she would keep her charge as far away from Iden Peverell as was humanly possible given the narrow confines of the vessel.

Ariadne stifled an ironic laugh. Actually, were the truth to be told, she was nearer to tears than to laughter. She had met Mr. Peverell for the first time early that morning when he had come to the Purple Crown to greet his charges or, more specifically, his burdens! Again, she was exempting Minnie, who in addition to being easy on the eye, would do her best to be helpful. However, she did not need to be particularly imaginative to realize that a man such as Iden Peverell could find little pleasure in the company of two singularly unprepossessing females, one of them old enough to be his mother and the other . . . well, she was not young enough to be his daughter since he was twenty-seven. Ariadne grimaced, wishing, and not for the first time, that she was Carola Caulfield and a beauty!

If it had been last year and Carola were confronted with Mr. Iden Peverell and facing the prospect of two-month voyage to Greece, the end of that period would not have been in doubt. Rather than being the wife of Lord Brynston, she would have been calling herself Mrs. Peverell.

Ariadne conjured up a vision of Carola's red-gold curls and sea-green eyes. The one waved above a beautiful white forehead and the others were set beneath brows darker than her hair. Carola's eyelashes, similarly dark, were long, her nose was straight, there was an enchanting dimple at the corner of her mouth, and her figure was excellent.

She cast a disparaging look at her own figure, hidden beneath her cloak but plump all over! If she could only have been taller, it might not have mattered, but she was small. She had a double chin, puffy cheeks, and pimples! Furthermore, if her forehead was wide and intelligent, it, too, was spotty and only added to the breadth of her face. Her eyes were her best feature. They were dark blue and her hair was blue-black, a combination of coloring called Irish. Ariadne's mother had been a quarter Irish and a beauty. Her father had often commented on that while sadly looking at his daughter, causing her to deeply resent the mother she had seen only in portraits. Lady Caswell-Drake had expired within an hour of her birth.

To do him justice, Sir Arthur did not hold his wife's demise against his only child. He was fond of her and he was also proud of her intelligence, but what did intelligence matter to a gentleman other than her father? Carola was not in the least intelligent and she had been wed within two months of her arrival on the London scene!

True, her dearest friend was not entirely pleased with that undoubted triumph. Her last letter, which had arrived shortly after Sir Arthur's missive bidding Ariadne to join him in Greece, had contained an invitation to stay with Carola at Brynston Towers in Lincolnshire.

"Can you imagine," Carola had written with very black ink on a paper which bore smudges suggesting tears, "not three months wed and I am Breeding! And Willie says that I cannot come back to London until such time as I have Dropped the Brat!"

That, of course, was unfortunate. Carola had been enjoying her Season, but she had been no less pleased than her mama when she had captured an extremely eligible earl. Lord Brynston was nice-looking as well, but he was not a patch on Mr. Iden Peverell!

Ariadne closed her eyes against the retreating shoreline and implanted Mr. Peverell's face against the resulting darkness. His features were noble, she thought. In fact, she could compare them to the plaster head of Michelangelo's David that occupied a prominent place in her father's library. He had the same broad forehead, the same large eyes, the same full mouth, and did the statue have a cleft chin? She could not remember, but Mr. Peverell did. He also had dark wavy hair, startlingly bisected by a white streak positioned near his widow's peak. He was beautifully proportioned. His shoulders were wide, his chest broad, his waist narrow, and his legs shapely. It was well Carola had not met him. She would have felt even more frustrated than before—Ariadne was sure of that. However, her friend's frustration could never have equaled her own!

"And this, Mr. Peverell, is Miss Ariadne Caswell-Drake," her aunt had said in her deep, commanding voice, which always added an extra quotient of importance to any introduction.

"Ariadne," he had repeated. "We ought to be sailing by the Isle of Naxos. 'Tis a pity we are not." He had smiled, a smile that had not reached eyes that remained somber and brooding.

Ariadne groaned. Overwhelmed by shyness she had not given him a single indication that she had known what he was talking about. She had also felt sorry for him. There were lines etched into his forehead and around his mouth, more than there should have been for one yet in his twenties. He looked dreadfully unhappy and she had been miserably positive that her presence on board would not help to raise his spirits. On occasion, she could be amusing. She amused her father and he, at least, appreciated her intelligence, something her aunt decried.

Certainly, she had not displayed an iota of that touted intelligence this morning. Struck by Mr. Peverell's handsome face and princely bearing as well as by his evident unhappiness, she had not been able to mutter more than an acknowledgment of the introduction. She barely remembered what he had replied, something about welcoming her aboard *The Argonaut*. He had been equally polite to Mrs. Gore and evidently quite unaware of the latter's chill, disapproving glance.

Miss Gore heartily endorsed Lady Lovett's opinion of Mr. Peverell. She, too, had heard of his adventures or, as her aunt dubbed them, "misadventures" in India. Once he had left them, she and Lady Lovett, equally unmoved by his handsome melancholy presence, had launched into another dissertation on the subject of Sir Arthur's inexplicable decision to let his daughter sail so far in such dubious company. Both ladies had rounded on Ariadne, sternly adjuring her to remain as far away from that reprehensible rogue as was humanly possible.

Thinking of those reiterated stipulations, Ariadne smiled ironically. If Mr. Peverell were, in the course of the voyage, to approach her more than was absolutely necessary, she would undoubtedly swoon with shock. She loosed another groan as she remembered his pronunciation of her name— "Ariadne." He had spoken it with a touch of amused surprise. She had no difficulty understanding why. Ariadne did not suite her. It was a name that implied beauty. It had a lilt and a charm that she did not possess.

The real or, rather, the original Ariadne, of course, *had* been abandoned on the Isle of Naxos by the adventurer Theseus, who had ill-repaid her for the help she had given him in the destruction of her hideous and monstrous half-brother, the Minotaur. However, she had been beautiful—for had she not been rescued and espoused by Dionysus, God of Wine?

Ariadne put a plump hand to her bosom and sighed deeply. The burden of not being beautiful and of having spots had never been so heavy! It lay on her spirits like a pall. Indeed, she felt even worse than she had when contemplating a Season when she, attending balls, would have been relegated to the company of other girls as ill-favored as herself. In common with them, she would have spent the entire evening sitting in spindly chairs hopefully eyeing young men without partners or enviously watching their more favored sisters as they whirled around the floor.

Not even the glowing prospect of avoiding that particular fate by joining her father in Athens and using what he had described in his last letter as "your knowledge and fine Taste, my Love," could please her. She had a swift and envious glance at Miss Gore, whose given name was Jane. It suited her. It would have also suited *her*, Ariadne. At this moment in her life, she wished that her father had remained at home overseeing his lands or, if he needed to join the ranks of the collectors, concentrating on Italian paintings or Austrian music boxes.

She caught suddenly at a nearby rope, wincing as its rough, hairy texture bit into her hand. The ship had suddenly descended into a gully and now it rose up again, forcibly reminding her that she was no longer on land. She shot a look at Minnie and found to her surprise that the girl was no longer there. A giggle alerted her to the fact that she was not far away. Gazing in the direction of the sound, she saw Minnie talking animatedly with one of the sailors.

A startled moan beside her brought her attention back to Miss Gore. Ariadne winced as she noted that the chaperone was looking very ill. Her narrow face was drained of color—at least her usual color—and appeared yellowish-green. Her eyes were closed and one hand was pressed against her flat chest.

"Oh, dear, I believe you must be feeling the motion of the boat," Ariadne said commiseratingly. "Might I help you to your cabin?"

"You should . . . I . . . you . . ." mumbled Miss Gore.

Ariadne shot another look at Minnie, who was still talking, or rather flirting, with the sailor. She decided against summoning her. Grasping the chaperone's arm, she said bracingly, "I think you'd best go to your cabin."

"You must all go to your cabins," amended a voice behind her. "We are in for some rough weather, I fear."

Startled, Ariadne turned to find Mr. Peverell a few steps away. Had he been there all along and she unaware of him? She could not dwell on that at present, not with Miss Gore making ominous gagging noises. "I wonder . . . should we not take her to the side of the boat first?" she asked.

He cast a knowledgeable eye over the chaperone. "Possibly, but you . . ."

"I do not think we need concentrate on me, Mr. Peverell, not immediately." Ariadne clutched Miss Gore's arm.

"I expect not," he agreed, taking the unhappy woman's other arm. "I will see to her," he added dismissively. "You'd best go to your cabin, else you'll run the risk of being equally ill."

"No, I shan't," she contradicted. "I have never been seasick. Come," she added hastily as Miss Gore made another even more threatening sound.

They reached the railing just in time and Mr. Peverell, putting a steadying arm around the chaperone, stared at Ariadne with a certain amount of surprise and even some respect. "Have you been upon the open sea, then?" he asked.

She nodded. "In the midst of a squall—the Irish sea," she clarified. "Everybody, even Papa, was feeling queasy, but I was not."

"You are indeed fortunate," he commented. "Let us hope that your luck continues."

Later, as she sat by Miss Gore's bedside waiting for Minnie, who would soon relieve her, Ariadne could at least congratulate herself on proving her point and, at the same time, causing Mr. Peverell to unbend, at least slightly. However, what small satisfaction she could derive from that had been largely negated by the swiftness with which he had left them once he had escorted the suffering chaperone and herself back to the cabins. If she wanted to be totally miserable she could also dwell on his largely impersonal attitude. Beyond congratulating her on her strong stomach, he did not seem interested in her at all and, though he had been unfailingly courteous, she had the feeling that he might even resent her presence on board his boat.

That she had read Mr. Peverell's feelings accurately might have strengthened Ariadne's belief in her powers of deduction, but it was just as well that she had not been party to a conversation currently taking place on the bridge between Mr. Peverell and his old friend Captain Robert S. Wellstood.

"How could I have done otherwise?" he was demanding rhetorically. "Sir Arthur's an old friend of the family and she's his only chick, poor creature."

"Females!" the captain, a man of thirty-five, commented. There was a world of meaning and experience in his disparaging tone.

"Yes." Mr. Peverell fixed his brooding gaze on the far horizon. "Only *she*, Radha, was different. She wanted to see Greece, you know. We discussed it before . . ." he swallowed painfully, ". . . before she died."

Captain Wellstood's blunt, sun-reddened features registered more concern than Mr. Peverell had received from either friends or family. "A great pity, Iden."

He received a grateful glance. "Only you understand, Rob. I ought not to be seeing Father. It's unfair to her memory, when you think of all he said and wrote on the subject. Unfair and unfaithful!"

"He's old," Wellstood said gently. "You are the one surviving child . . . and also his one hope for posterity."

"Posterity!" Mr. Peverell snorted. "That hope cannot be realized. I could no more contemplate another marriage or children than . . . With Radha dead, I'll not marry again, I can assure you."

The captain gave him a long look, saying after an even longer silence, during which time he had puffed contemplatively upon his pipe, "You say that now, lad, but—"

"Now and *forever*!" Mr. Peverell retorted passionately. "All other women pall beside her. I wish you might have known her, Rob. She was so incredibly beautiful." He shuddered. "She would have been married to that toad Narayan if I'd not persuaded the Maharajah that I intended to wed her. We were so happy. She . . . there was no one more gentle, more . . ." His brow darkened. "I could have strangled Lady Lovett and that other ill-favored crone, Miss Gore, looking at me as if I'd committed murder! 'Twas the same in Calcutta, all those I used to call friend, treating me as if I'd descended into hell! Hell? Hell is where Radha is not." He cast a despairing glance at the sky.

"One day—" Captain Wellstood began.

"Do not tell me that one day I will recover and settle down to wedded bliss with some female of the likes of little Miss Caswell-Drake. *Ariadne*, if you please! That homely little brown wren is named Ariadne. Sir Arthur could not have hit upon a worse choice! And she does not get seasick. That has already been proven."

The captain appeared understandably confused. "Can you be regretting that, Iden?"

Mr. Peverell flushed. However, he said candidly, "On one count, yes. Mind you, I do not actively wish the poor child to suffer such discomfort, but at least it would keep her in her cabin and prevent me from remembering that when I first planned this voyage, I meant to have Radha at my side."

" 'Tis a shame," the captain said, sounding as if he meant it. "Well, it's only two months, lad. You'll not need to see her once you've delivered the chit to her father."

Mr. Peverell rolled his eyes. "May the gods send us strong winds to hasten us upon our course and bring us quickly to our destination," he said feelingly.

"Not too strong, Iden," the captain amended.

"On the contrary," Mr. Peverell cried with the despair that was never quite absent from his tones. "Let Poseidon and Aeolus stir the sea and send a tempest to bear us to the coasts of Attica." He glared at the vivid Cornish skies.

Chapter Two

"Two months," Ariadne muttered. She added dolefully, "and only three days out. That will leave us twenty-eight more days before we reach Greece." She cast an apprehensive glance about her, hoping no one had heard this observation. As an only child, often left to her own devices, she had a habit of talking to herself out loud.

Having been assured that no one had heard her, Ariadne, standing by the rigging on the larboard side of the ship, drew a deep breath, gratefully inhaling the cool, sea-scented air. She found it definitely preferable to that which had filled her nostrils for the last two hours. Her initial pleasure in the voyage had dissipated considerably and that even before losing sight of the harbor. Miss Gore was so very seasick and since she had no abigail, she had to be tended by Minnie and Ariadne. Though Minnie had protested this arrangement, saying bravely that Miss Caswell-Drake should not be encumbered by the care of her chaperone, she had looked both pleased and relieved to learn that she was not to bear the entire burden on her slim shoulders.

Thinking of Minnie, Ariadne smiled but also sighed. The girl's appearance could not but stir some envy in her breast. Minnie was so delightfully slim, and very pretty too, with her heart-shaped face, her huge blue eyes, and her clusters of golden curls.

Astonishingly enough, Miss Gore did not like her, declaring that she was too pretty by half and, if she were not careful, destined for a Bad End. Though questioned as to what end that could be, the chaperone had not elucidated, saying crossly that it was just as well Ariadne had no inkling of the pitfalls lying in the path of the well-favored. She seemed to believe that the lower classes were particularly vulnerable to these.

"The devil's gifts must be despised," she had concluded.

Ariadne grimaced. If beauty were a devil's gift, she would have been the first to stand outside the gates of Hades with her hand out. A second later, she was a little frightened by that blasphemous sentiment. Yet, it would be lovely to look like Minnie, who elicited sighs, winks, and whistles from the crew every time she stepped out on deck. She had already ignited what an authoress connected with the Minerva Press had described as "the flame of love" in the breast of one Edward Quigley, the handsome young second mate. As for Minnie herself, she blushed a lovely color every time she saw him. To Ariadne, that indicated a second flame possibly burning in her breast since the girl was largely oblivious to other expressions of approval from the crew.

Thinking about Minnie, Ariadne was half pleased that Miss Gore was not able to accompany them during their strolls on deck. She would certainly be looking down her long nose at Minnie and muttering that she would come to Grief even before the vessel arrived at its final port of call.

"Good evening, Miss Caswell-Drake."

Ariadne turned and had a startled look for Mr. Peverell. "Good evening, sir," she said, wishing that her heart did not leap to her throat every time he addressed her.

"I've not seen you this day," he continued. "One hopes that you have not succumbed to the motion of the ship, after all?"

"Oh, no, sir. I have been caring for Miss Gore, who has."

"So I apprehended." He regarded her curiously. "And might one inquire why you have assumed the burden of her illness, when your abigail—"

Anticipating his question, she broke in, "Oh, Minnie's shared a great part of the burden, sir, but I cannot leave her to it entirely, when she's never been on the open sea and Miss Gore is so horrid to her."

"Horrid, is she? I should think she'd be grateful for the attention."

"I expect it's difficult to be grateful when one is feeling so poorly, sir. Possibly, you have never been seasick?"

"I have been, of course, years ago."

"I, too, years ago."

"But not anymore?"

She had already told him that she never got seasick but, of course, he could not be expected to remember that. "No, not anymore," she said.

"Well, that's fortunate, else Miss Gore would be in truly sore straits and Minnie, too, and may I say I find your attitude toward your abigail singularly considerate."

Ariadne flushed with pleasure. "You are kind to say so, sir."

"You are kind to be so, Miss Caswell-Drake." His melancholy features were briefly lighted by his smile. "I hope that Miss Gore will not be ill too long. Once she acquires her sea-legs, she ought to be better."

"I expect she'll be even better once we touch land again. Gibraltar is our first stop, is it not?"

"Gibraltar," he corroborated.

"Or," she added, "Calpe."

He regarded her with some surprise, "Ah, you know the myth, how Hercules going to Gades—which I am sure you'd call Cadiz—tore asunder the two rocks standing before it, and they became known as the Pillars of Hercules?"

"Or Heracles, if one is going to Greece," Ariadne dared to say.

"Heracles, it is, Miss Caswell-Drake. Have you also studied the Greek classics? I understand your father's well versed in them."

"Indeed he is, sir. I am less so, although I have read the poems of Hesiod and Sappho. And also the plays of Sophocles."

"In the original Greek?"

She nodded. "Papa insisted that I learn it."

He smiled his approval. "You are to be congratulated, Miss Caswell-Drake. I am sure that there are few females so erudite. And do you know of any the modern Greek tongue?"

"A little, sir."

"Your father has prepared you well for this expedition, I see."

Before she could reply, a young sailor joined them. "Sir," he said.

"Yes, Haines?" Mr. Peverell turned to him.

"The captain would like a word with you, sir."

"I will come at once. I hope you will excuse me, Miss Caswell-Drake?"

"Of course, sir."

"And I charge you, do not stand on deck too long, 'tis turning cold."

"I shall not, sir." She smiled at him and as he moved away, she was regretful but, at the same time, pleased that he had gone. It was difficult to converse casually with one for whom she had developed so strong a regard. Indeed, such were her feelings for him that she was highly grateful that they had met in the twilight when he would not have been able to see the heightened color on her cheeks and, she feared, her forehead. She had also managed to conceal that shortness of breath that overtook her each time she saw him. She shook her head, wishing that her equilibrium would reassert itself—particularly since the object of her awakening passions was supremely oblivious of them and would have been most amazed not to mention amused were he to have so much as an inkling of them. This he must never have, she thought fiercely, even if it meant denying herself the immense if brief pleasure of his society. However, this alternative was not one she chose to contemplate. Yet, she would have to contemplate it and even face it—for her chaperone must soon recover from her malady. Everyone did. Then, Miss Gore would not only watch her like a hawk but would descend upon her with the single-mindedness of that bird of prey, effectively separating them.

Tears squeezed out of Ariadne's eyes. She wished that she had never come upon this voyage, never encountered this man, whose dark unhappy countenance troubled her dreams and who was beginning to occupy most of her thoughts—to such little purpose! Once they arrived at their destination, she would never see him again or, if she did, they would no longer share such close quarters. Upon this miserable reflection, she ran her hands over her face and shuddered. Never had her pimples seemed so large or so profuse! She could compare them to the stars that sprinkled the night sky. It did seem unfair that she should be burdened with this extra affliction when her mother had been so noted a beauty. Could the late Lady Caswell-Drake have conquered Mr. Peverell's heart? It did no good to speculate upon such matters. It only served to increase her misery. She stared at the sea which, at this hour, seemed more than ever the color of the darkening sky, and wished futilely that they were already in Greece, and contrarily that the voyage would never end!

Ariadne had occasion to remember and to regret that wish as well as to hope for a wind that would fill the sails and send *The Argonaut* swiftly skimming across the waters that lay between herself and their destination, for in four days time, Miss Gore, looking yellow and wizened but proclaiming herself entirely recovered, spent the greater part of every day with her on deck. This morning was a case in point. In the last half hour, she had delivered caustic opinions about everything from the motion of the ship to Minnie's growing and ill-advised friendship with young Mr. Quigley to Ariadne's brief exchanges with Mr. Peverell, one of which she had just interrupted without even the pretense of an excuse.

Ariadne's remonstrance that her father obviously approved her acquaintance with the son of his old friend Sir Marcus only served to anger Miss Gore.

Drawing herself up, she said icily, "Unfortunately, your father and yourself have lived a life far too free of Society's Restrictions, a situation to which he has hearkened but far, far too late. However, the fact that he *has* hearkened to it goes without saying, else he would not have acted upon your aunt's advice and availed himself of my services. A young lady, my dear Ariadne, avoids every appearance of evil. She does not, certainly, encourage the attentions of a gentleman with so malodorous a reputation!"

Ariadne avoided reminding Miss Gore that "attentions" was hardly descriptive of the sort of communion she enjoyed with Mr. Peverell. She said merely, "Once in Greece, Mr. Peverell and his father may be joining us in an expedition to Delphi."

Miss Gore raised a protesting hand. "I cannot think," she retorted sharply, "that your father would include you in any expedition of which Mr. Peverell is a member. I, for one, will strongly advise against it. Sir Arthur will heed me, I am sure of that. Your aunt has explained that he truly regrets not having provided you with a more conventional upbringing. She has said, furthermore, that he is most eager for you to take your proper place in your world."

Ariadne made no response. She wondered if it could possibly be true that her father had communicated such a desire to her aunt. Possibly, he had suffered a change of heart and decided that, after all, he had been remiss in not observing the proprieties attendant upon the raising of a daughter. Still, that did seem unlikely since he had always scoffed at what he termed the "dullness" of "your average female."

"Education, Ariadne," he had proclaimed on more than one occasion, "is desirable whether it be in a man or a woman." He had also advanced the unorthodox theory that a female's brain was the equal of that belonging to her male counterpart. "See them floating in brine, my love, as I have when visiting the dissecting chambers of a hospital. Were the jars not labeled, I would have been unable to tell one from the other. The convolutions are the same and I am of the opinion that wits are like plants. They need only the proper tending to grow strong."

Ariadne wished she dared quote that remark to her chaperone, but several weeks in Miss Gore's company prevented her from this particular indiscretion and fortunately a sudden dip of the vessel caused that lady to put a hand to her heart and say nervously, "I do think we ought to go below, my dear."

"Yes, Miss Gore," Ariadne agreed with an inner sigh. There were times when she could hardly wait until they reached the shores of Greece, and this was one of them. She darted a glance at her companion's hatchet-sharp profile and wished strongly that her father had not allowed himself to be influenced by the promptings of her aunt regarding a suitable chaperone. She blushed for her other wish, which was that the lady was still a prey to mal-de-mer and she able to tread the streets of the approaching port in the dubious but delightful company of Mr. Peverell.

It was a wish she had good cause to remember when, on the following day, only Captain Wellstood, Mr. Davies, his chief officer, and young Mr. Quigley came ashore. Mr. Peverell, she noted to her regret, was nowhere in sight. However, despite that disappointment, she could not help but be intrigued by the island of Gibraltar which, Captain Wellstood explained, was shaped like a sleeping lion. "Of course," he had added, "you can only see that shape when you are approaching it. More specifically, 'tis known as The Rock."

The city itself was a mile from the port and located at the bottom of that towering chunk of granite which did, indeed, bear some resemblance to a pillar and which bristled with fortifications.

Because of the crowds, the captain suggested that they would be better off not trying to haggle for one of the battered vehicles which would bring them into the main square. "Pirates," he said, half-humorously, "are not unknown to these shores and I am of the opinion that these, er . . . charioteers must be among their lineal descendants. They are not above charging exorbitant rates and halting midride to demand more. 'Tis but a mile and a little over to the center. I think we'd best walk."

Predictably, Miss Gore protested his suggestion. Fortunately, she was soon in agreement that the crowds swarming about the docks were daunting enough to preclude remaining in that vicinity any longer than necessary. She was rendered particularly nervous by the numbers of idling soldiers who strolled about ogling such females as either disembarked from incoming vessels or seemed indigenous to the area. Seeing Minnie singled out for this exuberant masculine attention, Miss Gore sharply reproached her for flirting with them. Her accusation brought tears to Minnie's eyes and a black frown to Mr. Quigley's brow. He stepped forward but, fortunately, his protest was anticipated and silenced by Mr. Davies.

Words also rose to Ariadne's lips, but she managed to swallow them. It was no time to quarrel with the chaperone. Captain Wellstood had said he would take them to the Almeda, a public garden. The contrast of such an oasis with this crowded, noisy pier was infinitely beguiling. Consequently, she merely patted Minnie's arm and, remaining at her side, made her way along the fortified stone and concrete walk that brought them to the dusty road leading into town.

More than dusty, it was badly mired and, of course, drew more complaints from Miss Gore. Fortunately, the captain was able to find a short cut to a destination which elicited a cry of pleasure even from Miss Gore as she gazed on a stretch of green grass, brightly colored geraniums, red, pink, and white oleander bushes, and other flowering plants. As they neared the gardens, Ariadne's attention was captured as much by the pedestrians as by the beckoning floral beauties. She might have been at a costume ball, she thought, seeing such strange garb worn so casually. Minnie was similarly fascinated.

"Cooee, Miss Ariadne," the girl murmured. "Look at 'im w'i that little red cap so close on 'is 'ead."

"And look at those flat yellow slippers so many people are wearing," Ariadne said. "And the soldiers. I wonder how many regiments are represented here?"

"Mr. Quigley 'as said . . ." Minnie cast a look over her shoulder at the three men walking behind them, ". . . that there be—"

"Minnie," Miss Gore interrupted coldly. "I am going to sit under that tree over there." She indicated a white marble bench. "And I want you to fan me. I find myself extremely warm and exceptionally weary."

The abigail tensed. A mutinous look passed over her face. She opened her mouth and closed it, her years in service obviously precluding the protest that she was not there to wait upon the chaperone.

" 'Tis Minnie's first time ashore," Ariadne said quickly. "I will fan you, Miss Gore."

"There's no need for that," Miss Gore snapped. She directed a poisonous look at Mr. Quigley. "Minnie knows where her duties lie."

It flashed through Ariadne's mind that her chaperone hated the girl. Undoubtedly, she was jealous of her glowing beauty and also of the attentions she was receiving from the young seaman. Against her will, she felt a certain kinship with Miss Gore. She, too was ill-favored and it was very difficult not to envy one who had received such lavish gifts from nature. However, since Minnie had not ordered her looks from a beneficent creator, she ought not to be penalized for their possession. She said firmly, "Minnie, I am sure, wishes to see some of the town and Mr. Quigley is willing to show it to her. Consequently, I have already given her my leave to go. I will fan you, Miss Gore."

Miss Gore raised angry eyes to Ariadne's face, but an argument would have been futile. She said merely, "Very well." A second later, she snapped, "I thank you!"

"But Miss Ariadne," Minnie protested feebly, "I do think I ought to remain—"

"Mr. Quigley is waiting for you, Minnie," Ariadne said firmly.

With a movement closely resembling a skip, the girl abandoned any further arguments and joined her swain.

"You spoil them," Miss Gore commented crossly, "when you are so lax with the lower classes. They do not appreciate your permissiveness, I can assure you. They only sneer at it and laugh at you behind your back. I wonder your father has not told you that."

"Papa has said that all human beings have a duty to provide comfort for each other," Ariadne responded coolly. She was extremely glad that Miss Gore had never met her father. Though Sir Arthur might easily have delivered himself of such a sentiment, to her certain knowledge he had not. Mindful of her promise, she added, "You'd best sit down now."

"Miss Caswell-Drake?" Captain Wellstood moved to her side. "Would you be minding if Mr. Davies and myself were to leave you and your chaperone for a short time? You'll be quite safe in the gardens and we have . . . an errand to perform for Mr. Peverell."

"Not in the least—" she began.

"Quite safe!" Miss Gore broke in. "You are proposing to leave two females here in a strange place—"

"Miss Gore," Ariadne interrupted, "I am sure we will

take no harm. Look . . ." She pointed at a group of women seated on a bench a few feet distant. "I cannot think that Captain Wellstood means to leave us for very long."

"Oh, no, Miss Caswell-Drake," the captain assured her. "We will be back in the quarter of an hour, no more."

"Have we your word on that?" Miss Gore demanded.

"You have, indeed, ma'am." the captain assured her.

"Very well," she said grudgingly. "I expect you may go."

"Thank you, Miss Gore," Mr. Davies said respectfully.

A few moments later, Miss Gore, finally ensconced on her bench, said as she watched the two men join the crowds on the street, "No doubt they have gone for a drink. I can only hope that they'll not keep us sitting here until 'tis time for the ship to lift anchor!"

"I do not think they would," Ariadne said. She produced her fan. "Why do you not close your eyes against the glare of the sun. I am sure 'twill make you feel more the thing."

"I wish it might," Miss Gore sighed. She did close her eyes, adding, "I cannot expect to feel well until we have the promise of dry land for more than a day. Five more weeks . . ." She heaved another sigh.

Ariadne stifled a burgeoning groan. Five more weeks of Miss Gore's companionship was something she preferred not to contemplate. Yet, despite her dislike of the woman, she did feel sorry for her. She was such a joyless creature. She seemed to take no interest at all in her surroundings. Had Sir Arthur been with her, he would have insisted on walking all around the town. He would also have scaled The Rock. She glanced up at it wistfully. There would be a wonderful view at the top. The sea would be spread out like a blue carpet and across from Gibraltar lay the coast of Africa, visible, she knew, from that height. Her father would not have let her leave the island without seeing it. In fact, he might be extremely disappointed that she had not availed herself of the opportunity.

Her hand was becoming tired from the motion of fanning. She glanced at Miss Gore and found that her head had drooped and that her mouth was half open. In that same moment, she heard a small snore. The woman had fallen fast asleep!

Ariadne put the fan down and shook her cramped wrist. It was extremely warm in the gardens. She wished she might walk about and see something of the town. She had a moment's envy of Minnie, leaning on Mr. Quigley's strong arm as they looked at whatever there was to see in the way of small shops and public buildings or even the military excavations on The Rock. Certainly, the sights that must be filling their vision were more interesting than her immediate surroundings. Green grass and flowers were all very well, but they were hardly new or different. She wondered how much time had elapsed since the captain and Mr. Davies had left them. Unfortunately, she had forgotten to pin on her watch.

Distant shrieks of laughter reached her. She looked across the park and saw children playing. She could envy them, too. It would be great fun to roll on the grass or toss a ball back and forth. It would be more fun to wander through the town or, better yet, climb to the top of The Rock. Ariadne cast a look around the gardens and, as she had anticipated, she did not see the captain or his first mate. Her father *would* be disappointed and even annoyed if she did not avail herself of the opportunity to see as much of this great fortress as she might. She was absolutely certain of that!

Impulsively, she rose. The streets leading to the top of the hill were fully visible from the gardens. They were extremely steep. In fact, some of them were merely flights of stairs. They were also some distance away, but that presented no barrier to one who, in the company of her father, had walked for miles in search of hut circles on the Devonshire Moors and Roman ruins in Wales.

In another few moments, Ariadne was out of the park and following the crowds that hurried like ants in a hundred different directions. If she received any interested looks, she was not aware of them; she was intent only on her destination. She had chosen a street that rose practically perpendicularly at its furthermost extremities and, in a few moments, she was beginning to feel the steep grade on the backs of her legs. She presumed that this was due to the fact that for the last three weeks her only exercise was strolling on deck. All of a sudden she thought of Mr. Peverell or, rather, she concentrated on him. She really did not need to think of him. Ever since she had first seen him, her mind had been divided into compartments, some big and some small. He occupied a very large compartment, her father occupied another, and, oddly enough, her long-anticipated journey to Greece was squeezed into a much smaller space, one it shared with a feeling of regret that once they disembarked at Patras she would see much less of him.

"And where are you bound, all by yourself, little lady?"

A voice, practically in her ear, startled Ariadne. She came to a stop and looked up hastily at a tall, elderly man in a red jacket and kilt which, of course, meant he was a member of a Scottish regiment. His gold epaulettes signified that he was an officer, though at his age, it seemed unlikely that he could still be on active duty. She liked his face. He had a broad forehead topped by grizzled hair which must once have been red. His cheekbones were high and there were smile lines around a firm mouth. His eyes, under tufted red-gray eyebrows, were very blue. His expression was benign and his manner polite. It was quite safe, she decided, to answer him.

"I thought to see the top of The Rock," she said shyly.

"A worthy ambition," he commented. "But should you be going all that distance alone?"

"I expect not," she admitted candidly. "But my chaperone's asleep and even if she were not, I should never have been able to coax her up this incline. And my father has said I should visit as many points of interest as possible on my way to join him in Greece."

"I see, and I agree with him. I am also glad that you have a chaperone, but," he regarded her sternly, "I do not think you should have left her. Still, since you have, you must let me accompany you to your destination." He glanced upward at the remaining stairs.

Ariadne regarded him dubiously. He was not only elderly, he was very thin and might be frail. "I intend to go as far as possible, sir."

"I have anticipated that. I am, by the way, Alexander

MacKenzie of the 93rd Highlanders. I have been stationed on this island for one and thirty years."

"Oh!" she exclaimed. "You must have been here at the time of the Great Siege?"

"Not quite." His lips quirked into a rather rueful smile. "Unfortunately, I arrived ten years later."

"I would not think that unfortunate, sir—it must have been terrible, the constant bombardment and the lack of food or water."

"Soldiers learn to expect hazards, my dear. I *was* here, however, when Lord Nelson's ship, the *Victory*, was anchored off-shore."

"Oh," she said. "In July of 1805 on his way to Trafalgar."

"Precisely."

"And did you meet him, sir?"

He shook his head. "He did not come ashore."

"Oh, I had forgotten that. Papa was most dreadfully cast down over his death."

"As was all of England." He nodded.

"It was a more personal loss for Papa. He had met him quite often in Naples—at the home of Sir William Hamilton."

Her companion's eyes widened. "He was most fortunate. May I know your father's name, my dear?"

" 'Tis Sir Arthur Caswell-Drake and I am Ariadne Caswell-Drake, sir. I fear I have been remiss in not introducing myself ere this. Do you know Papa?"

"By name, yes. In common with the late Sir William, he is a collector of paintings and other artifacts."

"That is true, sir," she said in some surprise. "I shall have to tell Papa that he is famous, though probably 'tis his collection that is really famous."

"Quite right, my dear. And all the more reason why his daughter should not be wandering about this town by herself. But I should not scold you. You'd not be Sir Arthur's child, were you not anxious to take in as many sights as possible. Shall we go onward?"

"If you, please, sir," she said eagerly.

"I do please. 'Tis not often I can move in such illustrious society."

"Oh," she blushed. "You are funning me."

"On the contrary," he said gently. "I meant it, every word."

Some fifteen minutes later, Ariadne, much winded, stood at the top of the street, staring out across a wide expanse of bay to a white town Mr. MacKenzie had just identified as Ceuta. "And," he continued, "that high limestone cliff is Abyla, the Mount of God or the second Pillar of Hercules."

"Oh," she breathed. "That is Africa, then."

"Africa," he corroborated. "And there, through the straits of Gibraltar, came the Moors, swarming onto this Rock and thence into Spain. And before them the Phoenicians, braving what all had thought to be the very boundaries of the earth— beyond which lay the dark river called Lethe, whose waters brought forgetfulness to the Dead who crossed the Styx with Charon. And—"

"Miss Caswell-Drake!"

Adriadne turned swiftly and was startled to see Mr. Peverell, red of countenance, toiling up the steps. "Oh, dear." She glanced up at her companion. "I wonder how he knew where to find me?"

"A friend, my dear?"

"He . . . 'tis his yacht that is taking us to Greece, but I cannot understand how he came to discover me. He was not with us when we left the ship!"

"Well, he has rectified that omission," Mr. MacKenzie commented. He added, "I find myself exceedingly grateful for my multiplicity of gray hairs. Else, I should be quaking in my boots, I am sure, for he looks very angry."

"I cannot imagine that you would ever quake, sir," Ariadne assured him. At the same time, she found herself a prey to that aforementioned condition. Mr. Peverell was almost upon them and his expression was thunderous. In another second he had gained the step just below them and, glaring at them, he panted, "Might . . . I . . . understand . . . what you . . . you are doing . . . here in the . . . the company of . . . of. . ."

As he paused for breath, Mr. MacKenzie said calmly, "Colonel MacKenzie of the 93rd Highlanders, sir. I understand that you are Mr. Peverell, the owner of the yacht bearing this young lady to join her father in Greece?"

"I am, sir." Mr. Peverell looked startled and, at the same time, considerably mollified. "Colonel Sir Alexander Mac-Kenzie?" he inquired.

It was the colonel's turn to appear startled. "The same," he averred. "However, I do not believe—"

"Your reputation, Sir Alexander," Mr. Peverell interrupted, "has spread beyond the gates of Gibraltar." He added respectfully, " 'Twas very kind of you to accompany Miss Caswell-Drake."

The colonel had a smile for Ariadne. "It was not only kindness, sir. I have found her a most rewarding companion."

Ariadne flushed. "You exaggerate, sir. 'Tis I who have been rewarded."

"I do not exaggerate," he contradicted. "I have enjoyed both the climb and the conversation." Fastening his vivid blue gaze on Mr. Peverell, he added, "I expect you will want to escort her back to the ship?"

"Yes, 'tis time and past that she returned, Sir Alexander." The look he bent on Ariadne had turned censorious. "Her chaperone is exceedingly anxious about her."

"Oh, dear, has she awakened then?" Ariadne cried.

"Did you think she would not?" Mr. Peverell demanded chillingly.

"I . . . oh, dear." Ariadne swallowed a sudden lump in her throat. "I've not been gone long, have I?" she asked in a small voice. "I vow it cannot be above a half hour."

"Five minutes would have been too long, and you've been missing at least an hour! And—" Mr. Peverell broke off. Turning to Sir Alexander, he said, "Miss Caswell-Drake is not yet a seasoned traveler, as you must realize."

"That is obvious," Sir Alexander returned. "However, it is also obvious that she is an innocent."

"I am aware of that, sir. And had I been with them . . . but unfortunately, I was not," Mr. Peverell said tensely. "But enough, I will not tax you with my recriminations. If her chaperone is not to have the vapors, I think we must go."

"Of course," Sir Alexander responded. "I think, too, that she cannot but profit from the experience."

"I am sure she will. However, she has been extremely

fortunate in her choice of companion. I do thank you, Sir Alexander.''

"Again, I must impress upon you that I am delighted to have been of some help.'' He turned to Ariadne again. "I hope, Miss Caswell-Drake, that I will have the opportunity of meeting you at another time—will you be visiting our shores on your return journey?''

"I am not sure, sir, but I hope we will.'' She smiled up at him.

"Will you be coming with us now, sir?'' Mr. Peverell inquired.

"No, I think that having gained this summit, I shall linger here for the nonce. I do not often find my way up to these heights and 'tis a most stimulating view. One forgets, you know.''

"I do understand, sir.'' Mr. Peverell gazed out across the bay. "I do agree with you. 'Tis very stimulating, indeed. I will bid you good morning, sir.''

"Good morning, Mr. Peverell,'' Sir Alexander responded.

"Good-bye, sir,'' Ariadne said softly. "I do thank you.''

"It was a great pleasure, my child.''

As she started down the stairs, Ariadne was conscious of a strong desire to put as much distance between herself and her companion as was possible. Unfortunately, she dared not hasten down that steep incline. Instead, she was forced to go very slowly while in back of her, Mr. Peverell, maintaining a stony silence, stepped on each tread as she left it. By the time they had reached level ground, her heart was beating heavily and hovering somewhere in the vicinity of her throat. Though there was sound all around them of marching feet on the pavement, of a distant bugle, of shouts and cries and wheels rumbling over stones and horses neighing while dogs barked in seemingly a hundred different voices, Mr. Peverell remained ominously quiet, a quiet that seemed to rule out all other noise. Turning to him, she said in tones she could not keep steady, "How . . . how d-did you . . . you h-happen to . . . to f-find me?''

"By the sheerest accident,'' he said coldly. "I thought you must have gone either up or down. I decided that you might have gone up and by the greatest good fortune, I was ascending a parallel street when I looked across and, through a gap in the crowds, glimpsed you." He suddenly caught her by the shoulders and actually shook her. "How could you be such a fool?" he cried. "Have you no sense of propriety or common sense? Or more to the point, how could you go off by yourself in a strange town—a port town, where the dregs of all nations roam? Can you not imagine the dangers awaiting you?"

She looked up at her companion's flushed features. Words bubbled up in her throat but it was a moment before she could reply. "I have some knowledge of those dangers, sir, but I doubt that such persons would be interested in me."

He did not contradict her. He said caustically, "You have heard of being held for ransom, I expect, Miss Caswell-Drake. *They* might be extremely interested in gold."

"Yes, I expect they would," she agreed in a small, mortified tone of voice.

"Furthermore," he continued inexorably, "Miss Gore is nearly prostrate. It was unkind of you to place her in such a position. If I'd not found you, she would have been blamed for your disappearance!"

"Well, you did find me," Ariadne said, her heart plummeting to her shoes. He was not concerned about *her*. He only cared for Miss Gore. It was on the tip of her tongue to tell him that the chaperone would not have welcomed his concern. However, a glance at his stony face informed her that such information must be kept to herself and, of course, angry as she was, she would never want to wound him by a description of Miss Gore's sentiments.

As they reached the garden, she braced herself for the inevitable scolding but Miss Gore, on seeing her, let out a small shriek and looked at Mr. Peverell with actual tears in her eyes. "Oh, you have found her. I am so relieved! My dear, dear child, to go off by yourself here of all places! I pray that nothing untoward has happened . . ."

"Nothing at all *untoward*," Mr. Peverell emphasized. "Miss Casswell-Drake was fortunate enough to meet with Sir Alexander MacKenzie, a colonel in the 93rd Highlanders. He is a famous man, I might add. A brave soldier. He escorted her to the top of The Rock, which was where I found her. Providence was looking after her, I think.''

"Well, that's a mercy," Miss Gore commented.

"Indeed," he agreed.

Looking from Miss Gore to Mr. Peverell, Ariadne was extremely surprised by their unusual accord. She had the impression of words exchanged silently—a message, in fact—and all at once, she guessed what must be troubling the chaperone. "Gracious," she said, "did you think me in danger of being ravished, Miss Gore?"

"Ariadne!" Miss Gore took a step backward, staring at her in horror.

"But I assure you, I was not," Ariadne continued. "And I must tell you that Papa has told me how I can protect myself against—"

Miss Gore had turned a bright and unbecoming puce. "Not another word!" she said chokingly. "Not another word, I charge you! The idea of mentioning anything so . . . so indelicate in front of . . . of . . ."

A smothered sound from Mr. Peverell brought Ariadne's attention back to him. He, she noted in some surprise, was almost as flushed as Miss Gore. His eyes, somber no longer, were bright with amusement. Meeting her gaze, however, he smoothed out a burgeoning smile. "I think that we'd best go back to port."

"Yes, yes, at once!" Miss Gore exclaimed. "And I will have something to say to you, Miss Caswell-Drake, when we arrive, something of great moment, I assure you!"

A gibbering sound coming on top of her words startled them all and the chaperone uttered a small shriek as a brownish ape suddenly appeared from behind a bush and as quickly disappeared.

"Gracious, that must have been a Barbary Ape!" Ariadne exclaimed.

"It was indeed, Miss Caswell-Drake." Mr. Peverell nodded.

"Horrid creature!" Miss Gore exclaimed.

Ariadne, meeting Mr. Peverell's eyes and finding them alight with amusement, wondered if the thought which had just occurred to her had also entered his head. She was sure of it when he threw a side glance at Miss Gore who, at that moment, bore a most surprising resemblance to the creature in both face and voice.

Encountering the chaperone's darkling glance, Ariadne swiftly composed her features; she knew she would be roundly scolded when they returned to the yacht, but that silent exchange was, she decided, more than enough compensation for what must surely follow!

Chapter Three

"Piraeus!" Captain Wellstood regarded Mr. Peverell with considerable surprise. "I thought you had it in mind to head for Patras."

"I have decided I would like to cruise among the islands," Mr. Peverell explained. "I met little Miss Caswell-Drake last night, looking wistful, as well she might since the Gorgon refused to let her go ashore at Malta or Zante. I tried to persuade the woman that I would see that she remained in my view at all times, but those assurances, I fear, did not work in her favor. In common with many of my countrywomen, she holds me in anathema."

"She is a most unpleasant creature," Captain Wellstood observed. "And she is being unnecessarily strict with the poor girl. I hold myself partially to blame for that."

"You?" Mr. Peverell demanded. "Why?"

"We should not have left her alone that day in Gibraltar. Our return was delayed because we lost our way, as you know."

"As well blame Miss Gore for falling asleep," Mr. Peverell said ruefully. "However, Miss Caswell-Drake should not have wandered off by herself. Still, 'tis my notion she is being punished less for that infraction than for her frankness."

The captain laughed and then sobered. " 'Tis a pity more females are not similarly well-informed."

"I think they are," Mr. Peverell mused. " 'Tis the fashion to hide it. Where ignorance is bliss, 'tis folly to betray one's wisdom, if I may paraphrase Grey. Radha would have laughed. She did laugh at the 'false faces English wear,' as she put it." He frowned and then, after a moment, he added, "But be that as it may, I think we might take an extra day and sail past Naxos for our little Ariadne."

"You've come to like the chit, I see." The captain gave him a narrow look.

"I do find her refreshing," Mr. Peverell admitted. "She seems to scorn the devices that females are so fond of employing while in masculine society. She says what she thinks and she's never afraid of stating an opinion. On the few times we have conversed, I have found her quite intelligent."

" 'Tis a pity she is not more attractive," Captain Wellstood commented.

"Alas, yes. She is no beauty. Poor child, she has attractions that go beyond beauty, but I fear these will not be appreciated by the man who ultimately weds her for her—fortune."

"Mayhap there'll be someone who will prefer brains and a sense of humor to beauty."

"Perhaps so," Mr. Peverell said dubiously. "Unfortunately, there are those spots. More seem to appear each day. They quite disguise such attractions as she does possess. Her eyes, for instance, are large and a lovely color of blue. Her nose and mouth are well-shaped, but that complexion! She looks almost as if she had contracted a permanent case of the measles."

"I agree," the captain said. " 'Tis well that she is an heiress."

"Very well, but I still say that gold ought not to be the yardstick by which she is measured." Mr. Peverell shrugged and sighed. "However, neither you nor I are capable of altering those standards—so let us bring a little happiness into her life and take her past that fabled isle which, I know, she is longing to see."

"Very well," Captain Wellstood said. "I'll chart the course."

Sitting in the dining salon which served as recreation room during the day, Miss Gore, leaning weakly against the back of her chair, glared at Ariadne. "If you'd not mentioned the islands, we should be on dry land by now! Oh, God!'' she suddenly groaned at a downward swoop of the vessel. She seemed no less happy when it rose again. She directed a second glare at Ariadne. "We could have been in Patras,'' she amplified, and closed her eyes. Minnie, too, was looking pale as *The Argonaut* continued its irregular course through the storm which, just before sunset, had come roaring out of nowhere.

With a narrow look at her companions Ariadne, who found the wild weather exciting rather than daunting, arose and staggered toward the door.

"Where are you going?'' groaned the chaperone.

Since the truth would only have netted her another argument, Ariadne said, "To my cabin.''

Miss Gore nodded and groaned a second time at an even greater heave of the vessel.

At least, Ariadne decided a few minutes later, she had not told Miss Gore a complete falsehood. She *had* gone to her cabin to snatch her hooded cloak, not that it would be much use in keeping dry aloft. The rain was pelting down, the waves were mountainous. In fact, they seemed high enough to engulf the craft and send her to the bottom. Yet, even with the decks awash in seawater, the wind howling like a pack of Furies, and the moon appearing and disappearing, rather like the storm-tossed craft on which she stood, as wavelike clouds scudded across its bright surface, she found these warring elements preferable to the stifling heat of the hold.

She wondered where Mr. Peverell was and suffered some feelings of regret. Miss Gore's accusations were true. He *had* changed course so that she might see the Greek Islands, in particular Naxos, largest of the Cyclades. They had been on their way to its rocky shoreline when the storm struck. Had they been blown very far off course? She had no right to be experiencing the disappointment she was currently feeling. Undoubtedly, her father could arrange an expedition to the island. But seeing it with Sir Arthur would never be as exciting as having Mr. Peverell as her guide. Still, if they had not changed course, they would not have been battling Poseidon's forces at this present moment. While she did not

fear defeat—the vessel was well-constructed and this was not
the first time they had encountered rough weather—she had
no doubt that once they reached port, she would be in deep
disgrace. Undoubtedly, she would be hearing about her "folly"
in implementing this unscheduled detour for the rest of her
stay in Greece. And it had *not* been her idea! True, she had
expressed a wish to see the islands, but Mr. Peverell had
initiated the change. She sighed. Undoubtedly, he was regretting his kindness now. She wondered where he was. There
was no guessing. He could be any one of the men rushing
back and forth on the streaming deck. Probably he was beside
the captain on the bridge.

A streak of jagged lightning followed by an immense crack
of thunder shattered her thoughts. Water was bubbling up
over her feet, the wind tore at her cloak and buffeted her
body. Had she not been clinging tightly to a rope at the side
of the vessel, she might have fallen.

"What are you doing here?" someone yelled angrily. "Damn
and blast it, get below!"

Ariadne, looking up into Mr. Peverell's momentarily moon-
brightened countenance, loosed her clutch on the ropes. "I
. . ." she yelled, but could say no more as the vessel dipped
and a wave came up, sweeping her from the deck and into the
water. She had a sensation of going down, down, down, and
being twisted and flung about by contrary currents. Water
seeped into her nostrils and into her mouth, stifling the
scream that rose in her throat. Then, she was breathing again,
and gazing upward she saw the moon with a watery nimbus
about it, as if it, too, had fallen beside her into those roiling
waters!

There was sound in her ears and something was clutching
her. She tried to shake herself free but could not. She looked
wildly about her but could see nothing! The clouds had
covered the moon's face once more. What had caught her? A
horrid explanation came to her. There were octopuses in
these waters and squid. Mr. Quigley had told Minnie about a
monsterous squid called the Kraken. It had arms twenty-five
feet long and it was known to drag seamen from the decks of
ships and, after squeezing them to death, devour them! And

now one of these creatures had seized her and was dragging her down! She screamed and struggled against the hold. More sound was in her ears but she was not being dragged down, she was being held aloft and now the moon emerged from its bank of clouds. Its brightness illuminated the churning waters and, incredibly, she saw the face of Mr. Peverell and knew that it was he who held her.

"You . . ." she was able to enunciate. "Why?"

He had no answer for her. He merely clutched her, holding her up. No, he did seem to be saying something, but his voice was borne away by the shrieking winds. It flitted through her mind that she would drown, she and Mr. Peverell together. And then she stopped thinking for she was being pulled down again. But she could not abandon herself to the raging sea. She could swim, she had to make the effort! She tried to strike out and in that moment, something struck her and she knew nothing more.

There was sand in her mouth, sand in her hair, and a coating of sand on her bare feet, her legs, and even her thighs under her sea-stained muslin gown. Her throat was parched and there was the acrid taste of salt in her mouth. She had swallowed quantities of the "wine-dark" Aegean. The water had been painfully pumped out of her by the man who lay a few feet away, his dark head pillowed on his folded arms, oblivious of her, unaware that the full moon was down and the sun climbing toward its zenith or, if she were an ancient Greek, Helios was guiding his plunging steeds on their daily journey across the heavens.

Ariadne shook her head, wondering how she could think of something so irrelevant to her situation. She sent a look about her at low, cave-punctured cliffs, at water-pitted rocks, at shell-strewn sands, and wondered how they had survived their plunge into those roaring waters and, even more miraculously, the perilous swim to shore. She had no recollection of that swim. She had been unconscious and had not revived until the moment when she had felt the rhythmic pressure of Mr. Peverell's hands on her ribs and herself coughing and spluttering as the water bubbled forth from her mouth and nose. She did not want to think about that and nor did she want to dwell on the previous evening, but she could not push the fragmented images from her mind. Concurrent with these was a great wonder. She ought not to have been able to think at all! She ought to be lying on the sea bottom.

" 'Of his bones is coral made,' " she whispered, wondering where she had heard that line before. She traced it to Shakespeare's play *The Tempest.* " 'Full fathom five thy father lies . . .' " and how many fathoms would she have sunk before she lay caught among the seaweed on the ocean floor? She shuddered, remembering the huge wave that had swept her from the deck in the midst of her burgeoning altercation with Mr. Peverell, who had subsequently joined her in those tempestuous waters! Had he leaped in to save her life or had he been washed overboard by that same wave that had engulfed her? It did not matter. He was with her and he *had* saved her life, striking her on the chin when she had made her futile attempt to swim toward a shore she could not even see. Probably he had thought she was struggling against him. Her father, who had taught her to swim, had told her that such actions had caused the death of persons who might otherwise have been saved.

Her father!

Tears filled Ariadne's eyes. What would he think once Captain Wellstood told him that she had been drowned, and Mr. Peverell also? Sir Marcus Peverell was also in Athens. She hated to contemplate their needless misery. Yet, that would be at an end once they reached the mainland—and where were they at this present moment?

She stared out at the sea, bright and placid under the mid-morning sun. The squall might never have occurred. There was, however, no sign of *The Argonaut* in that blue distance. She had a horrid feeling that their disappearance might not have been discovered until the storm died down. And there was no telling where they were! Once more she looked about her at scraggly bushes pressed against cave-punctured cliffs. There were some large rocks at the water's edge and earlier she had taken a walk along the shore but though she had gone a considerable distance, she had seen no sign of human habitation.

In common with Defoe's Robinson Crusoe, they might have been cast ashore on some desert island! And did that imply . . . she refused to follow that line of reasoning to its illogical conclusion! They must be on one of the islands of the Cyclades, and when Mr. Peverell awakened they would find their way back to some settled part of the area and to people who would sail them to the mainland!

She cast another look at Mr. Peverell and frowned. She had been unwilling to disturb him, reasoning that he needed his sleep after his battle with the elements, but he had shifted his position and the sun was beating fiercely down on his upturned face. His skin was already deeply tanned, but he might yet suffer a bad burn or even sunstroke were he to remain there. Moving to his side, she gently shook his shoulder. He moved restlessly and muttered something. Then, more clearly, he said, "Radha . . . Radha . . ." His eyes opened and, staring at her confusedly, he said, "Where is she? Radha?"

Her concern increased. Already, he must be feeling the effects of that fiery sun! She said concernedly, "You'd best get to the shade, Mr. Peverell. 'Tis too bright by half, the sun. I should have aroused you earlier." He was looking at her so blankly that she wondered if he understood what she was saying. With considerable trepidation, she added urgently, "Do you understand me, sir? Do you not remember what happened last night?"

"Last night . . ." he repeated vaguely. "Fell . . . into the sea." He blinked and the vagueness suddenly vanished. He regarded her intently. "And so did you, Miss Caswell-Drake."

Ariadne nodded. "I fell first," she emphasized. "I . . . I must thank you for saving my life." She swallowed, adding miserably, "I am only too aware 'twas my folly precipitated this situation."

"Precipitated, indeed." He sat up, staring at her, a frown in his eyes. "Why did you come up on deck in the midst of such a squall? What could have possessed you?"

"I . . . needed air. 'Twas monstrous close below, but I never dreamed . . ." Tears filled her eyes again.

"I beg you'll not weep!" he said sharply. "Weeping will

not mend matters and nor will my accusations. We must concentrate on our present plight, and I do thank you for rousing me before I received any more sun." He rose stiffly. "I had a coat. I cannot think where it went. You still have your cloak, but your shoes . . . where are they?"

"They came off in the water."

"With my coat, which was too much of a hindrance for swimming. I . . . remember now." He glanced ruefully at his thin muslin shirt, which was torn in several places. His next glance was for the cliffs. "Oh, Lord," he muttered, adding, "Well, at least we're alive." He emitted a harsh laugh. "I had wanted to die, but it seems that the Fates have something else in store for me. Actually, I am not sorry. Travelers do not often return from Poseidon's lair, but you and I have accomplished the voyage and 'tis well to see the sky from this particular vantage point."

"You . . . you had *wanted* to die?" she questioned.

He stared at her oddly, as if he was seeing her for the first time. "I suppose you'd not understand that, my dear—and nor need you." He paused, then continued in a more gentle tone of voice, "I've not asked you . . . how you are faring, my poor child?"

Ariadne swallowed. Of late he had taken to addressing her as "child," and she was positive that he thought of her as years and years younger than himself. However, her feelings for Mr. Peverell were not childish. He had only to smile at her and she experienced symptoms that heretofore she had known only from Carola's description of her feelings upon first seeing Lord Brynston. She had dreamed about Mr. Peverell at night, too, just as Carola confessed to doing.

"Sometimes, I have hated to wake up," her friend had confided.

She, herself, had experienced a similar disappointment upon awakening and encountering Mr. Peverell on deck, regarding her coolly and dispassionately, rather than with the ardent gaze he had visited upon her in her dreams. Nothing could be cooler than his present gaze—and he had asked her a question and she was taking her time about giving him an answer. She said, "I am very well, thank you," and was both surprised and indignant to hear him laugh merrily. She said stiffly, "I do not understand . . ."

"I am sorry," he said. "Pray accept my apologies, Miss Caswell-Drake, but 'twas the formality of your answer coming upon a silence that was beginning to give me concern." His smile vanished. "You are really 'very well'?"

She laughed too. "I really am, Mr. Peverell. Aside from a few bruises, I am quite myself."

"And a very brave self that is," he commented. "Any other female would have been treating me to a royal fit of the vapors!"

"I do not know about that," she said in defense of her sex. "However," she added mischievously, "I can think that Miss Gore might have been rather discommoded."

His laughter rang out again. "Save me from Miss Gorgon!" he cried.

"Oh!" Ariadne clasped her hands. "And is she not? Papa could never have agreed with my aunt as to her choice of chaperone and . . . oh, dear!" She gave him a stricken look. "She will be distressed once she meets him and must tell him I am dead . . . and your father, too."

"Yes," Mr. Peverell said soberly. "We must hurry and get back to civilization—such as it is in this part of the hemisphere."

Ariadne glanced up at the barren cliffs. "I wonder where we are?"

"We were nearing Naxos at sundown," he reminded her. "But the storm might have blown us off course. Still, we can be positive that we are on one or another of the Cyclades, and not stranded like Robinson Crusoe."

"Why I thought of him, too!" Ariadne exclaimed.

"One naturally would," he said. "But I can promise you, Miss Caswell-Drake, that our sojourn here will not run into years or even weeks. I would guess that we'll be arriving on the mainland in a day or, at the most, two."

"Do you really think so?"

He nodded. "The Greeks are a friendly people and, fortunately, I can speak their language and explain our situation.

We have only to reach a village, which we will probably do today. And tomorrow . . .''

"We might be in Athens?" she said eagerly.

"Or on our way. Are you hungry?"

"Hungry?" She gave him a startled glance. "I'd not thought of food. I am not hungry at this present moment, but I expect I shall be."

"And I," he smiled at her. "We'll need to search for edible plants and fruits. Oranges and pomegranates grow wild, but it is late for the latter. And . . ." he gestured at the sea, ". . . we can probably catch fish, if necessary."

"Without a rod?" she demanded.

"I was not actually thinking of the sea. There'll be freshwater streams and pools further inland and I can snare trout with my hands."

"You can?" She gazed at him admiringly.

He grinned. "I learned the trick from a poacher. It has often stood me in good stead. However, it might not come to that. We'll probably reach a village this afternoon or even earlier."

"If we do not, there are olive trees in Greece. Some of them grow wild, I've heard."

"They do. However, we'd best not sample their fruit. Have you ever eaten an olive that has not been cured?" As she shook her head, he continued, "You'd not want to repeat that experiment. 'Tis like eating a green persimmon."

"Oh, I've done that." She grimaced. She added, "I do not think we ought to be discussing food. I think we must find out where we are, if possible. Do you not agree?"

His eyes gleamed. "I do. And I must beg your pardon for having introduced that dangerous subject in the first place."

"You must be hungry." She gave him a stricken look. "Oh, Mr. Peverell, will you ever, ever be able to forgive me? All this is my fault. If I'd not come up on deck . . ."

"Ariadne, child . . ." he put a comforting arm around her shoulders, ". . . you'd no notion that anything like this would come to pass any more than I could know that the wave would engulf us both as I scolded you and caused you to loosen your grip on the rope. In those circumstances, we were both at fault, but 'tis far too late to cry over spilt milk. You have suggested that we try and ascertain our location and we can do that only by walking or . . ." he eyed the cliffs dubiously, ". . . climbing, depending on how far these extend along the shoreline."

The pressure of his arm and his use of her given name, strange in her ears but delightful, as well, were enough to deprive Ariadne of speech and even locomotion for the nonce. Fortunately, this euphoric sensation was soon dispelled by common sense and the depressing realization that he thought of her as a child. She longed to cry, "I am not a child. I am seventeen, sir, an age when my mama married. She died before her twenty-first year!" Of course, she could say nothing of the kind, not to a man whose own wife had died young and only a short time since, but that was not the only reason why she must hold her peace. She would be out of her role. Men made declarations. Women accepted them. At least, some women did. She was quite unable to imagine Mr. Peverell or, indeed, any gentleman favoring her with such a declaration.

She moved away from him, saying quite calmly, "Should we walk or climb, do you think? There seem to be plenty of tocholds on the cliffs."

"I think we ought to skirt them," he said. "I would rather try and see what we may find on shore."

"I did walk along the shore before you woke, Mr. Peverell. I saw very little save more cliffs."

Concern was written large on his countenance as he said reprovingly, "You should not have gone anywhere without me, Miss Caswell-Drake."

She longed to beg him to use her given name again, but she said only, "I did not go far and I am here, safe and sound, as you see."

"You have been fortunate," he began, "but—"

"Have we not both been fortunate, Mr. Peverell," she interrupted with a little shiver. "We could so easily have been at the bottom of the sea."

"True," he agreed soberly. "But obviously 'twas not part of nature's design for us."

His use of the term "us" provided another thrill for Ariadne. She could not even be concerned over her plight with this man beside her, this man whom she loved so deeply, so hopelessly. Never by look, gesture, or word could she reveal anything of what she felt for him. In these unhappy circumstances, she could only be pleased that when she said, "I expect we ought to be on our way," she sounded quite matter-of-fact.

"We should be going," he agreed. "The sun's already warm. Come midday, we'll not be able to bear its rays. Here in Greece, the goatherds drive their flocks into caves until two or three in the afternoon. We'll need to follow their example." He glanced down at her bare feet, adding concernedly, "I wish you'd not lost your shoes."

"The sand is soft." She shrugged.

"But we might not be able to keep to the shore. Still, I can plait some straw into sandals for you."

"Then I will be a true Greek!" She smiled up at him.

He smiled back at her, admiringly now. "You are certainly game, Miss Caswell-Drake."

"You've already given me your opinion of vaporish females, sir. I'd not dare fall into such folly."

"That, my child, is quite true," he said with mock sternness.

Ariadne bit down a small sigh, wishing . . . but it was no time to give rein to these foolish and futile fancies. She could only be glad that he had no way of reading her mind. She would never want him to guess that rather than being concerned over their situation, she was entirely happy because they were together. Worse yet, she would have been even happier had they, like Robinson Crusoe, been stranded on an unknown island where ships never came.

Though it had not yet reached the mid-heaven, the sun was uncommonly bright and warm. Perspiration rolled down Ariadne's body as she trudged along a shore grown much rockier than before. They must have been walking for at least two hours and, as yet, she had seen nothing but cliffs, higher than those which had loomed over the spot where they had come ashore. Huge sea-carved boulders stood like pillars at the water's edge and the waves, coming up between them, bubbled into rock pools. Looking at them, she was particularly glad that the stormy waters had not carried them here, where they must have been dashed to pieces! As she followed Mr. Peverell, carefully avoiding the sharp, rocky protuberances scattered along the shoreline, she started to stop on a large, flat moss-green rock only to have it slip out from under her. Caught off-guard, she stumbled and fell on the wet sand, laughing as the supposed rock, thrusting out thick, scaly legs, crawled slowly away.

"Oh," she cried and, in spite of knees scuffed and bleeding from the sharp pebbles, she continued to laugh.

Mr. Peverell hurried back to her side. "What is it? Did you hurt yourself?"

"The rock . . ." She giggled. "Only it was not a rock."

He gave her a wary glance and had another for the sun. He would have spoken but Ariadne, anticipating his question, shook her head. "I am neither sunstruck nor moon-mad," she assured him. "Look, there it goes!" she pointed. "I thought 'twas a rock but it proved to be a tortoise!"

"A tortoise?" he repeated. "Where is it?"

"There . . ." she pointed.

"Ah, it's quite large," he said thoughtfully. "We might kill it. The flesh is rather rubbery, but—"

"No!" Ariadne jumped up. "It looks like a cross old man. I . . . I would feel like a cannibal!"

His lips twitched. "My dear Miss Caswell-Drake, we castaways might have no choice."

"Please," she begged. "Let it alone."

"Very well," he relented. "But we may regret it. Are you not hungry by now?"

"Not for tortoises," she said with a small shiver. "But I am passing warm and a little thirsty."

"I am extremely thirsty and I am sure you must be the same." He glanced upward. "There are trees on the tops of the cliffs. There may be streams, as well. I think we must retrace our steps and find a place where we can climb more easily. You need not worry about falling—I will be close behind you. And we'll be able to rest up there, as well."

"In a cave like a goat?"

"Like two goats." He grinned. "And I will find us something to eat. I cannot promise bread and cheese, and since you disdain tortoise . . ." He looked down and then frowned. "Good God, Miss Caswell-Drake, what have you done to yourself?"

Following his glance, she saw that there was blood on her dress. "I do not know . . ." she began, and tried to push his hand away as he lifted her skirt. "Please, sir."

Ignoring her protest, he said sharply, "Your knees. You've scraped them badly."

"Oh, that." She shrugged. "I did not know they were still bleeding. It happened when I fell just now. 'Tis nothing."

He actually glared at her. "If there is anything I cannot abide, 'tis misplaced courage. We are not in the middle of St. James Square. There is no physician to come and visit you. If you were to get dirt into these scratches it might be extremely dangerous." As he talked, he was ripping off a strip from his shirt. Wadding it up, he dipped it into a rock pool and kneeling beside her, he began to swab her knees.

"Oh dear." Ariadne's blush deepened. "You must not . . ." She tried to move away from him. "I can do it, you know."

"I beg you'll not put on these missish airs with me, my girl!" he exclaimed. " 'Tis not my intention to ravish you, I can assure you. But I would like to prevent infection. I cannot think that even the Gorgon could protest that!"

"But . . . but you've used your shirt," Ariadne said concernedly. "I could have torn a strip from my gown. There's more of it. Oh, dear!" she added as he ripped yet another strip from his shirt and began to bandage her knee.

"You will need your gown to preserve your modesty. As for me, I have none." He smiled up at her now. "I am sorry I scolded you, little Ariadne. I was worried—but after this, you must tell me when anything's amiss, will you promise me that, please?"

For some odd reason, she felt like crying, but she was able to swallow the rising lump in her throat. "I will promise and gladly, Mr. Peverell. However, I did not even know that I had hurt my knees. I was thinking about the . . . the tortoise."

"The tortoise preserved!" He flung out his arms in a mock dramatic gesture and laughed at her. "You are a delightfully refreshing child, do you, know, Miss Caswell-Drake?"

"I thank you, sir," she said in a small voice, "but if . . . if you'd not mind . . ." She paused nervously.

"What must I not mind, Miss Caswell-Drake?" He cocked an amused eye at her.

"I . . . I would much prefer to be addressed as Ariadne." She regarded him anxiously, wondering if he would approve this breach of etiquette but, of course, he *had* already used her Christian name.

His eyes, so somber in repose, suddenly gleamed with humor. "You are extending me this privilege?" he inquired solemnly.

"I am," she murmured shyly.

"I am honored Miss . . . er, Ariadne, especially since 'tis one I'd usurped already and without permission, the which, of course is unforgivable!"

"I did not think the less of you for it, Mr. Peverell," she said on a breath.

"Then, I am forgiven?"

"Of course, Mr. Peverell."

"So be it. If I am to be allowed to call you Ariadne, you must not continue to address me as Mr. Peverell. My given names are Marcus Iden Anthony David Peverell. And so that I will not be confused with my father, he and my close friends have always called me Iden."

"And I may, also?" Ariadne felt warm and cold at the same time, as if, indeed, the privilege he was granting her were far and away more important than the one she had just extended to him, as if, in fact, some manner of barrier that had existed between them had been removed forever!

"You may, Ariadne," he nodded. "And do let me hear you say it, please. Surely you need not stand on ceremonies with a fellow castaway?"

"I will, then . . . Iden," she said, and impulsively put out her hand.

He clasped it warmly. "Good," he said, and releasing her hand, he added, "We are friends, Ariadne."

She produced a rather tremulous smile but did not trust herself to say anything more, lest her voice quaver. She was almost as content as if that warm handshake had been a warmer embrace. That, she knew to her sorrow, would never be forthcoming. Even in his dusty breeches, scuffed boots, and torn shirt, even with his jaw coated with the dark fuzz of a sprouting beard, he was the most handsome man she had ever seen. The most handsome, she thought ecstatically, and the kindest, and she must cherish these hours, perhaps these days with him, for once they reached the mainland, they would be but a memory. Beauty must needs seek beauty, and if he ever fell in love again, it would not be with the likes of her!

"Ariadne, beloved of Dionysus, come," Iden prompted. "Let us retrace our steps and see if we can find a cave. Later, I will go forth and look for food and, I promise, 'twill be neither tortoise nor turtle!"

Chapter Four

The cave lay halfway up a cliff and gave the impression of having been carved by the action of a nearer sea, the waters of which had pitted its rocky sides and smoothed the floor. The cave mouth was an irregular gash, large on one side and narrow on the other. Wind-stunted bushes partially covered it and the way up to it was accomplished by a series of toeholds and through the grasping of various small plants and roots, sticking out of the dry, crumbly soil. Since it was not far from the beach, access was easy and before departing on what he had dubbed a "foraging venture," Mr. Peverell had piled grasses inside for Ariadne's comfort. He had ordered her to remain there and rest.

She had promised she would, but she was privately positive that she could not rest, left alone here, even though she believed him when he insisted that the cave was safe. It was not long enough to suggest an inmate dwelling in its depths or large enough to tempt another traveler, should there be one in the immediate vicinity. Rest would not come easily to her because he was gone and a lively imagination peopled the wilderness with wolves and snakes. She did not rule out Turks, even though Mr. Peverell had assured her that there were not many of these on the Aegean islands, there being very little to tempt them in such primitive regions. However, despite her procrastinations, she rested and, in fact, to her subsequent chagrin, she fell deeply asleep. She must have slept for a long time because the sea, bright when she had settled down, was darker now and the sun lower in the sky. And where was he? He must have been gone several hours! Where had he gone? Oughtn't he to have returned by now?

Her heart, seemingly escaped from its moorings, pounded heavily in her throat as a variety of possibilities presented themselves to her—all of them frightening.

He could have fallen, been set upon by bandits, bitten by a snake, stung by a poisonous insect, attacked by a wolf, or, more logically, he could have lost his way. Of course, he might also have discovered a village and, at this very moment, he could be negotiating for someone with a boat to bring them to the mainland. They might be in Athens by the morrow. No, that was not likely. They would probably have to wait until the following day, and she could not be sorry for that. To be with him was all she craved, and where was he? She tensed, hearing an unfamiliar sound. Someone was whistling. It was a tune she recognized! Her memory supplied the words of a song sung by the highwayman MacHeath of *The Beggar's Opera*.

> How happy could I be with either
> Were t'other dear charmer away!
> But while ye thus tease me together,
> To neither, a word will I say.

She crawled to the mouth of the cave and saw him come striding up the beach. She flushed. He was stripped to the waist and carrying a fish in one hand and, in the other, what remained of his shirt, tied into a bundle. "Mr. Peverell!" she cried gladly.

He looked up, his dark eyes reflecting his smile. "Miss Caswell-Drake!" He bowed.

"Iden," she amended.

"Ariadne," he bowed a second time. "You see me loaded with the spoils of the hunt and also with good news."

"Good news?"

"I have seen windmills in the distance. We are, I would assume, no more than a half-day's journey from human habitation!"

"A half-day?" she repeated with a glance at the darkening sky.

"Tomorrow morning, early, we'll commence our journey.

Tonight, we will retire betimes in anticipation of a longish walk. Did you sleep while I was away?''

"I did," she said.

"Good child, and how are your knees?''

"My knees?" she repeated blankly.

"Do they smart? You fell hard.''

"Oh, no, I had quite forgotten.''

He looked both surprised and gratified. "My congratulations, Ariadne. You are an ideal castaway!''

She flushed with pleasure. "But 'twas nothing," she said deprecatingly. "Oh, I am glad to see you back," she added, and blushed. "I mean . . .''

"I am very glad to be back," he assured her. "I do not mind telling you that I managed to lose my way two or three times. Fortunately, one cannot lose sight of the sea. Now . . . will you come down or shall I help you?''

"You need not.''

He eyed the face of the cliff. "On second thought, I think I must.''

" 'Tis not necessary, sir," she insisted. "Papa and I have been in all manner of seemingly inaccessible spots looking for Roman relics and the like.'' She slipped out of the cave and backed down the short distance, easily finding toeholds in the soft earth. However, just before she reached the bottom, he caught her in his arms and set her down.

"There you are, my dear.''

"I thank you . . . oh!" she exclaimed, seeing a long red scratch on his arm. "However did you come by this?''

" 'Twas nothing." He shrugged. "An encounter with a twig, the which I punished by breaking it off, which must teach it a lesson it will not soon forget!''

She laughed and then looked at the fish. "How did you ever manage to catch this?''

"Did I not tell you about my friend the poacher?''

"You caught it by hand . . . from the sea?''

He shook his head. "No, as I anticipated, there are streams of fresh water in yon wilderness above. I found this basking in a pool, which is another reason why I was gone longer than I'd anticipated. I, alas, am far less expert than he—the cunning rouge.''

"But you accomplished it, sir," Ariadne said admiringly, and flushed, remembering at that moment that Miss Gore had called him a rogue. She frowned disliking the chaperone even more. No one could be less a rogue than Mr. Iden Peverell, she was sure of that!

"I expect you are wondering how we will cook him?" he said.

"It had not occurred to me," she said. "But . . ." she swallowed, "how will you cook him?" She could not keep a touch of anxiety from coloring her tone. Oddly enough, she had not been hungry before, but with Iden returned and safe, she was suddenly ravenous. She was also thirsty.

"I have, by great good fortune, a tinderbox that the waves did not purloin but," he looked at her concernedly, "I think before we start dinner, I must put these supplies in the cave and take you where you may have a drink of water. I know how I felt when I saw that cool stream bubbling over the rocks. Come. We'll find a place where 'tis easier to reach the cliff-top. And once your thirst is slaked, we will return for a feast of the gods!"

"A bacchanalian feast?" she inquired.

His laugh rang out. "Not quite." He turned a roguish eye upon her. "Have you any notion of what that implies?"

"Do they not serve wine? I mean, 'twas in the honor of Bacchus, the Roman Dionysus, was it not?"

"Of course . . . Bacchus and Ariadne, my sweet innocent, and may you always remain in that enviable state," he teased. "Now come, let us find the stream before it is too late and you will have expired from thirst."

There seemed to be something unspoken hovering in the air between them. Ariadne tried to remember exactly what a bacchanalian feast was—she had the impression that it must imply something more than merely tasting the juice of the grape—and was slightly annoyed, wishing that he did not think of seventeen as seven and herself as not yet freed from the schoolroom. Yet, at least they were friends, and that was almost enough.

"Come, my sweet," he said, extending his hand.

She grasped it and was again prey to sensations she was heartily glad he could not divine.

In the middle of the night, Ariadne woke to the rumble of thunder and stared into a darkness, turned Stygian; in another second, however, the blackness was shot with moonlight amid a vast tapestry of stars. There was another roll of thunder and again there was darkness as immense clouds obscured the moon. She hoped that the sound had not awakened her companion. He needed his sleep and besides, the possibility of a new storm must distress him. They would not be able to travel in the rain and it would be another day before they reached his windmills, another day of anxiety for her father and Sir Marcus, too. Actually, it would be more than *one* day because who knew how long it would take them to reach the mainland?

"Radha . . . Radha . . ."

She turned in the direction of Mr. Peverell—Iden, she must remember to call him. Iden, lying a short distance from the mouth of the cave, was muttering that word or name. It must be a name. With a pang, she guessed it was the name of his wife.

Radha.

It sounded strange to her ears, but the girl had been an East Indian. She must have been beautiful too. Ariadne could not imagine that Iden would be attracted to a female who was not as beautiful as himself. She pressed her hands to her face and was surprised to discover that her skin did not feel as bumpy to the touch. Her forehead seemed much smoother and so did her chin. Were her spots going away? Carola had told her they probably would and her father had insisted they would. She had doubted both of them, thinking they meant only to be comforting.

A sudden crash of thunder startled her. It had sounded very close! Iden groaned and muttered, but said nothing. He had not awakened. She was very glad of that. He needed his sleep and so did she. She closed her eyes to the inevitable and expected sound of rain. She hoped that it would cease before morning or, at least she ought to hope that, and should not long for another day in his company or wish that she might spend all the days of her life with him! It was also wrong of her to be glad that he was no longer married. That implied that she was also glad that his poor young wife had died. She shivered a little at that—it was almost like ill-wishing a departed spirit. However, if the girl he had lost were alive, she would never have met him, never been with him here. She could feel sorry for Radha, who had lost him so quickly. Yet, perhaps she ought to feel sorrier for herself, who did not have him to lose. Once they returned to Athens, she would undoubtedly never see him again. No, he would be joining them on the expedition to search for artifacts—but would he want that now? She doubted it. Tears rolled down her cheeks and, thinking of that other Ariadne, she could share her anguish. She, too, would soon be abandoned and there would be no beneficent god to give her another haven!

By noon of the following day, Ariadne had reason to wish that she had never hoped for more rain, at least not in Greece, where prayers to the deities did not always remain unanswered. The rain was still descending and so heavily that it looked like a sheet of solid silver. Yet despite the steady downpour, Iden, after watching it for some two frustrating hours, had said, "We'll need some manner of food, my dear. I will have to do more foraging."

"But what can you find in this weather?" she had demanded. "You'll only catch your death of cold."

" 'Tis still warm," he had pointed out. "There are roots and seaweeds such as we had last night. That will give us some sustenance. We will need our strength for tomorrow."

"I hope the rain will have stopped by tomorrow," she had said, and meant it.

"I think it will. This is not England. The rain gods of Greece are a lazy group. As you can see, Zeus has already ceased to startle us with thunderbolts. Thor would still be hard at it. Consequently, we can hope that Helios will be wheeling out his chariot by daybreak."

Upon this facetious observation, he had gone and he had not yet returned. How much time had elapsed? She was not sure. Two hours? Three? Again her powerful imagination was conjuring up perils. He had spoken about losing his way yesterday. Today, it would be even easier with the rain pelting down and obscuring or even transforming familiar landmarks. It must have washed lots of earth from the cliff that held their cave. There was also the chance that he could slip in the soft earth and fall into the sea and be swept away by the stormy waters.

In that moment she heard voices. She could not make out the words, but they seemed to be coming closer. She tensed and crawled away from the opening, not wanting to be seen by whoever might be approaching. Into her mind popped the uncomfortable possibility of Turks. Iden had assured her that there were not many upon the islands but, she remembered, there were probably a few. Or . . . her mind offered the possibility of bandits. She edged back toward the mouth of the cave. They would not be able to see her behind these bushes and—her thoughts ceased abruptly as she caught the familiar sound of Iden's voice. He was speaking Greek! His observations were being answered by unfamiliar voices also in Greek. He was accompanied by another—no, two other men—and now she saw them clearly. They were in peasant garb and Greek, she was sure of that. They were also smiling, which suggested that they were friendly, and they were looking in her direction. Mindful of her tattered gown, she backed away, groping for her cloak.

"Ariadne!" Iden called, and was up the side of the cliff and into the cave in a trice. "My dear," he continued excitedly, "we have passage to the mainland! My companions are a pair of fishermen. They were out in a small boat and, like ourselves, they were blown off course. I helped them get to shore and calk their boat. They're grateful and have promised to bring us to Piraeus once the storm's subsided. Meanwhile, they'll take us to their village which, by great good fortune, is not far from here!"

"Oh," Ariadne clasped her hands. "That is lovely."

"I knew you must think so, my poor child." He smiled broadly. "And I must tell you, my dear little Ariadne, that we are, indeed, upon the Isle of Naxos!"

"Are we! You'll never say so!" She burst into delighted laughter in which he, too, joined.

The village, a matter of an hour's walk over rough ground, lay halfway up a hill, steep enough to be termed a miniature mountain. A scattering of small whitewashed houses flanked muddy streets, in which a large assortment of fowls wandered back and forth clucking and squawking. Dogs of mixed breeds occasionally chased them but mainly limited themselves to barking at the strangers. Numbers of women, many wearing black, appeared at windows and in the streets as Ariadne and Iden, flanked by the fishermen, who answered to the names of Hector and Dimitri, walked up the hill.

Aware of their curious gaze, Ariadne strained her ears to try and catch what they were saying but could understand no more than a few words of a language distorted by their regional dialect. She did gather that they were curious and, possibly, suspicious. However, Hector, who seemed to be a person of authority, uttered a string of words that appeared to soothe them and, at the same time, pique their curiosity. A number of men, youths, and small boys gathered about them all speaking at once.

Iden glanced down at Ariadne. "They suspect us of being Turkish spies." He grinned.

"Oh, gracious!" She regarded him in alarm.

"Do not worry, child," he murmured. "Hector, here, will vouch for us."

The group confronting them had looked angry and fearful, but suddenly they relaxed and burst into a mixture of laughter and exclamations of surprise as Hector, with gestures, evidently described their accident and subsequent plight over the last two days. Ariadne heard her name repeated by several of the men, accompanied by more laughter and some curious glances directed at Iden. Then Dimitri strode to an old woman who stood watching them from the doorway of a nearby hovel. He spoke to her and she nodded several times. Coming back, he spoke to Iden, who also nodded and turned to Ariadne.

"We'll have food and lodgings for the night with yon lady.

Her name, I might add, is Hecuba, but I doubt that she is wed to Hector here."

"They have the old names, then," Ariadne breathed. "I had not expected that."

" 'Tis about all they have been allowed to keep in five hundred years of Turkish occupation," Iden said grimly. "We are fortunate that the Turks do not think these islands worthy of their attention. But come, you must be weary and we have a hostess now, who is ready and willing to give us bed and breakfast. I am sure both will appeal to you."

Her feet were aching and she was hungry, but she managed to smile up at him. "I am not really very tired. 'Tis all so very interesting."

He put an arm around her and gave her a little squeeze. "I suspect you of prevarication, my sweet Ariadne, which is not necessary save in polite society. However, I do commend you on your bravery. 'Tis something I'll not soon forget."

Dimitri beckoned to them and Ariadne, following Iden, found herself oddly depressed by his comment or, rather compliment. It implied something she did not care to contemplate but, which, she knew was imminent and inevitable— their coming separation. He would not forget her bravery, he had said. He would, however. And he would forget her, as well, once they were back on the mainland. She looked up at the sky, turned red in the glow of a descending sun. All unnoticed by herself, the rain had stopped and there would be nothing to keep them from leaving on the morrow.

"Watch your step. The ground is strewn with rocks," Iden cautioned.

She flushed. Again she had been lost in thought and now they were at the threshold of a tumbledown little cottage and the old woman was smiling and uttering a stream of words which, again, her dialect rendered incomprehensible. They entered a large room, simply furnished with a long trestle table and a few battered chairs. There was a second room and in it was a huge old bed. Looking from Ariadne to Iden, she muttered a few more words and went out.

"Oh, Lord." Iden looked at Ariadne with rueful surprise. "I fear that they imagine . . ."

"'Tis not hard to ascertain what they imagine," she said.

"I ought to have told them that you were my niece. It never occurred to me that they would believe otherwise."

"Nor to me!" she hastened to assure him. "But you must take the bed. I will sleep—"

"On the floor, of course." He laughed at her. "You will sleep on the bed, Ariadne."

"Oh, no, Iden," she protested. "You need your rest."

"I will do very well on the floor," he insisted. "It holds no hardships for me. 'Tis considerably less pebbly than the cave. I beg you'll not dispute with me on this, for your arguments will not prevail. Besides, Madame Hecuba has promised us supper as soon as we are settled. I am hungry, are not you?"

"Very!" she exclaimed.

"Then, come."

Though it had surprised Iden, it was not surprising to Ariadne that their hostess and probably the two fishermen who had rescued them naturally assumed they were wed. Supper over and Iden down the hill conferring with Hector and Dimitri concerning tomorrow's voyage, Ariadne stood a few steps beyond the doorway to the cottage watching the villagers as they toiled up and down the steep hill. Some of them were girls, younger than herself, but in company with men who were obviously their husbands. One of the girls, shy, pretty, and fairer than her fellows, looked to be no more than fourteen or fifteen but she was already heavy with child. She paused a few feet away from Ariadne, regarding her with timid curiosity. Then, she was joined by a young man, who put an arm around her. The look they exchanged was warm and loving.

Flushing, Ariadne turned away. She felt lonely and bereft. On the morrow, she and Iden Peverell would be bound for Piraeus and their separate lives.

She was still thinking of that loving young pair when, at length, she settled down on the bed and looked at Mr. Peverell, wrapped in a blanket on the floor beside her.

He grinned at her. "Good night, Ariadne."

"Good night, Iden," she murmured, and was glad that he

fell asleep so quickly. Just for the nonce she could pretend . . . but it was a dangerous pretense, one that brought tears to her eyes and a touch of anger as she stared at his moon-gilded countenance and whispered defiantly, "I am *not* a child, Iden, and I love you!"

Ariadne had wept until she had no tears left, until her eyes were dry and aching. She had cried most of the three nights that had passed since she had arrived in Athens. Now, standing white-faced and tense in the small room that served as Sir Arthur's library, she confronted her grave-faced parent and actually wrung her hands. "I hate her," she said passionately. "He's not a rogue. He did not t-touch me. 'Tis all her fault!"

Sir Arthur held up his hand, "My love, this most unfortunate situation cannot be blamed on Miss Gore."

"No," Ariadne said, dully now. "I am mainly to blame, am I not. I never thought—"

"No more did I," her father interrupted. " 'Tis only when Miss Gore told me what was being said . . ."

"And I am sure that *she* agreed with their every word and called him, 'rogue' to all who would listen to her!" Moving to Sir Arthur, she clutched his hand. "Must I be here when they come? Oh, how, how can I face him or his father, knowing it was all my fault? Papa, I swear to you that he was the very soul of honor. And why would he not be? How could anyone think otherwise? Even if he were a rogue, which he is not, they must realize that he could never, never think on me as an object of desire! He thinks of me as a child. That is how he addressed me at all times—as child, child, child!" She stamped her foot. "Oh, I do not want to see him again. How can I face him? He'll not want it, I can assure you. Oh, 'tis all spoiled, and how you and Sir Marcus can insist—"

"My dear, that is enough," Sir Arthur broke in a second time. "We *must* put a good face on this matter—else your life will be blighted. Miss Gore, much as you may dislike and dispute her, is quite right. Unfortunately, young Peverell does not have the best of reputations and neither of you will be able to escape unscathed from this situation if proper steps are not taken. You will not be able to hold up your head in society. Already the trouble has begun. There were invitations—one from Lord Willoughby, an old friend of mine, who wished us to attend a dinner tomorrow. His wife has accompanied him to Greece and she has sent word that they will be unable to receive you.''

''I do not care a fig for them!''

''No more do I, and I am quite disappointed in Willoughby, but his attitude is a barometer of that which already prevails in Athens.''

''I do not care,'' Ariadne cried passionately. ''I do not care if I am never seen in society!''

''You are angry and hurt, my love, but you must care. This is your world. This is young Peverell's world, as well. Can you imagine that he wishes to be known as a despoiler of innocence? He is the last of his line, my love. He owes it to his heirs—''

''How can anyone imagine that he would want to despoil me of my innocence!'' Ariadne wailed. ''I tell you he does not think of me that way. And he is not a rogue. He married an Indian girl. I expect Society would have preferred it if he *had* despoiled *her*. That he did not renders him disreputable. It is all so confusing, and so utterly, utterly ridiculous!''

''Yes, I agree that it is ridiculous. I am quite sure that he does think of you as a child. 'Twas how he talked when he brought you here. However, as Miss Gore has pointed out, you are old enough to be married, and since he has agreed to marry you—''

''He cannot *want* to marry me!'' Ariadne moaned.

''He understands that after two nights in an island cave with a girl of seventeen, he has compromised you beyond all possible doubt,'' Sir Arthur said sternly. ''We can only be grateful that he has recognized his responsibility in this matter.''

Ariadne thrust her hands against her burning face. ''I will not marry him,'' she cried passionately. ''You cannot force me to it. You cannot!''

''That is enough,'' Sir Arthur said in tones so stern that she could scarcely believe that they were issuing from the mouth of her usually indulgent father. '' 'Tis all arranged. The ceremony will take place this evening.''

"No, I tell you, no, no, no!! You may . . . may scald me with boiling water, you may drown me in the sea, but I will never wed him, never, never, never!" Ariadne fled from the room and down the hall to her chamber. Opening her door as far as it would go, she slammed it shut with all her might before throwing herself onto her bed and bursting into anguished sobs.

'' 'Tis all my fault,'' she groaned. "All, all, all mine, and to . . . to repay his kindness so cruelly! If only I'd thought, but I never dreamed, never, never, never dreamed . . .''

Images Ariadne longed to expunge from her memory flowed inexorably before her inner vision. She could see herself and Iden aboard the small craft with its purple sail, a boat resembling an illustration from a book of mythology as it skimmed over the dark blue waters toward Piraeus. Iden had been helping the man sail it and she had been sitting toward the prow, gazing at the nearing shore. She had been, she recalled, more than a little regretful because their glorious adventure was drawing to a close. Yet, at the same time, she did long to see her father and alleviate his anxiety. He would, she knew, be suffering greatly over the supposed death of his only child. Iden, too, was anxious to assuage Sir Marcus's similar grief.

Then, they had arrived in port and there had been other English people present. Some among them were not new to the place. Word of the tragedy aboard *The Argonaut* had reached them and, upon learning the identity of the ragged pair who had disembarked from the small fishing sloop, there had been great excitement and numerous ladies had rushed to comfort her and to listen to the story of her rescue.

Another groan escaped Ariadne. In her mind's ears, she could hear herself gleefully explaining how they had reached Naxos; she had described the cave and Iden's finding them food. Had she called him Iden? She had. Had she actually compared herself to the stranded Ariadne of old being rescued by Dionysus, God of Wine, a libidinous diety whose reputation was far from spotless? Miss Gore had told her there were certain salacious sallies circulating through British enclaves in Athens regarding Dionysus and comparing him with Mr. Peverell in ways that added an extra degree of prurience to her experience. More tears filled Ariadne's eyes.

The door opened and Ariadne knew it was Minnie come to dress her for her wedding. Without looking at her, Ariadne groaned, "Oh, God, Minnie, why did I say anything? He might think I deliberately tried to . . . to make him m-marry me. Oh, God, I wish I were dead. I will never wed him, never in life. I will tell him so!"

"And he will ask you why you are so reluctant little Ariadne?"

A cry, half-muffled by her pillow, escaped her. Ariadne turned and looked up into the face of Iden Peverell. "Ohhhhh," she moaned again. "Ohhhhh, Iden."

"Child." He sat down on the edge of the bed. "Am I such a dragon, then?"

"A dragon?" She stared at him confusedly. "No, I did not mean *that*. But they insist that you . . . that we . . ." She broke off, staring at him woefully.

"They say we must be married, yes." He added with a whimsical smile, "We, you understand, are confronted by a Cerberus wanting a sop or, if you prefer, a triple-headed Mrs. Grundy, who is shaking the banner of Public Opinion in our faces."

"How can you make light of it?" she cried. "You cannot agree with Papa or . . . or Sir Marcus!"

"As to that, we will discuss it presently, but first I want you to wash your face and change your gown. Then, you must meet me in the hall within twenty minutes or however long it takes. I would like to take you for a walk. Your father has told me you've not yet seen the Acropolis."

"No, but . . ."

"Then, we must rectify that omission immediately. You should not have been here two days without visiting it. Fie, and you a Greek enthusiast, child."

She blushed. "I have not been out much," she mumbled, adding hastily, "I . . . I've not been feeling the thing, but I am better now."

"I am glad of that, my dear." He rose. "I will be waiting for you." He patted her on the shoulder and left the room, closing the door softly behind him.

Her mind was in a turmoil. The encounter she had so dreaded had passed off more easily than she would ever have deemed possible! She had, she realized, been terrified of meeting him again and reading accusation in his eyes, accusation and anger, if not downright fury at the position in which she, with her artless confidences, had placed him. Yet, he had seemed marvelously unaffected by their predicament. He had actually suggested a walk. He had not appeared to realize that the reason she had not yet visited the Acropolis was that she feared to meet English travelers. According to Miss Gore, there were quite a number of them in Athens. Some, like her father, were there to purchase antiquities while others were in the diplomatic corps and still others were there for pleasure. Again, according to Miss Gore, they were all acquainted with her scandalous adventure or, as the chaperone waspishly put it, "misdaventure."

Yet, here was Iden, willing to fly in the face of propriety by inviting her to come with him on a walk to the Acropolis. What could be his purpose? Surely, he did not intend that they should marry—no matter what her father said. No, he must have some other scheme in mind, but what? There was but one way to find out. She must steel herself against possible or rather *probable* snubs and accompany him. At least, if they did meet other English travelers, she would be with him and the slights less difficult to countenance. She slipped out of bed and rang for Minnie.

The way to the Acropolis was steep and her companion had warned Ariadne that it would be disappointing to view the ravages caused by centuries of battles as well as the depredations committed by professional and amateur souvenir hunters. "Yet," he had concluded, " 'tis one of the sights that cannot be missed. I had promised myself to visit it at the earliest possible opportunity—and with you, my companion in misery."

"But it was not all misery," she had dared to say, before realizing that he was not talking about their sojourn on Naxos but rather of their present situation. She had subsequently fallen into a silence he had not attempted to break, as they walked toward the hill with its massive crenelated walls over which the broken pillars and shattered roofs of the once-mighty buildings could be seen.

Yet, if she did not speak, her mind was crowded by conjecture and, at the same time, another part of it was detached enough to observe her companion and contrast his present appearance with his previous guise. In common with herself, he had retrieved his luggage from *The Argonaut* and nothing could have been brighter than the polish on his Hessian boots with their shining gold tassels. His dark hair was newly cut and again, or rather, as always, she admired that startling white streak which, her father had said, had not been caused by grief but was, instead, a birthmark. His high shirt collar was stiffly starched. His cravat was most intricately tied, and his claret-colored coat became him beautifully. His stockinette trousers clung to his well-shaped legs and he wore a curly brimmed beaver. To her eyes he was dazzlingly handsome and she felt uncomfortably dowdy beside him, who should have been accompanied by, at the very least, an Incomparable! Instead, he was walking beside a short girl in a plain muslin gown, wearing a wide-brimmed bonnet to shade a face she wished were hidden by a veil! Her only consolation was the fact that in the wake of the sunburn she had suffered on the island, her spots had almost disappeared! Her skin was darker, something Miss Gore decried, but it was almost clear! She wondered if he had noticed, and doubted it. Her musing was interrupted by the sudden appearance of Lord and Lady Ventriss, he a distant relation of the British Counsul. The couple were also friends of her father and had, on occasion, entertained him and herself at their estate in Berkshire. However, on this afternoon, they, neither of them, appeared to recognize herself or her companion, even though Mr. Peverell, who seemed also to know them, tipped his hat and murmured a greeting.

"Miles, dear," Lady Ventriss said to her husband, "do hurry, we should be home before noon." She deftly stepped around Ariadne and, followed by her spouse, who looked a bit more red-faced than he had before, went on down the hill.

"I suppose," Ariadne said in loud, carrying tones, "that she would have preferred it had I drowned."

To her surprise, her companion threw back his head and laughed merrily. "Or, as an alternative, been swallowed by some sea serpent? I am sure of it, my dear."

Ariadne laughed, too, but sobered quickly. "It was all my fault. If I'd had any sense—"

"Shhhh." He put a finger to her lips. "That water has already flowed beneath a bridge. Come, we are nearly to our destination." He indicated the hill. "It is unfortunate that the theater which lay there . . ." he pointed to a mass of ugly wooden shanties, ". . . is covered by those Turkish hovels which have sprung up like wild mushrooms."

"Toadstools," Ariadne corrected with a grimace as she looked at narrow alleyways filled with refuse and thronged with screaming, scrawny, dark-haired urchins, battered cats, and mangy dogs. She remembered having heard that the Turkish faith, forbidding all artistic representations of the human face, had moved some of its adherents to smash the visages of the Greek statues and bas-reliefs.

"They have no right here!" she said passionately. "They should go back to Turkey. Arrogant butchers!"

"You are right about that, my child, but . . ." Mr. Peverell guided her along the path toward the gates leading to the top of the hill, "I beg you will not air your opinions while we are in their hearing. Some speak excellent English."

Ariadne gave him a stricken look. His advice reminded her once more of her unwise description of his gallantry after their descent into the sea. "I am inclined to talk too much." She sighed. "But," she clutched his arm and looked up at him despairingly, "there is no need for you to suffer because of my folly. Oh, Iden, what are we to do?"

"We are to look upon what is left of these wonders of antiquity, my dear. Come."

There were Turkish guards at the entrance to the ruins, but Iden surprising Ariadne with his glib command of the Turkish language, brought her past them swiftly and in another few minutes they had gained the top of the hill.

The ground, she noted with regret, was strewn with stones, some of them were recognizable fragments of pillars and even of statues. She was even more regretful to find a Turkish mosque situated behind the pillars of the Parthenon.

"They had no right to put it there. 'Tis a desecration and . . ." She paused as she met Iden's eyes. She sighed. "You see, I am in the habit of speaking before I think, but," she added dryly, "I need hardly explain my failings to you."

A gleam of amusement brightened a gaze which had been very sober. "No, we know each other very well, I think, better than 'tis given to most who contemplate marriage."

She stared at him in utter shock. "You cannot *want* to marry me!" she cried.

He was silent a moment. Then, he said slowly, "No, child, I do not *want* to marry anyone, but marry I must. I have responsibilities and not only to you but to my family. I am an only son, an heir to considerable property and to a proud name. My father is old. He will not wed again and 'tis his dearest wish that the line continue." There was a bleak lool in his eyes as he added, "I have not always been a good son, but I have found that I do love my father and if I can grant his wish, I shall. You, my poor child, are in need of a husband. More specifically, you are in need of me to offer for you." He paused, and then continued, "I wish I could tell you that I am in love with you—but you are intelligent enough to realize that I am not. Also you cannot but be aware that love is not a prerequisite among us. We marry for family and for property. If we are fortunate enough to find someone with whom we are compatible, we are indeed blessed. I might mention, also, that my mother was not even consulted as to her preferences when she was promised to my father. It was a long-standing arrangement between their families."

"Papa has told me 'twas the same with him," Ariadne murmured.

"Yes, that happens more often than not. As I have said, love is seldom a consideration in our marriages, but compatibility is certainly to be desired. You and I have weathered a very difficult three days and I believe 'tis safe to say that we are and will be compatible."

"Oh, yes," she breathed.

"Then," his gaze grew intense, "you are not unwilling to be my wife?"

Words crowded to her lips, all the words of love she had longed to lavish upon him but, of course, she dared not utter them, not now. He did not love her. However, something Carola had once told her popped into her mind. She had been speaking of Lady Angelica Fairmont, a mutual friend who had been forced to marry an earl who had wanted the match even less than herself.

"And can you imagine?" Carola had said gleefully, "they adore each other. They are scarcely to be separated." She could think of another even more pertinent example. Her father had adored her mother so completely that he could not bring himself to marry again or even to take a mistress! She said with a calmness that belied her interior excitement, "I . . . I would not be unwilling."

"I see." He cleared his throat. "There is one thing more I must needs tell you, little Ariadne. We must wed, I think, but beyond that, I cannot go, as yet. I will be your husband in name alone for a certain period of time. You must know that I have suffered a great personal loss . . ."

"Your bride," she whispered.

He nodded and cleared his throat a second time, "My heart as well, I fear. It went with Radha. Her name was Radha, she was called after an Indian goddess, and was one in every sense of the word. I will not be able to replace her in my heart, I must tell you that. And I cannot be with you . . . immediately. You will remain here with your father and return with him to London. I have received messages from Calcutta which demand my presence at Hydrapore, a small Indian state. I have, as I think you are aware, a connection with the East India Company, and it is imperative that I leave very soon. I do not think that my business in Hydrapore will take longer than three or four months. However, it is necessary to take into account the time spent in traveling. A voyage from India to England takes at the very least four and a half months. Consequently, I think we must say that I will be gone the better part of a year. After that, I will remain in

England and we will contrive to be happy—if you agree to wed me in these circumstances." He took her hand. "Will you marry me, Ariadne?"

His words had meant very little to her. He was going away and a year was not really a very long time—and meanwhile, she could be with her father, here in Greece. She said softly, "I will marry you, Iden."

He bent and kissed her on the cheek. In a low voice, he said, "I am honored." He added, "Now, my dear, shall we stroll about and enjoy the Parthenon?"

"I should like that above all things," Ariadne said huskily.

PART II

Chapter One

Save for a few spindly chairs, the drawing room at Brynston House was nearly empty of furniture but, as a harried young footman remarked to a passing abigail, " 'Tis a wonder the place don't bust its seams wot wi' so many o' *them* present, 'n more to come's the word."

The abigail favored him with a lofty stare. "The thing's that you comin' up to London from the country, you ain't used to a proper rout, Charlie. 'Er ladyship's 'ad more 'n these wot are 'ere, I can tell you."

"Well, per'aps, but I don't know 'ow they makes themselves 'eard, such a babblin' as goes on. In fact, I could be in the Tower o' Babel itself, as was wrote up in the Bible."

His comment was overheard by Sir Iden Peverell who, in company with Sir Anthony Radcliffe, a friend from his years at Cambridge, had just come to the entrance of this crowded room. "The Tower of Babble indeed," he muttered in his companion's ear. "The lad's quite correct." He moved back into the hall, adding, "Stay with me a few moments before we plunge into that maelstrom." He cast a dubious eye at the assembly of fashionably garbed and for the most part distinguished-looking people, the "cream of the ton," according to Sir Anthony. This designation, however, held little interest for Iden. He had come in search of his wife who, according to her flustered companion, Miss Lottie Kingsmith, was present. He had a rueful glance for Sir Anthony. "I ought to have brought the Kingsmith woman with me—for I fear I will have some difficulty finding little Ariadne in there. I expect she must have changed in four years."

"Four years," Sir Anthony said disapprovingly. "Yes, I

do think that highly possible, Iden. 'Tis a long time to remain away."

"I am quite aware of that." Iden frowned. "And yet, that time seems to have sped past on winged feet. And actually, I had meant to return before this—but 'twas not possible. The affairs in Hydrapore were in a tangle."

"Is that not always the way with Indian affairs?" Sir Anthony demanded.

"At least in Hydrapore," Iden admitted ruefully. "And yes, I would say that 'tis a microcosm of all India. But be that as it may—my work's nearly at an end. One more journey and I am out of the Company." There was a tinge of regret in his tone as he continued, "I had planned to settle down with Ariadne. I must say I did not anticipate her request for an annulment."

His friend gave him a narrow look. "Did you think of her at all?"

"I did." Iden spoke defensively. "I wrote to her."

"As often as you wrote to me?" Sir Anthony inquired.

"A little oftener, but, as you know, there were times when 'twas impossible to write."

"I understand—but did she?"

"Well, I could not be too explicit in my letters—one never knows how many eyes will see them. I expect I have no leg to stand on when it comes to the annulment. 'Tis rather a pity. I know I must have hurt her grievously by my seeming indifference. And she was a taking little thing, not at all pretty, but intelligent. I did like her, but, of course, that was as far as it went. I expect I cannot blame her for wanting to change partners, as it were."

"And who is her second choice?"

"As to that, we might as easily call him her first choice since, as you know, this marriage was thrust upon us by circumstance. But to answer your question, I do not know the name of my successor. She only mentioned 'a serious attachment.' She seemed mainly intent upon assuring me of the proprieties of an annulment as opposed to a divorce."

"And you say she is here?"

"So I was informed by Miss Kingsmith. I had told Ariadne

that I would wait upon her today, but I was late in arriving last night and slept late—so that when I came to the house, she was gone, having had this prior engagement. I am glad of that. She does seem to be getting about—judging from the numbers of invitations I found on the hall table. I feared that she might be very lonely after her father's death last year. I wish you knew her, Tony."

"I wish I did, too, but I have been living mainly in the country. I came to London only to discuss some matters with my man of business."

"No, that is not true," Iden contradicted. "You came because of kismet, or at least that is what they would say in India. 'Twas kismet provided you with an invitation to this rout and set you down upon the steps just as I was arriving with all manner of excuses upon my trembling lips."

Sir Anthony's gray eyes gleamed with laughter. "I accuse you of prevarication, Iden. I am sure those lips have never trembled!"

"They have and would have, facing Lord Brynston without a card to his rout. I am much in your debt, Tony."

"I have been in yours from time to time." Sir Anthony spoke warmly. He added, "You are looking well, Iden. And . . ." He broke off. "But here is our host."

"Sir Anthony." A tall young man with a pleasant face brightened by a welcoming smile, bore down upon them. " 'Tis good to see you, man. You've made yourself too long a stranger to this town. Is it so much more pleasant in the country?"

"I am beginning to find it thus, Brynston. I would like you to meet Sir Iden Peverell, who has just come back from another country."

"Peverell." His lordship's eyes widened and he looked at Iden with some interest. "That name's most familiar to me. You'd not be related to Mrs. . . . er Lady Peverell, who is a particular friend of my wife's?"

"I am of the opinion that I might be," Iden began, only to have a harried young woman come to his host's side and mutter something in his ear.

"Oh, Lord," Brynston groaned. "I am wanted. If you will

excuse me. And please, will you both not join the fray?'' He waved a hand at the crowded drawing room and, taking the young woman's arm, he hurried away.

''Your kismet is working again.'' Sir Anthony grinned. ''If your lady's a friend of Lady Brynston, I have a passing acquaintance with her, too. I will have her point out your wife—that is, if you do not encounter her first.''

Iden favored him with a rueful glance. ''It occurs to me that we ought not to be meeting in such a manner. I blame my impatience, but it has been four years, though until this moment, they have, as I mentioned to you, seemed no more than their equivalent in months. I wish I were at liberty to explain myself more fully, but unfortunately, I am not.''

''I imagine I understand.'' Sir Anthony gave him a long look. ''I have heard some odd rumors about those who are in the employ of the Company. But come, my dear fellow.'' He placed a compelling hand on Iden's arm.

Conversation in that vast room rose and fell like the tides of a mighty ocean, or so it seemed to Iden, who had been so long removed from London gatherings. Footmen bearing trays of ices or glasses of champagne moved among the assembled company. Occasionally he glimpsed a familiar face, but for the most part he was among strangers. He was beginning to wish that he had not obeyed the impulse he had mentioned to Sir Anthony. It was not right to seek out his poor little wife here, where his presence must give rise to considerable speculation and, for her, embarrassment and possibly anger.

He sighed. In the last year, he had been more and more eager to return to England. He was tired of India. The heat, the milling and fractious native population, the constant dangers to which he, by reason of his work, was constantly subjected had been very wearying, and now that he had accomplished what some members of the Company did not hesitate to term ''a miracle'' in Hydrapore, he wanted to shake its dust from his heels. He longed for the peaceful life he had once disdained. More to the point, the agonizing grief that had possessed him upon the death of Radha had, much to his surprise, faded to the point that the prospect of settling down with Ariadne was no longer onerous.

He remembered her as a singularly understanding girl. She was also brave and uncomplaining. Those were good qualities in a wife and if she were rather plain, that did not matter, either. Character was more important than beauty, for the former existed far longer than the latter. And, as he remembered telling her, the fact that they were compatible was also important. They had been most compatible, he recalled. It was a great pity that he had not made more of an effort to see her in the intervening years. It would have been difficult, given the time it took to travel to and from India, but it might not have been impossible. He wondered whom she had found to fill his place? Was her decision irrevocable? He wished he might see her now—but now was definitely not the time, and it would be better if he were to leave and visit her on the morrow. Impulsively, he turned and as he did, some of the liquid splashed from his glass. He heard a feminine voice say angrily, "Oh!" And then she added, "Sir!"

Iden turned hastily and found himself looking at a young woman who at that moment was futilely dabbing at a large red blotch on a pale blue gown which, he noted in that same instant, was shades lighter than the deep blue eyes she raised to his face. For a split second, he was speechless with a combination of shock and embarrassment, for she was quite the most lovely female that he had seen since the death of his wife. She was reasonably tall and very slender. Her hair, he noted appreciatively, was blue-black and wavy. Her eyes were slightly slanted, her mouth was red and full, and her complexion ivory pale. He could not keep staring at her, particularly when she was glaring at him. He did not blame her. The blotch on her gown was his doing, however inadvertent. "I am so sorry, ma'am," he said apologetically. "I was not aware that anyone was standing so near me. I pray I have not ruined your gown. But I fear I have and do hope you will let me replace it."

Her eyes narrowed and, much to his regret, her anger appeared to increase. However, she said merely, "My gown, sir, is not ruined beyond the ministrations of my abigail. Consequently, I thank you for your offer, but 'tis not necessary."

"I hope that is true, but if it is not, I beg you will give me your direction. I will write to you and perhaps you will let me know—"

"My dear, and Iden, well met, my dear fellow! You are returned, then." The speaker, a tall, fair young man, moved to the girl's side and smiled brightly at Iden.

"Sir Robert Heath!" Iden exclaimed in some surprise, but swiftly reminded himself that it was at least ten years since last they had met and circumstances do change. Obviously, Sir Robert's own circumstances had vastly improved. He wore garments that could only have been fashioned by one of London's fine tailors. The colors, gray and dark blue, complimented his complexion and his vivid blue eyes. His gaze seemed steadier than he remembered and there was no trace of the nervousness that some attributed to his always being a step ahead of his creditors and others to the fact that there was a streak of madness in his family. Be that as it may, he was evidently a most particular friend of the young woman, for her anger had abruptly faded and she was favoring him with a bright and, to Iden's mind, rather intimate smile. It was obvious that Sir Robert's undoubted charm had won him a real prize this time.

"It is good to see you again, Sir Robert," Iden said politely, if not truthfully. "You are looking well."

"I am well, Iden, particularly well now that you are returned!"

Iden regarded him with no little surprise. Though they had known each other tolerably well at Cambridge and though he had been one of several to fund Sir Robert when he was short of money, they had never been close enough to warrant so joyful a greeting—and how did he know that he had been out of the country? That was not difficult to guess. They had some friends in common. And since it behooved him to be polite he said with an assumption of cordiality, "I thank you. 'Tis pleasant to be in England once again."

"Robert," the young woman said peremptorily, "I see dear Carola over there. I've not spoken to her yet. I think . . ." She raised her eyes to Iden's face. "If you will excuse us, sir." She had another glance for Sir Robert, who seemed confused. "Come." She caught his arm and seemed on the verge of actually pulling him away.

"But, my dearest Ariadne," Sir Robert protested, only to have the young woman loose her hold on his arm and actually glare at him.

"Ariadne!" Iden said blankly. "You'd not be my . . . my. . ."

"Yes, Iden," she said icily. "I am your . . . wife, for the nonce. I am sorry that I failed to introduce myself immediately, for I did recognize *you*. However, though you need not concern yourself about my gown, we do have other matters to discuss and these, I think, must be in the presence of my solicitor and my fiancé, Sir Robert here."

"You!" Iden stared at Sir Robert. He said incredulously, "You are planning to wed my wife?"

Sir Robert reddened and said with considerably less cordiality, "In view of the circumstances attendant upon your marriage and its aftermath, I hope you will offer no objections."

Before Iden had an opportunity to reply, Ariadne said caustically, "How can Iden object, Robert, when we are giving him the freedom he must desire so ardently and without the onus of a scandal, since all here are cognizant of my situation." She raised stormy blue eyes to Iden's face. "I was told you were searching for me, sir. I imagined you wanted to fix a time for the meeting I have mentioned."

Iden had a sudden vision of a famous painting of St. Stephen, reproduced in a book of drawings he owned. It showed the saint uncomfortably pierced by arrows in several vital spots. He had no difficulty in relating the image to his present condition even though he must needs admit that some of those arrows were the result of his own untoward actions and consequently released by his own bow. However, this was not the time to think in metaphors. In fact, his thoughts were in such a turmoil that thinking or, rather, pondering must be put aside until such time as he was better rested and alone. He said, "Yes, I should like to meet with you, Ariadne. However, I think we should also talk privately."

"Do you indeed, sir?" she questioned crisply. "I, on the other hand, find myself in disagreement. I am of the opinion that anything we might need to say to each other can be done in the office of my solicitor. If you will be kind enough to tell me when you are free, I will make the necessary arrangements. I will, of course, require *your* direction so that I can send a message stating the time and place."

"I am at your disposal," Iden murmured.

If the look he received from Ariadne's brilliant eyes had been a bolt of lightning, he would have been slain in an instant, he thought regretfully. She said, "And you, Robin."

Sir Robert flushed. "You know that I am always at your beck and call, my dear."

"Very well, since Iden must have a great deal to occupy his time, he being so rarely in this country, I think we should schedule our meeting for eleven o'clock tomorrow morning. Would that be convenient, sir?"

"Of course," Iden replied. "You have but to give me his name and his direction."

"His name is Henry Lanyon and his offices are on Fleet Street Number 9," she said crisply. "If you will excuse us, sir, I must join Carola." She turned away and, followed by Sir Robert, who had a slightly nervous smile for him, moved through the gathering and was lost to sight.

Iden, looking after her, had sensations similar to those he had had when he had received a hard blow in his solar plexus. There was the same breathlessness and the same chaos in his brain coupled with an inability to concentrate on the matter at hand. He took a deep breath and, releasing it, took another, before turning toward the door. However, even before he had taken a step toward it, he remembered Sir Anthony. He ought to find him, but he was in no condition to search for him amid this gathering. He had to get out, out into the fresh air! He sent a harried glance around the room and fortunately found Sir Anthony standing a few feet away, chatting with an older woman who, even more fortunately, moved away just as he reached them.

"Tony," Iden muttered, "I must go. Would you mind coming with me?"

Sir Anthony regarded him with some concern. "You look a bit pale, Iden. What's amiss? I hope you've not been taken ill?"

"No, I have, however, sustained a shock."

"Really? Might I ask what happened?"

"I will tell you once we are away." He cast a harried glance toward the door.

"Were you able to find your wife?"

"Yes," Iden said impatiently. "I have spoken to her. We'll meet tomorrow with the happy bridegroom-elect and her solicitor. That is the plan."

"I see, then what's amiss?"

"Will you come with me so that I might tell you? I would prefer to have you come with me to Grillons, where I am staying."

"Do you not have a house here in London? I thought—"

"I do," Iden interrupted. " 'Tis on Charles Street, but it has been closed since the death of my father." His face darkened. "The letter informing me of his demise did not reach me until five months after he breathed his last. I did not even know that he had been so ill—but I presume my lady-wife thought that my failure to attend him could be attributed to sheer negligence!"

"You are sounding uncommon bitter, Iden. Am I wrong in assuming you had words?" Sir Anthony regarded him quizzically.

"*She* had words, Tony. I listened. I'll tell you the whole of it, but please let us take our leave."

Staring into the flames that blazed in the fireplace of his cozy parlor at Grillons Hotel, Iden finished relating his encounter with the young woman who had proved to be his wife.

Sir Anthony broke the short silence that followed by saying, "I saw a tall and most beautiful girl in a pale blue gown. From your description, I am sure 'twas your wife. One could not miss her."

"True," Iden groaned. "Who would have thought . . ." He ran a hand through his hair, tugging at the white lock, a habit with him when disturbed. "God, it brings to mind those old tales of changelings."

"But changelings were ugly . . ."

"Exactly. It's as though she had been spirited away to fairyland at birth and brought back by some miracle, but I grow unkind. My wife—I am talking about the child I wed—was below average height, she was spotty as to complexion though her features were good—but why go on? The transformation is remarkable. She was angry because I failed to recognize her—but how could I have recognized her?" There was a plaintive note in Iden's voice.

"By returning to these shores more often," Sir Anthony murmured.

"Lord, Lord," Iden sighed. "My sins of omission have come home to roost, right enough. And now she'll wed that damned loose screw, Sir Robert Heath, blast his eyes. Can she not see that he's naught but a fortune hunter?"

"I do not know as I would term him a fortune hunter now," Sir Anthony said.

Iden glared at him. "And how would you term him, might I ask? You knew him at Cambridge, too, and how often did you lay out your blunt to keep him from Debtor's Prison? And do you remember the occasion when he, in all seriousness, insisted he saw a ghost in King's Chapel?"

"He was a bit imaginative," Sir Anthony agreed. "However, I understand he has expectations, a rich uncle. And I've never known him to pursue an heiress for his own gain. That he's a spendthrift's true enough, but you mustn't let your jealousy cloud your vision."

"I am not jealous!" Iden flashed. "I am merely being protective. Whether he intends it or not, Robert will spend her money as he did his own—and his expectations cannot approach her fortune, which is immense!"

"Then, it should be immense enough to sustain Sir Robert," Sir Anthony said reasonably.

"Tony, whose friend are you—mine or Robert's?"

"Yours, of course, Iden. I am but playing devil's advocate."

"I beg you'll cease that game. I cannot like it." Iden leaped to his feet and took a turn around the room. "Oh, God, what am I to do?"

He received a pitying look as Sir Anthony said, "I do not know, Iden. If only it had not been four years."

"I tell you . . ." Iden began and stopped. "If only she'd let me see her. She used to care for me. It was very evident. But now she looks upon me as if I were her enemy!"

"I am not trying to play devil's advocate when I tell you that your actions or rather the lack of them are to blame for that."

"I know . . . I know . . ." Iden groaned. "I cannot offer you any arguments on that score. But look at it from my perspective, Tony. Four year ago, I was close to despair. Radha had died after six short months of happiness. She was my first love and, I thought, my last. I never expected to be attracted to another woman. Then, there was the voyage, the accident, and I was on an island with a child—"

"Four years ago," Sir Anthony interrupted, "she must have been seventeen or eighteen. I judge her to be twenty-one or -two, now. Consequently, she was not a child, Iden."

"No, she *was* seventeen, but she seemed much younger than her years. She didn't kindle any flame of desire in my breast, I can tell you! She was, however, bright and, on occasion, amusing. I liked her. I've told you that. Then, we were rescued and she chattered about our experiences to the point that she would have been completely ostracized from society had I not given her my name."

"The which you must have resented."

"Yes and no, Tony. I did not want to be wed, but my father favored the match and so did Sir Arthur. I was positive that no one could ever take Radha's place in my heart, certainly not little Ariadne. However, she came of good stock and I thought that in time I'd be pressed to wed in any case because of my responsibilities as the only son of the house. Therefore, I yielded to argument readily enough. I liked her and we were compatible. I told her I would not be able to assume the role of husband immediately."

"You did not, I imagine, explain that you would have to wait four years."

Iden shook his head, "No, of course I did not tell her that. I anticipated . . . but why go on." He sighed. "If only there were more time—but tomorrow at eleven, I am expected to resign my rights. *Tomorrow*, Tony, and she'll not see me before or after the appointed hour."

"You could storm the citadel," Sir Anthony said facetiously.

"I wish I might."

"Unfortunately, the days when you could put a lady-fair across your saddle bow and gallop into the night are gone."

"They are, yes." Iden groaned.

"Yet, you seemed resigned to the idea of an annulment not two hours since."

Iden reddened. "I did not know that she had chosen Sir Robert two hours since. If she had informed me as to his identity, I might not have been so sanguine."

Sir Anthony emitted a short laugh. "I put it to you, Iden, that two hours since you were not only uninformed as to your successor's identity, but you'd no idea your wife had emerged from her chrysalis and developed butterfly wings."

"I will not deny it. She *is* uncommonly beautiful." Iden had a despairing look for his friend. "Tony, she has something of the quality of Radha! Her coloring is similar, too, save that Radha's eyes were dark. Radha's skin was golden, but not much darker than that of Ariadne. And there is something about her . . . God, must I give her up without even a chance of getting to know her?"

" 'Whoever loved who loved not at first sight?' " Sir Anthony murmured.

"Do not shame me with Shakespeare!" Iden said testily.

" 'Tis not Shakespeare, 'tis Marlowe. *Hero and Leander* to be exact, though I believe Shakespeare quoted the line in *As You Like It*. He had a habit of quoting or borrowing, as the case may be."

"Blast you! Can you think I want to discuss literature?" Iden growled.

"Very well, we'll talk of Ariadne, who is not Radha, Iden. And beauty is as beauty does. She does appear to have a bit of a temper."

"She's spirited." A gleam of amusement lighted Iden's somber eyes. "I do not like her any the less for that. Regrettably, I deserve the reception she accorded me. However, in my opinion she is far too spirited for the likes of Robert Heath. He seems completely under her thumb. Damn, I will not stand idly by and see her wed that . . . that poor excuse for a man. She's my wife, and possession's eleven points of the law!''

"Until eleven o'clock tomorrow morning," Sir Anthony reminded him.

"I will not meet her tomorrow morning," Iden retorted. "I'll send a note explaining that, after all, 'tis not convenient. I will insist that we meet in private."

"Supposing she refuses?"

"I'll make my agreement to the annulment a factor in her acquiescence. I'll further explain that I'll not countenance the presence of a third person at our meeting."

"I fear she'll not receive that demand with equanimity."

"I am sure you are right." Iden's eyes were sparkling now. "However let me give you another quotation, 'Nothing ventured, nothing gained.' "

Chapter Two

"My dearest love!" Lottie Kingsmith, a frail, pale woman of some forty summers, ran a nervous hand through her faded blond hair. She turned even paler as a china vase shattered against the serene marble countenance of one of the two caryatids bearing on their heads the wide marble mantelshelf over the fireplace in the library of Lady Peverell's London house.

The hurler of that ornament glared at her. "How dare he?" she demanded roundly. "But . . ." she stamped her foot, "I should not be surprised. Do not," she snarled, "do not, I charge you, pick up the pieces."

"But my love, it could be mended."

"I do not want it mended. Let it remain as shattered as my so-called marriage! 'Tis not *convenient* for him to meet me this morning! How dare it not be convenient for him to meet me after . . . after . . . Oh, it does pass all understanding! He *agreed* to meet us. He gave me his word! Damn and blast him, how long will he continue to cast his shadow across my life? How long, I ask you?"

"I am sure I do not know, my love, but—"

"How could you be expected to know? Do not be ridiculous, Lottie. 'Twas a rhetorical question!" Ariadne took a turn around the room. "The audacity of the man. Do you note how he addressed me? 'My dear wife!' Wife, indeed!"

"He . . . he is within his rights, my dear," Miss Kingsmith began.

"I beg you'll not prate to me of *rights*!" Ariadne cried furiously. "He renounced those rights three years ago, when he failed to return after his stipulated year!"

86

"He explained—"

"Oh, yes, he explained, did he not? I expect poor Papa told you of his letter saying that he must needs be away a little longer due to the . . . the turmoil in the province of . . . of wherever he was at the time. We will allow him three more months for his so-called peacemaking efforts. We will not allow him three years and three more months. That we will not do, Lottie."

Meeting a vengeful blue glare, Miss Kingsmith said placatingly, "He must have had his reasons, my love. He seems a very well-spoken young man." She quailed at fresh fire from Ariadne's eyes, but figuratively girding her loins against this blaze, she dared to add, "And I thought him uncommonly handsome, also."

"I cannot agree with you!" Ariadne snapped. "What a romantic idiot I must have been, idealizing that scoundrel. Everyone was agreed that he was a rogue, you know. I happen to think that his appearance has changed considerably and *not* for the better! He's much darker than I remember. I cannot abide dark men, as you know. And he looks much older, also. There are deep lines on his forehead and around his eyes. Of course, he is not young. He can give me ten years."

"Thirty-one is not particularly old, my love. He's about the age of Sir Robert, I think," Miss Kingsmith murmured.

"He is a year older than Robert and looks as if he were at least five years his senior. 'Tis a miracle I recognized him!"

"He is quite distinctive-looking, I think," Miss Kingsmith dared to comment.

"You are besotted, Lottie. One can meet his like on . . . on any London street and . . . ." her bosom swelled, ". . . he ruined my gown. Rosie says she can do nothing with it!"

" 'Twas an accident, my love."

" 'Tis not an accident that he seems bent on ruining my life, as well," Ariadne said with a logic her companion found more than a little questionable. "Does he intend to keep me waiting for another four years before I can finally be free of him?"

"My dearest, you are being unreasonable. He only asked to see you in private."

"I do not see why he must needs see me in private. I do not want to see him at all!" Ariadne stamped her foot. "How dare he make demands on me? He did not even know me, Lottie!"

"Well, my love, you have changed—and considerably—in the three years that I have known you. You are much taller—"

"Spare me a recital of the differences. He ought to have known me and would have known me if he had had the decency to come home any time in the last four years and three months! He did not even return for his poor father's final illness!"

"Well, I expect that it took a long time for the news to reach him, my love."

"Possibly! I will allow him that, but as for the rest . . ." Ariadne's indignation increased. "Oh, Lottie, how dare he come here and make these arbitrary demands. He is totally without principle! The sooner I am freed of this odious encumbrance, the better it will be for me!"

"Then, I suggest you accede to his request, my love."

"No," Ariadne cried. "I do not want to see him alone. Why does he demand it?"

"My dearest, I suspect you of being purposely obtuse. It has been four years and a little over, after all, and doubtlessly he has a great many things he wishes to discuss with you, in private. I cannot see that that is so very hard to understand."

"I do not wish to hear anything he has to say," Ariadne retorted. "I do not trust him!"

"Ar-i-ad-ne!" Miss Kingsmith turned a shocked face toward her. "I know that you are angry with Sir Iden and I will never dispute your reasons for that—"

"I am less angry than indifferent," Ariadne interrupted.

"Be that as it may, my dearest, you've no reason to distrust him. And he is still your husband!"

"I beg you will not continue to refer to a relationship that has no basis in reality. Oh, God!" Ariadne ran her hands through her hair. "I expect I must needs grant his request. But I cannot imagine what he wishes to say to me. I assure you 'twill be nothing I wish to hear! However, if only to expedite matters for poor patient Robert and myself, I will write to him." She moved to a small rosewood desk and, sitting down, she added, "You need not remain here, dear Lottie. Why do you not go and have some tea?"

"As you wish, my love." Miss Kingsmith glided out of the room and sank down in a chair just beyond the door. The session with Ariadne had been very wearing on one who was, in temperament, pacific. In fact, she wondered at the audacity that had prompted her to argue with the girl. On another occasion, her retiring nature must needs have asserted itself and put a bridle on her tongue. These were, however, unusual circumstances!

Though it had been reprehensible of Sir Iden to remain away for so long a period of time, there *were* reasons for that. There was his connection with the East India Company, something she did not quite understand but which, she had heard, did have its dangerous aspects. There was also the fact that he had been constrained to offer for one whom, according to Sir Arthur, he considered a mere child and, Miss Kingsmith recalled, a rather unprepossessing child at that!

She had no difficulty in understanding this point of view. Having replaced Miss Gore some three years and two months ago, she was still amazed at Ariadne's late and lovely blooming. In that space of time, she had changed almost completely. She sighed. It was a great pity that Sir Iden had not been present to witness the unfolding of a blossom that bid fair to be plucked by another. She grimaced, thinking of Sir Robert Heath.

Even given her own lively prejudices against Sir Iden, she could not help contrasting the man with Sir Robert. If they had been dogs, she could envision Sir Iden as a fearless hound and Sir Robert as a poodle, "all bark and no bite." The phrase drifted across her mind and her anger at Sir Iden's cavalier treatment of his wife took a different turn. He ought to have returned earlier if only to save her from the likes of Sir Robert, whom she could not admire. He was too soft by half. Ariadne already had him under her thumb. She could prevail upon him to grant her every wish. Despite his expressed disapproval, he had consented to take her to the masquerade at the Italian Opera House this very night. And on other occasions he had, though under protest, accompanied her to equally questionable places such as Vauxhall Gardens and even to a Mill!

Furthermore, there was a certain nervousness in Sir Robert which put her on edge. She could not explain it, but she could not like it, either. And—her thoughts were brought to an abrupt conclusion as Ariadne, an envelope in hand, came out of the library.

"Ah, there you are, Lottie," she said. "I have agreed to see him at three this afternoon—here and without the presence of Sir Robert. Does that satisfy you?"

"I believe that is the wisest course, my love," Miss Kingsmith murmured, thinking privately and regretfully that Ariadne's acquiescence, given under duress, would mean very little when they finally confronted each other.

A few minutes before her meeting with Iden, Ariadne, waiting in the library, was once more ablaze with resentment. Feelings buried for the last three years had surfaced again, bringing with them the memory of the agony she had endured as day followed day without so much as a word from her "husband." Her late Aunt Isabel had called his behavior typical, saying that one could expect no more from a rogue of his cut. Her father, his own indignation increasing, had vainly tried to comfort her, to no avail. Only time could and *had* done that, and a life she had thought at an end had renewed itself, bringing it the intelligence that she was beautiful!

The realization had been very slow in arriving. For a long time, she hated her face, thinking it was her appearance that had driven Iden away. However, the actions of certain females who had called themselves her friends had helped to change her opinion. Helena Seabright, second only to Carola in Ariadne's lexicon, had not wanted to be seen with her in public, not after the time she had asked Ariadne to drive in Hyde Park at the fashionable hour of five in the afternoon and, much to Ariadne's amazement, a great many young men had ridden past Helena's barouche, their eyes on *her*. They had not seemed interested in Helena at all!

She had had much the same experience with Isobel Stanton, but, of course Isobel, once voted an Incomparable, had been

breeding, and consequently she had looked rather puffy about
the cheeks and there had been circles under her eyes. But
after the child, a son, was born, Isobel had remained cool and
so did other ladies, but each time Ariadne rode in the Park or
appeared at a rout or a ball, gentlemen clustered about her,
seeming not to mind that she was Mrs. Peverell. Ariadne
flushed, recalling the many veiled advances she had received.
Once, staying at an estate in the country, she had been
obliged to enlist the aid of Rosie, the abigail who had replaced Minnie (married now to her Mr. Quigley), to thrust an
enterprising gallant out of her bedchamber.

Robert, she thought lovingly, was different. He had never
made any improper advances. He had respected her from the
first and she, who had believed herself steeled against love,
had begun looking forward to his visits and deeply resenting
the other females with whom he danced at Almack's and
elsewhere. However, he had seemed to prefer her above all
others and that, coming from a man so attractive and so
popular with other ladies, had been balm to her wounded
vanity. In the last eight months, she had finally come into her
own and she fully believed it had been Robert's unabashed
adoration that had helped her to overcome her deep sense of
inferiority. He seemed to crave nothing so much as to be with
her. Yet, he was totally circumspect, never overstepping
boundaries set down by society, this even though he had
directed many an ardent look at her and had said on more
than one occasion that he longed to be more than her friend.
And now, due to Iden's belated return, he could be—and why
was this man, who had proved beyond all possible doubt that
he cared nothing for her, erecting these barriers?

"Why?" she muttered aloud, and took a nervous turn
around the room. If Iden felt nothing for her, she felt even
less for him. Indeed, she had the strange idea that she had
been split in two like a worm beneath a scythe. It was said
that when such a thing took place, two worms appeared to
exist, each wriggling off in an opposite direction. It was not a
pretty analogy, but it was apt. She had no connection with the
girl who had shared that cave with Iden Peverell four years
back and before he was an hour older, the man who called
himself her "husband" would know that.

Just for reassurance, Ariadne moved to the mirror that hung over the mantelpiece and stared at her image. She had dressed with care in a new gown, a turquoise blue kerseymere with the fuller body that was popular this season. She wore a gold necklace and dangling gold earrings, which with her ebony locks gave her an almost gypsy-like appearance, Miss Kingsmith had said dubiously. She had added that they were most becoming and had opined that Ariadne was looking her best. Now, staring into the glass, she, telling herself that she was not being conceited but merely truthful, could agree with Miss Kingsmith. Indeed, she was positive that she had never appeared to better advantage! It was lovely to be taller, too. She was almost at an eye level with Iden. She had noticed that yesterday afternoon. He would not be able to look down on her as he had four years ago—four years and three months ago—and he would never, never be able to address her as "child"!

There was a tap on the door. Ariadne stiffened and, much to her annoyance, swallowed a lump in her throat before calling, "Yes?"

The butler opened the door. "Sir Iden Peverell, my lady," he announced.

"Please show him in, Creswell," she said coolly.

A moment later, Ariadne was confronted by Sir Iden, who was looking very handsome in a dark brown coat, elegantly tied cravat, buckskin breeches, and dark brown boots. His dark hair, bisected by that white streak, had, she noted, a few tendrils that were similarly white, but the lines around his brown eyes that she had seen the previous night were gone. He looked much better rested and, damn him, he was smiling at her cordially. "My dear Ariadne, how well you are looking. 'Tis a most becoming gown." He bowed over her hand, brushing it with his lips, and then straightening, he stared around the room. "I see some of the sculpture you acquired in Greece, but not all of it."

"No, not all of it," she acknowledged. "Those few pieces you chose before you left us I have donated to the British Museum."

If she had hoped to wound him, she was unsuccessful. His

expression did not change. "I am sure they must have been grateful for the gift."

"They expressed their thanks. However, I am sure you have not come to discuss sculpture with me."

"No, I have come to see *you*," he said. "I hardly know how to begin."

"There is not much reason for this meeting, Sir Iden," she cut in.

"Surely, you need not address me as Sir Iden, Ariadne."

"You have come into the title," she said coldly.

"I have, yes, but we know each other better than that."

"Do we? Last night you failed even to recognize me, Sir Iden."

"You have changed considerably, my dear Ariadne. You notice," he smiled, "that I refuse to address you as Lady Peverell."

"That is as it should be, sir, since I shall not be using that title much longer. I am quite determined on the annulment. I feel that I have waited long enough."

He sighed. "As to that, Ariadne, I am indeed sorry that I was unable to return to London at an earlier time. However, I must explain that my next voyage to India will be my last. I am determined on leaving the service and I shall settle here in England. I had hoped that you . . . that we might be able to resume our marital status."

"Resume, sir?" she cried indignantly. "How might one resume that which has never existed?"

His steady gaze flickered and, for the first time, he seemed less at ease. "I once told you, I think, that I could not immediately assume the role of husband."

"And I accepted that," she flashed. "However, I do not accept three letters in four years! And—"

"There were more than three!" he exclaimed.

"If there were, they went astray. Your letters, those I did receive, were very interesting and informative, sir. I learned a great deal about bazaars and native costumes as well as elephants white and gray. There were also amazing portraits of Indian potentates. They were the letters one writes to a niece or a nephew yet in the schoolroom. I had left the schoolroom by the time I embarked for Greece aboard *The Argonaut*. I was not a *child*, I was seventeen which, if you will remember, was the reason you were constrained to give me your name, even though I told you 'twas not necessary. Well, I have since learned that I was in error. It was, indeed, necessary. With it, I had an entree to society. I am grateful for that, sir. It has enabled me to meet the man I love and intend to wed once the annulment is granted. I thank you for your acquiescence upon the occasion of our return to the mainland from Naxos.

"However, I find myself no longer in need of this beneficence and consequently, I would be pleased if we could come to an agreement as soon as possible. Sir Robert grows impatient, and surely you must concede that eight months is long enough for him to wait!"

Iden's smile had vanished. He looked grave and, Ariadne noted, regretful. That surprised her but, she reasoned, perhaps the late Sir Marcus Peverell had not been as wealthy a man as her father had seemed to believe. Probably it would be very difficult for her so-called husband to relinquish her properties. Of course, he would keep the dowry, but he might have spent that already. He said, "I know Sir Robert Heath."

"So he has told me. You were at Cambridge together."

"Yes, that's true." He paused. " 'Tis a pity your father died within two years of your return from Greece. If he were alive he might have—"

"My father was not in your corner when he died, if that is what you are suggesting, sir."

"No, that is not what I was suggesting. I was suggesting that your father might have given you some advice about the choice of a husband."

Ariadne's eyes widened. "Are you daring to . . . to criticize that choice, sir?"

"Sir Robert is not a wealthy man, Ariadne. He—"

"I know he is not a wealthy man," Ariadne said freezingly. "However, he is not wedding me for my inheritance, as you so delicately suggest. If he had wanted an heiress, he might have married the Honorable Angela Barret, who is not only beautiful but the sole heiress to . . . But we waste words, sir.

Robert loves me and I love him, *passionately*. In fact, I am exceedingly grateful that you did not assume your so-called obligations, because think what must have occurred had I met him after rather than before your return? I have, in fact, saved us all from a very nasty scandal!''

''If I had been here . . .'' Iden began, and then paused and shrugged. ''Very well, Ariadne, I will cease to interfere with the course of 'true love.' You may have your annulment. I am at Grillons. Make your arrangements with your solicitor and I will meet with you.'' He bowed. ''I will take my leave.'' Without waiting for her response, he wheeled and strode out of the room, closing the door softly behind him.

Stunned by the swiftness of his acquiescence, Ariadne felt very strange. In fact, she felt rather hollow inside and a little dizzy, too. However, those feelings soon passed, leaving her . . . she was not sure what. She had an urge to run out and tell him . . . no, not him, she was rid of him forever. She wanted to tell Lottie, but not yet. No, she would despatch a note to Robert first. He was extremely anxious over the outcome of her interview with Iden. He had been much against it, saying that Iden would, no doubt, attempt to blacken his name. She had assured him that nothing Iden could say would carry any weight with her. She moved to her desk and, taking out a sheet of paper, sat down and began to write.

Iden Peverell, closing the library door behind him, strode into the hall and in a few moments was outside on the sidewalk. He had turned in the direction of the cross street when a hand was put on his arm and his name uttered in quavering accents. Looking down, he recognized Miss Kingsmith's timorous countenance, rendered even more apprehensive at this particular moment. ''Sir, a . . . a moment of your time, I beseech you,'' she breathed.

''Miss Kingsmith!'' he exclaimed. ''Pray what is amiss?''

''Oh, sir . . .'' She cast a furtive look over her shoulder at the house. ''Please do walk up the street a short distance with me. We must not be seen standing *here*.''

Though he was hardly in a mood to be amused, he could not forebear a smile at a maneuver that smacked of the clandestine. "Very well, Miss Kingsmith," he replied, and quickened his steps.

Waiting until they were what she evidently considered a safe distance away, Miss Kingsmith said, "This will suffice, sir. I will not keep you long, I promise you."

"I have time," he assured her. "My meeting with my . . . wife was brief."

" 'Tis your own fault!" she burst out. "Oh, why did you not communicate with her earlier, see her earlier? You might have saved her."

His eyes narrowed. "Saved her from what, Miss Kingsmith? I fear I do not understand you."

"From herself!" Miss Kingsmith spoke with a mixture of rue and pain. "She is so headstrong, so foolish. She takes such chances and will surely come to grief one of these days. 'Twas different when her father was living, but now that she's alone—"

"She'll not be alone for long," Iden interrupted. "She will soon be wed to Sir Robert Heath."

"Sir Robert Heath!" Miss Kingsmith actually snorted. "Can you think she will heed him? She has him wrapped around her little finger. Tonight's a case in point. Even though he strongly disapproves of the undertaking—he did argue with her about it—he has agreed to it. He rides with too loose a rein and will always let her have her head, no matter how high the fence."

"I fear I do not follow you, Miss Kingsmith. Are we discussing Ariadne or a fractious mare?"

"They are mighty similar, sir," Miss Kingsmith said miserably. "Fancy, he has agreed to take her to the Opera House Masquerade tonight!"

"No!" Iden exclaimed in a surprise edged by shock. "That is no place for her!"

"So I have told her and Sir Robert also, but she will go. They do have a box and I can only hope that she will remain in it."

"She should not be seen there!" Iden frowned. " 'Tis the height of folly!"

"I am sure that is what adds spice to the evening for her. She has even had a costume made."

"What manner of costume?"

"She will be going as a nun, but in a scarlet satin habit—and mask, of course. Sir Robert will be garbed as a monk in black satin. They will be leaving at eleven o'clock. And suppose they get separated—anything could happen." Miss Kingsmith raised her eyes to Iden's face. She repeated pointedly. "Anything could happen, Sir Iden."

"You are suggesting . . ." he began.

"I am suggesting, Sir Iden, that Sir Robert Heath is not the husband for her, not when she is already wed to someone who could control the reins."

"Control the reins?"

A faint color glowed on her pale cheeks. "In moments of stress, I fear I use expressions learned in my youth. Until he came to grief at too high a fence, Papa was a noted horseman—that is, when his pastoral duties did not occupy his time to the exclusion of all else." She added wistfully, "I often rode with him. But be that as it may, sir, you once saved Ariadne's life. 'Twill not be of much use to her if she must spend it with the likes of Sir Robert Heath—who is all show and no weight."

He regarded her quizzically. "Why do you have such a prejudice against him, Miss Kingsmith?"

"Because I know the shoals that can rise in the river and which can wreck a slender craft," she said with a bitterness that surprised and, at the same time, touched him. "I must tell you that though Ariadne may have changed outwardly, there is much about her that remains the same, if only it can be reached. Oh please, Sir Iden, if you have any feeling for her at all, do not let yourself be discouraged by her uncompromising attitude. You have hurt her grievously, but still I am of the opinion that—"

He caught her hand. "You need say no more, Miss Kingsmith. I do understand. I will think on all you have told me and meanwhile, I do thank you for it."

"I am very fond of Ariadne, sir. But, I have delayed you long enough." She turned away.

"Please, you must let me accompany you back to your house."

"No," she protested. "All things considered, sir, 'tis best I return alone."

He bowed and bore her hand to his lips. "Good afternoon, then, and thank you, Miss Kingsmith."

She gave him a shy and fleeting smile. "Good afternoon, Sir Iden." She hurried away.

Iden, turned thoughtful, watched until she was out of sight before hailing a passing hackney. "Grillons, please," he said, but a short time later he changed his request to an address in Bond Street.

Some twenty minutes before midnight, Ariadne, in her scarlet robes and black mask, clutched Sir Robert's arm tightly as they entered the brilliantly lighted confines of the Italian Opera House.

"Oh," she said excitedly. "*This* will certainly be enjoyable!"

"I hope so, my love," Sir Robert said dubiously. " 'Tis a very long time since I have attended one of these festivities. They can be very rowdy, you know."

"I do know, but," she smiled up at him, "I have you to protect me."

"Just so, my love." He drew her a little closer. "We must," he added nervously, "get to our box."

"To our box . . . immediately?" Ariadne regarded him in surprise. "Why?"

"I think 'twould be wiser to view this vast assembly from afar." Sir Robert was sounding even more dubious. "You have but to look around you, my love, and I am sure you must agree with me. I fear 'tis a very mixed company."

"I am looking and listening, too." She pitched her voice higher in an effort to vie against the sounds around her. The scene that met her eyes was actually rather daunting. There was such a mass of people around her and in an astonishing variety of costumes! Gypsies, monks, sailors, pirates, Turks, knights-in-armor, maidens from all periods of history, clowns, and Columbines as well as many in plain dominoes and masks. Several bands were ensconced at various parts of the house and when one stopped playing another began. Cotillions followed waltzes, waltzes gave way to country dances.

The boxes were full of merrymakers and some of them, she

noted, seemed very drunk. Though she had determined that she would not be shocked at anything she might see, she felt a flush mount her cheeks as she saw several young females flaunting the thin, clinging muslins popular at the turn of the century. These gowns were cut very low and dampened to reveal every line and curve of the figure. Some of the girls were unmasked, their faces were painted, and their movements deliberately provocative.

Against her will, Ariadne was repelled by the way they ogled passing gentlemen, sidling up against them and whispering in their ears. As she watched, one young man gave his charmer a slap on the buttocks which sent her into loud giggles between which she scolded him in the ugly accents of Tothilfields. However, she yielded quickly enough when he drew her onto the floor. Watching them, Ariadne wished she had not come. She hastily pushed that thought away. She did love to dance and she had a particular reason for dancing tonight. Joy! She was finally free of Sir Iden Peverell!

He had given in much more swiftly than she had imagined he would. Probably, he had expected she would be the one to yield. He must have been sadly discomfited to find that she no longer worshiped the very ground he walked upon!

Unbidden, she recollected their wedding. She had not been able to take her eyes off him, she remembered bitterly. She had reveled in his handsome face, his tall, stalwart body, and his air of distinction. He had been even more fashionably garbed than when he had proposed to her, certainly a great contrast to the rags he had worn on the island. She could not believe her great good fortune in being wed to one whom she had had no difficulty in likening to the Greek god who had rescued the original Ariadne from despair on Naxos. Yes, she had actually counted herself among the favored-of-fortune because, at the combined persuasions of her father and his own, he had actually consented to give her his name.

Standing beside him as the minister spoke the words that bound them together, she had never felt quite so plain and dowdy. However he, as if conscious of her state of mind, had given her a brief smile and said, "The blue of your gown is a perfect match for the sky and your eyes, little Ariadne."

She had thanked him shyly, with a mixture of awe and love, because her most precious dream had been realized. She had married the man she loved. Had she really loved him? No, not really! She had been the victim of a foolish infatuation with a figment of her imagination! She had coupled him with the romantic heroes she had found in the pages of the books published by the Minerva Press. She and Carola had been wont to devour these novels, buying two or three sets at a time. The man she had married was barely aware of her existence, and he had removed himself from her presence even before the sun set on their wedding day. Oh, he had come to see her the following day and the next. He had taken her to visit some of the ruins in and around Athens. He had gone with her and her father on a buying expedition to Delphi, and that had been her so-called wedding journey. Then, he had left for India while she and her father had roamed through Greece, as they had originally planned. There was the tightness of anger in her throat as she recalled the lengthy period when she had expected to see him again. How long *had* it lasted? A year? No, it had been longer—almost two years before she had begun to give up hope.

A story from the Arabian Nights came back to her: "The Fisherman and the Genie." She could liken her feelings to those of the latter. Encased in his bottle, the genie had longed for rescue and had vowed that he would reward his rescuer beyond his wildest dreams, but as the centuries passed and none came to free him, his wrath increased. Consequently, by the time that the Fisherman inadvertently opened the bottle, the Genie had vowed that only the death of his savior could compensate him for his lengthy imprisonment.

She did not wish for Iden Peverell's death—but some manner of vengeance had been in order and she felt the better for having achieved it. Yet, she wondered if "vengeance" were the proper term for what had taken place between them? The fact that he could blithely remain away for four years and three months and then come to claim her as if that period of time had been four months, was indefensible. However, it also suggested that though he might be surprised and even slightly miffed at her dismissal, he could not be too cast down. Probably, he would, on his return from India, offer for some other female. Judging from the admiring looks he had received on the afternoon of the rout, which she had noticed even in her state of anger, he would have no difficulty in securing a bride. However, be that as it may, she *had* given him some food for thought. He would go back to India with a bee in his bonnet or, rather, a gnat in his hat, and would that it could give him the sting he so richly deserved!

"My dearest Ariadne," Sir Robert said in tones much louder than was his wont, "did you not hear me?"

She started and said apologetically, "I beg your pardon, Robin. What did you say?"

"I said that I think we must go to our box."

"Not yet," she protested. "Do let's join the dancers. They are playing a waltz."

"Very well," he said reluctantly. "But when it is concluded, I beg you will let me take you upstairs. I cannot like mingling with these rowdy cits!"

"Oh, Robin." She put a hand on his arm. "I beg you'll not be a spoil-sport. 'Tis such a lark being here. And I imagine that behind these masks there are a great many of the ton present. I admit 'tis a bit rowdy and I'll not want to come here again, I promise you, but since we are here, should we not enjoy ourselves? And my freedom? *Freedom*, Robin, I am free at last. He has promised it."

"But will he hold to that promise?" Robert asked nervously.

"I am sure of it. Oh, do look at *his* costume," she added as a tall man, dancing with a girl garbed as Columbina, came near them. He wore a long cloak embroidered with the sun, moon, and stars in gold on black velvet. However, what had really caught her eye was his gold mask, which covered his whole face. He had topped it with a black skull cap. "I do believe he must be a soothsayer," she giggled. "I wonder if he will tell my fortune!"

"My dear," Sir Robert expostulated, "I believe he has heard you."

Ariadne blushed as the man, disengaging himself from his partner, came to her side. "Mademoiselle," he said with a strong French accent, "I am not, *helas*, the fortune teller, *mais* I would very much like to dance with you."

"Well, I like that, I just say!" shrilled the Columbina and forthwith whirled away from him.

"Sir," Sir Robert said sharply. "You are annoying the lady."

"*C'est vrai, mademoiselle?*" The soothsayer stared down at Ariadne.

Ariadne, meeting dark eyes glinting from slits in the gold mask, found his gaze a trifle unsettling, but she said merely, "You are not annoying me, sir, but as you see, I have a partner."

"Ah, for that I am sorry! *Tu es très belle et . . .*"

"Will you take yourself off?" Sir Robert's voice had grown rather shrill. "Or must I . . ."

The man turned to him. "Or you will run me through with your so sharp sword, monsieur? Ah, but the monks, they do not wear swords, *n'est ce pas*? Still, I will go. *Au revoir, mademoiselle.*" Moving away, he was lost among the dancers.

"Damn him." Sir Robert sent a lowering look after him. "I would very much like . . ."

"Oh, come." Ariadne laughed. "He only wanted to dance with me, which it seems you do not."

"I do, of course I do, my love, but 'tis so crowded on this floor."

"The waltz is nearly to the end. 'Twill be over soon and I promise you I will go to our box."

"Very well, my dearest," he said reluctantly and, taking her in his arms, joined the other dancers.

The floor was crowded but, to his credit, Robert did manage to keep from grazing the other waltzing couples. Ariadne smiled up at him. He was supremely graceful and his half-mask did not disguise the fact that he was also very handsome. She did wish that he were a little more masterful, but he had other qualities that pleased her. She did enjoy being with him. And she could count on his remaining with her, not dashing off across the world. He . . .

"Ah-oof!" Uttering a shocked exclamation, Robert unexpectedly stumbled and fell heavily against her so that Ariadne, taken unawares, lost her balance and was thrust against another couple, who were similarly thrown to the floor.

"Ooow, my 'ip, it be 'urt," the woman wailed as Ariadne, attempting to extricate herself from the fallen foursome, felt someone help her to her feet.

"Wot's this?" A man in a pirate's costume rose up, glaring at Robert, who was still prone on the floor. "Wot 'appened 'ere? You bosky?" Some other dancers had stopped midstep and were gathering around them, but most merely laughed and continued waltzing as if such occurrences were the rule rather than the exception, Ariadne thought ruefully as she stared confusedly at Robert, now rising.

His mask was half off and as he stood up, the pirate clamped a hand on his shoulder. "Wot d'yer mean, knockin' us down?"

"My good man," Robert said in a shaken voice, "I do not—"

"Don' yer 'my good man' me," the pirate growled. "Yer foxed!"

"Please . . ." Ariadne started toward them, only to be wrenched back by a hard grip on her arm. "Your friend, he will be in trouble, mademoiselle. Come . . ."

Startled, Ariadne looked up to find the man in the golden mask at her side. With a mixture of surprise and annoyance, she said, "I thank you for helping me to my feet, sir, but I must see to my fiancé."

"It is best he see to himself, mademoiselle." To her surprise and annoyance, he drew, or rather, pulled her back from the group that was growing in size as the belligerent man in pirate's costume confronted Robert. "Let us wait at the edge of the floor, *oui*? There is bound to be trouble."

His grasp was so strong and he sounded so insistent that she was beginning to be frightened. However, it would never do to let him guess her state of mind. Straining against him, she said imperiously, "I do not wish to go anywhere with you, sir. Now, will you have the goodness to loose me? If you do not, I shall scream!"

He laughed. "And who will hear you, mademoiselle? I will say that you are foxed, *oui*? Come . . . *maintenant* we will dance." Moving in time to the waltz, he pulled her into the midst of the other dancers, whirling her around so quickly that she hardly knew where she was. And suddenly they were at the edge of the floor.

"Help me!" she screamed loudly. "Robert, Robert, where are you? This man is abducting me!" Unfortunately, her captor's words had proved prophetic. One or two of that riotous crowd stared at them and then, laughing, turned away as he drew her toward a curtained alcove.

"Where are you taking me?" she cried, truly frightened now. He was so very tall and his grip on her arm was so strong. She screamed again and knew that her cry was lost amid the laughter and the music that echoed through the vast auditorium. Then they were in the alcove and the man who clutched her was saying, "A thousand pardons, mademoiselle, but I have no other choice."

"You . . . you are mad!" Ariadne quavered, and in that same moment felt a sharp blow to her chin. She knew a second of utter terror before bright spots danced before her eyes and darkness engulfed her, blotting out sound and thought as well.

Chapter Three

Ariadne, awakening to an unfamiliar but, at the same time, oddly familiar motion, opened dazed eyes on darkness and was completely disoriented. She had a vague memory of another awakening. Her chin had ached and she had been told to breathe deeply. She had done so and had smelled an odor for which she had no name. It had been heavy and afterward there had been dreams, vivid but jumbled, filled with faces resembling those one saw in clouds or smoke. These had changed with that same rapidity, but now that consciousness had returned, she recalled one face that did not change, could not change, because it was a mask, a golden mask, expressionless but terrifying! Then she recalled the dance floor at the Opera House and Robert's falling—so odd for him to fall, he who never made a clumsy movement!

A moan of terror broke from her as she remembered more, remembered the man in the cloak emblazoned with the sun, moon, and stars. *He* had worn the mask and he had hurt her—had struck her.

She raised her hand, or would have raised it but could not because it was tied down. She tried to move her feet but they, too, were tied—bound rather, bound together, and herself lying on something soft, a bed, but not a bed because it was rising and falling. And it was so dark—why was it so dark? And where was she? A cry rose in her throat but could not escape because there was something about her mouth. She was bound and *gagged*, and where was she and what was happening and why did she still experience that strange movement? It was a familiar movement. She had known it before, the rising and falling and with it a creak of timber—a ship?

Impossible! No, she could not mistake that movement. But she had to be dreaming! How could she be on a ship?

She was not dreaming. She was on a ship. There was a familiar odor in her nostrils: saltwater, brine. There was knowledge lurking on the edge of her consciousness. She did not want to understand what had happened, but there was no avoiding that understanding. She had been abducted by the man in the golden mask—the Frenchman! Why, why, why? Her terror mounted. Tears rolled down her cheeks. Fear became frenzy! She tried to move, but she was bound so tightly and she was stiff. She must have been lying here a long time. How long? Hours? Days? And why? Sounds deep in her throat struggled for expression but were muffled by the gag.

She stopped trying to make herself heard. And she must not give in to terror. That would avail her nothing. She had to think. Why was she here? She had been abducted. If she had been abducted, it must be for a reason. Money. Her captor was holding her for ransom. Yet, the motion of the vessel seemed to obviate that theory. If she were being held for ransom, would it not be in England? But she must be in England on some waterway. A lake? A river? The sea? And her captor—who was he? She knew no Frenchmen. That did not matter. He was in the pay of someone. Who? And how did he know she was at the ball? And . . . her thoughts came to a sudden halt as she heard a cheerful whistle. Someone was whistling a tune from . . . *The Beggar's Opera!* The words came back to her.

> How happy could I be with either,
> Were t'other dear charmer away!

A vivid vision occupied the space back of her eyes. A rocky cave and Iden . . . Iden coming toward her.

"No!" the protest rose and died in her throat.

Light pierced the darkness, she blinked against it. It was coming closer and a voice, a familiar voice, which should not have been familiar, not anymore, said:

"Ah, you are awake then! I had hoped to arrive before that happened so that I could loosen your bonds. You must not be frightened, as I fear you are. You have, I know, a vivid imagination. And I shudder to think of the images your present plight has evoked. Suffice to assure you that you are in no danger. You are aboard *The Argonaut II*, which is an even sturdier craft than her sister ship. Our destination is India. We should reach it in four and a half months, or, possibly, four and three-quarter months, depending on the winds and tides.''

She stared at him in a fury laced with horror. A spate of words rose in her throat and escaped as only an unintelligible sound.

The light he was carrying was a ship's lantern and the way he held it illumined his face from below, giving him an almost devilish expression. He was a devil. More words arose and died in her throat.

"I expect," he continued, "that you will have a great deal to say to me. You will have a great deal of time to voice your objections to my high-handed or, if you prefer, underhanded methods. However, since for the moment you are rendered speechless, I'd best proffer an explanation. And, before you accuse me of abducting you, let me remind you that I am your husband. Still, you need not fear that I will exercise the rights our relationship allows. I will never presume upon that—er, area, unless you give me permission.

"As to why you are here—'tis my feeling that you need time to think ere you enter into an alliance with a man who might break your heart and will certainly waste your patrimony. You have known Sir Robert Heath for eight months. I have known him far longer. You know only one side of him. I have had the opportunity to examine other facets of his character.

"I might add, my dear Ariadne, that I would not have resorted to this unworthy stratagem had I not been summoned back to India far sooner than I had anticipated. I must needs deal with a crisis at Hydrapore. 'Tis a very small state, but its ruler occupies a surprisingly strategic position at least as far as we of the Company are concerned, and I am urgently needed.

"I will leave you now—with the intelligence that I have

the friendliest feelings for you and wish they might be recip-
rocated. Fortunately, I am enough of a realist to understand
that that is unlikely. I do hope, however, that your anger will
not sustain you for the length of a voyage which will not be
without interest.

"Ah, yes, I expect you are wondering how I managed to
spirit you away from the Opera House. You made that extremely easy for me—or, rather, Sir Robert did, by commit-
ting the great folly of escorting you to that highly questionable
entertainment. None with the exception of Sir Robert was
likely to notice your outcries—not there. An opera house
masquerade, mademoiselle, it is no place for the so-well-
brought-up *jeune fille, n'est ce pas?*"

Hearing the accent coating his tones, Ariadne's simmering
anger increased to full boil. That she could only express it in
a short explosive breath caused it to sizzle the more.

Meanwhile, he continued blandly, "Anything can happen
at these ill-conceived events and, as you have learned, it has.
However, I fear that if I go on talking, you will accuse me of
gloating rather than attempting to fill you in on various
aspects of your situation. That is not my intent. And I did
promise I would take my leave. And given your present state
of mind, I'd best leave the task of freeing you to Minnie.

"Yes, she is here, and has agreed to come on this voyage
out of her respect for you and her loyalty to me." He turned
away, starting for the door. Then, stopping, he turned back to
the bed. "I expect you would like to know where we are. We
have recently left the port of Gravesend and are on the open
sea. It is near nine o'clock in the evening on May 17th, in the
year of our Lord 1818—and if you wonder how you lost two
days, I must explain that I was regrettably forced to resort to
substances that induce sleep." With a slight inclination of his
head, he strode to the door and went out, leaving her in
darkness once more.

Words piled into Ariadne's throat but emerged only as
another unintelligible sound. Anger, more than anger, total
fury, the more virulent because it had been denied expression, swelled Ariadne's bosom and shortened her breath.
Conversely, mixed with the anger was a feeling of relief—

some of her fears had been allayed. She had not been abducted by some sinister stranger. However, that she was not going to be held for ransom or destined for a worse fate did very little to alleviate her rage. After four years of neglect, this man, this utter villain, had had the audacity to step casually back into her life and coolly abduct her from the very arms of the man she loved and who, unlike him, loved her! It surpassed all understanding and, indeed, his machinations hinted of the arcane—for *how had he known where to find her?*

She had been in costume, too—and wearing a mask. Robert, too, had been totally disguised! How had he managed to penetrate these disguises? There was an explanation, but one which seemed highly unlikely. Could he have had a spy planted in her household? No, impossible! He would not have had the time to introduce such a person, and her servants had known her from childhood! There was, of course, Lottie Kingsmith, but Lottie had often bemoaned what she had not hesitated to describe as "your husband's inhuman treatment." Consequently, how . . .

Impatiently, she shoved that futile speculation from her mind. She could not dwell on the confusing aspects of her plight. No matter how the abduction had been accomplished, she was her so-called husband's captive and she was bound for India on a voyage that must needs take a full third of a year and more! What would Robert think? Poor, poor Robert, ignominiously knocked down and overpowered at the ball! He must be frantic and he would remain in that condition, too. She could not get word to him and she doubted strongly that Iden had informed him as to what had happened.

Ariadne groaned. Why had she not recognized Iden's voice? She had a reasonable answer for that. In addition to his assumed French accent, it had been muffled by his mask and, furthermore, she had not heard it in four years. If she was not being entirely accurate, she had not really listened very closely to him at the ball or, for that matter, during the course of their interview. She had been far more attuned to her own interior angers. Furthermore, it had never occurred to her that he would be at the Opera House.

How, how, how had he managed to discover her where-abouts? Once more she cudgeled her brain as to how, how, how he had been able to learn so much about her movements on the night of the ball. Those frienzied speculations came to an abrupt end as she heard the door creak open. Once more there was light, a bright patch of it, reflected on the wall.

Ariadne managed to turn her head and saw Minnie, her pretty features illuminated by the glow from another ship's lantern.

"Oh, it do be a shame, I think. You must be so uncomfort-able, Miss Ariadne . . . milady." She set the lantern on a nearby table and, producing a large shears, hurried to the bed. "You'll be loosed in a second, milady." Carefully she snipped at the cords that bound Ariadne's wrists. "Oh dear, oh dear," she murmured. " 'E did tie these tight." She moved to the foot of the bed. "An' your ankles, too, but I'll 'ave ye free in a jiffy."

Ariadne felt a surge of gratitude. She had not anticipated any display of sympathy. Minnie, however, had been a friend as well as a servant. Ariadne had missed her sorely after she left to marry Edward Quigley. Evidently, Minnie still re-mained her friend. A tendril of hope stirred in her mind. Was Mr. Quigley on board? Could he . . . could they be per-suaded to take her ashore in a lifeboat? Perhaps? She could reward them amply!

"There." Minnie freed her ankles. "Ye'll be that stiff for a bit," she continued with an indignation spiced with regret. "I didn't 'old wi' this, I didn't. I told 'im so, but 'e was that set on it. I never saw 'im near so determined before! An' if 'is plan 'ad gone awry, 'e 'd've been in real trouble, 'e would. But milady, wot was you doin' in a place like that?"

Muttering incoherently, Ariadne tried to pull down the gag, but it was tied too tightly and her fingers were numb.

" 'Ere, let me!" Minnie said hastily. "I be that sorry, milady. I don't know wot I was thinkin' of." Carefully, she cut away the gag. "There!" she said. "Now you're free. Ye'd best let me rub your 'ands." She caught them in her warm, strong grip.

"Oh, M-Minnie," Ariadne croaked. Her throat felt very

dry and she was slightly dizzy, too. Tears came into her eyes. She had not expected to weep, but they were angry tears, not tears of fright. Angry, too, was the plea she could not help blurting out. "Oh, M-Minnie, I . . . I beg you'll help me . . . I pray you, help me to get ashore. We cannot be far from land, not yet!"

"Oh, milady," Minnie shook her head.

"I beg you'll not address me as milady," Ariadne cried furiously. "I . . . I've no connection with this . . . this rogue I've not even s-seen for f-four years! Sure you must agree with me. You were always my friend, Minnie."

"Oh, milady, 'e couldn't 'elp bein' away." Minnie looked distressed. "Not wi' all 'e 'as to do."

"And what does he have to do?" Ariadne demanded sharply.

"I . . . I don't actually know, milady, but it be special an'—"

"Never mind!" Ariadne interrupted imperiously. "I do not care. Oh, God, that *villain*! How dared he do this to me? Abduct me . . ."

Minnie released Ariadne's hands and moved to her feet, rubbing her ankles. "I expect 'e couldn't think o' no other solution, milady. It were 'igh-'anded o' 'im, but 'e were called back so sudden-like."

Ariadne regarded her incredulously. "High-handed!" she exclaimed. "It was dastardly, criminal, indeed. To . . . kidnap me and d-drug me and carry me on board this vessel— and you call it merely 'high-handed!' Are you mad, Minnie?"

"But ye are wed to 'im, Miss Ariadne—milady, an' you used to like 'im more 'n 'alf," Minnie said earnestly. "I've said I didn't think 'e acted proper, but 'e 'as said as 'ow ye'd not listen to 'im, an' even I've 'eard about Sir Robert 'Eath, milady."

"You mean you've heard what Iden has said about him," Ariadne accused.

"Oh, no, Miss Ariadne," Minnie said earnestly. " 'Twas afore we went to Greece. I knew a girl wot worked for Lady Sarsfield 'n Sir Robert come courtin' 'er daughter, Miss Sarah, an' she sent 'im packin 'n said she wouldn't 'ave no fortune 'unter danglin' after 'er."

Ariadne glared at her and, doing a rapid set of calculations in her head, she said coldly, "That was five years ago. Sir Robert's fortunes have changed since then. And . . ." She paused, coloring, as she became aware of the implications inherent in her defense. She added hastily, "Also I cannot believe that he was pursuing an heiress merely for her fortune. Knowing him as well as I do, I am sure he must have cared deeply for her. He has hinted about some severe disappointments in love. This must have been one of them!"

"The master 'as said—" Minnie began.

"I do not care to hear what the master has said," Ariadne flashed. "I love Sir Robert m-more than . . . than life! Also I respect him. I . . . I do not respect Iden Peverell. I would never, never credit *anything* he had to t-tell me about my fiancé. He is a . . . a scoundrel and I . . . I hate him."

"Oh, Miss Ariadne," Minnie protested, " 'ave ye quite forgotten 'ow 'e saved yer life all those years back?"

"I have forgotten nothing!" Ariadne glared at her. "But the . . . the fact that he saved my life does *not* mean that it b-belongs to him. And for him, *knowing* my state of mind and . . . and *agreeing* to an annulment, which he *did*, Minnie, to . . . to play this dastardly trick upon me, when he has p-proved that he has no feeling for me . . . oh!" Wresting her ankles from Minnie's soothing hands, she said icily, "If you are his appointed emissary, I . . . I beg you'll go back to him and tell him that you have failed in your mission! Meanwhile, I shall not require your s-services. I . . . I am quite capable of attending to my personal needs myself. You may tell him that, too. No, on second thought, I shall convey that information to him myself, and more while I am at it!" Suiting action to her words, she leaped from the bed, but, unfortunately, her limbs, stiffened from two days of inactivity, failed to bear her and she fell flat on the floor.

"Miss Ariadne!" Minnie exclaimed in horror as she hurriedly knelt beside her. "Are you 'urt, then?"

"I . . . I . . . ohhhhhhhh!" To her surprise and subsequent regret, Ariadne dissolved into helpless tears.

"Oh, Miss Ariadne, child." Minnie stroked her disordered locks. "You must let me 'elp you up . . . come now."

Gently, she assisted Ariadne to her feet and, with a sustaining arm around her waist, she brought her back to the bed. "Yer that confused, milady, but ye'll be feelin' better come mornin', see if you don't. An' I'm not sayin' as that I agree wi' the master entirely, but 'e's not wot you think 'e is, I promise you. An' 'e 'as told me to tell you that if yer still set on weddin' Sir Robert once yer back in England, 'e'll not stand in yer way."

"He will not stand in my way!" Ariadne cried. "But . . . but I will be gone more than a year!" The enormity of the situation into which the perfidious Mr. Peverell had thrust her angered her anew. "I shall never forgive him, never, never, never whilst I live!" She sat up straight. "You may tell him that." She paused, staring into Minnie's concerned eyes. "But . . . but Minnie, I am sorry for all I have said to you. Do remain in my service . . . I need one friend aboard this . . . *prison*."

"Of course I will, milady. I 'ave promised I will, an' I know 'ow you must be feelin'," she said compassionately.

"I do thank you, Minnie," Ariadne declared, wondering bitterly what the abigail would think once she learned that one of her tasks would be to act as a lookout. She would require Minnie to let her know when Iden Peverell was on deck. At such times, she would not go aloft, and nor would she speak to him again. Words would avail her nothing, but her continued silence might prove quite effective as an expression of her disapproval.

The more she considered this decision, the more pleased she became. She would pretend that he did not exist, this man who had proved to be a brigand, a pirate , and a rogue, indeed! She was sure that her attitude must prove highly disconcerting to him. Notwithstanding his four-year absence, he must have believed she would either fly into his arms or grovel at his feet in an approximation of the abject adoration with which she had once regarded him!

"I'll be bringin' you some tea 'n toast, milady," Minnie said.

It was on the tip of Ariadne's tongue to say grandly that she wanted nothing to eat or drink, however she swiftly realized that that would not be in her best interests. It occurred to her that she had not supped for close on forty-eight hours and, if she were not precisely famished, the proffered sustenance would yet be welcome. "I thank you, Minnie," she said, and for pride's sake managed not to urge her handmaiden to hurry back.

Once Minnie had gone, Ariadne concentrated upon exercising her stiffened limbs and, as mobility tingingly returned, she took as much stock of her surroundings as the indifferent glow from the lantern would permit.

The cabin was surprisingly well-appointed. At present, she was occupying a large, comfortable four-poster bed with a canopy and a silk bedspread. There was a chest across the room and beside her was a mahogany commode. Two graceful chairs which looked to be Chippendale and a small bookcase completed the furnishings. Staring at the chest, she belatedly thought of garments and, glancing down, she flushed. She was wearing only a shift. Who had undressed her? Minnie, hopefully. And what would she do for garments, who had been wearing only that shift under her nun's habit? Would she be forced to go clad in scarlet satin for the whole of the voyage?

The whole of the voyage! Once more, the horror of her situation arose to infuriate and confound her, blotting out all other thoughts.

"What I would not like to say to him!" she muttered between her teeth. All the words she knew and should not have known, the expletives uttered by sailors and by servants, by their foreign equivalents overheard on her travels, were not enough to fully express her fury! Belatedly, she remembered that she had determined that she would not speak at all. There were difficulties attendant upon that decision, especially given her volatile disposition.

"I will do it!" she vowed again, her fists clenching and another desire filling her. How gladly she would have welcomed the opportunity of shoving both of them into his eyes. Yet, even as that enticing idea entered her mind, the ship heaved, sending her back against the headboard. As she clutched a bedpost, she heard the familiar howl of the sea wind. Evidently they had come into some heavy weather.

An unbidden and most unwelcome memory slipped its moorings in the back of her mind and she saw herself hurtling into a storm-tossed ocean. She would not, would not, would *not* think of the man who had flung himself after her, unmindful of his peril, and had held onto her and, as Minnie had not scrupled to remind her, had saved her life and, subsequently, her reputation by marrying her!

"Ohhhhh," Ariadne groaned. "I wish I had drowned first. If I had known then what I know now, I would have."

"No, you would not have," contradicted a still, small voice in the depths of her consciousness. *"Life has been very agreeable in the past three years. Especially since you are no longer repelled by what you find in your mirror."*

That was a truth she could not dispute. It *was* lovely to be slim and taller, to possess, in fact, a shape that mantua-makers praised, saying—and, she knew, not untruthfully—that it was a joy and a privilege to dress one who enhanced their creations rather than the other way around. Furthermore, she had been lately approached by a well-known artist who had wanted her to pose as Hebe, cupbearer of the gods, for one of his mythological canvases. She had agreed to the sittings. No one turned down a request from Sir James Carmody! Tears filled her eyes. He, too, would wonder what had happened to her.

All her friends would wonder and Robert, dearest, dearest Robert, would be in utter despair! Did he dream that he would not be able to see her for a year? Had Iden found a way to let him know? She tried to remember all he had said in the horrid, mocking tone of voice he had used while she lay helpless, trussed up like some fowl ready for plucking!

Bits and pieces of his gloating discourse came back to her, but such had been her churning state of mind that she could hardly remember his confidences and then, she shuddered, one phrase arose to obviate all the others. He had mentioned something regarding the rights their relationship allowed— *had he said that*?

Ariadne froze. What if he chose to exercise those rights?

Because of her so-called married state, she had had some very frank conversations with Carola concerning the ways of husbands. While her friend had not been entirely specific, she had said that some of these resulted in the act of breeding. In five years of marriage, Carola, much to her secret indignation, had become the mother of two boys and was currently expecting a third addition to the nest.

Children appeared to be the inevitable result of an experience Carola had described as "quite pleasurable." Much to Ariadne's annoyance, she had not, however, given her any pertinent details, saying archly that she would let Ariadne discover those for herself. She shuddered. Supposing that the next time she encountered poor Robert, she would be breeding? No, no, no, that would not happen! Fortunately, she could now remember exactly what Iden had said. He had told her he would not presume upon those rights unless she gave him permission.

"I will see him at the bottom of the sea, first!" she vowed. "And," she muttered furiously, "I will be even with him, too. He will live to rue the day he ever, ever brought me aboard." She was not sure how she could bring this condition about but, she reasoned bitterly, she would have plenty of time to think, plenty of time to evolve a plan, and, given her lively imagination, she was rather sure she would be the victor!

"There she is." Captain Wellstood, indicating the tall, slender cloaked figure standing at the railing, shook his head. Turning to Iden, who was beside him on the bridge, he added, "I am still hard-put to believe that they are one and the same. I do not think I have ever seen anyone so radically changed!"

"And in every possible way," Iden agreed wryly.

"I told you at the time that I doubted the wisdom of your action," Wellstood muttered. "I presume that you must agree with me by now."

"After only a fortnight? If I know anything about her temperament, she will not be able to maintain this stubborn silence much longer."

"But do you know anything about her temperament, Iden?" Wellstood inquired.

Iden was silent, staring at Ariadne. She held herself stiffly. Animosity fairly radiated from her. In fact, one of the younger members of the crew, a lad from Essex with more than a dash of gypsy blood, had muttered that in his opinion she had the evil eye. Though he did not hold with such superstitions, Iden could agree that she had the angry eye. It was even more difficult now to reconcile this tall, lovely young woman with the child he had known, the child who had not been a child save in his own mind. That was part of the problem. In the four years which, for him, had passed so quickly, he had actually thought of her as "growing up"—that is, when he had thought about her at all.

He *had* thought of her, he amended defensively, and flushed, recalling that in spite of his assurances to Ariadne, he had bitterly resented the convention that had forced him into that loveless marriage! In those early days, he had hastened away from his so-called bride because in his confused and still sorrow-laden mind, he had thought of himself as being actually unfaithful to his adored Radha. Yet, later he had found himself remembering their days on the island. She had been a pleasant companion and, as he remembered telling her, he had admired the fact that she had not treated him to the vapors. And, it had been very obvious to him that she was in love with him.

Regretfully, now, he wondered what would have happened had he returned earlier, before Ariadne's infatuation with Robert had reached full flower? It was useless to indulge in such speculations. He had not returned and she did fancy herself in love with that scoundrel!

No, he decided regretfully, Robert was not exactly a scoundrel. As Miss Kingsmith had implied, he was weak. And, remembering the ghost episode at Cambridge, was he quite sane? He was definitely high-strung but, still, his lineage was impeccable and given enough money to sustain him, he would be a good husband for any woman, and faithful, too. He was not a philanderer. He just enjoyed his creature comforts and, unfortunately, he was a spendthrift. Iden's lips twitched. Many natives of India believed in the transmigration of souls. If Robert had enjoyed a former life as an animal, he might easily have been a pampered pussycat. He had never been a man of action. However, Iden recalled, he could, when aroused, be moved in that direction. He had called someone out while they were still at Cambridge—this in defiance of the rules. Amazingly, Robert had proved to be an excellent marksman. He had shot his opponent in the right shoulder, thus avenging his honor without slaying him and having to leave England hurriedly.

Now Robert's honor, he thought ruefully, had been impugned again, and his affections as well. It was more than likely that upon their return to England he, himself, would be in receipt of a similar summons—only the target on that occasion would not be his shoulder but his heart! Determinedly, he pushed these speculations from his mind and, instead, contemplated the circumstances which had resulted in actions he was currently inclined to deplore. It had been Lottie Kingsmith who had persuaded him to—no, he was being unfair. His decision to abduct Ariadne had been predicated partially on his concern for her, true, but also out of regret, anger, and something else he hardly cared to consider.

Could a man who had once fallen in love at first sight with the beautiful Radha undergo a second experience of that nature, and at an age when he had believed his youthful fires banked? His common sense rejected so extravagant an idea. Yet, seeing Ariadne without recognizing her, he had reluctantly to concede that he had felt just such an emotion. And then to discover that this radiant young woman was the child he had married four years earlier, had been a rude shock, and one that carried with it attendant feelings that troubled him anew each time he saw her. Even at the end of this most frustrating fortnight, and with no encouragement at all, she continued to stir his senses, dominate his thoughts, and trouble his sleep.

Indeed, there were times when, lying awake in the hammock he must needs use since he had surrendered his cabin to her, that he had been hard put to keep his passions in check. Often he had envisioned himself storming into that same cabin and exercising the prerogatives of a husband. Fortunately, he had been able to subdue that most unworthy impulse, but fourteen days of chill glances and silent opprobrium were more disturbing than he cared to admit, even to himself. It was impossible not to compare her with the Ariadne he had once known. Was there not a possibility that the love she had once felt for him was merely dormant? Or was it completely gone?

If only he had gone back to England on leave. There was trouble in Hydrapore now that Kitrachandra, the Maharajah, was so ill and his relatives quarreling over the succession. However, he could have returned to England two years ago, but that would have meant coming to terms with his marriage and so he had not gone. He was paying for that decision now and the price was more costly than he had deemed possible. Given his arbitrary behavior and his long absence, he had provided Ariadne with some very salient reasons to loathe and despise him. Judging from her uncompromising attitude, she did. Or did she?

". . . . horizon, do you think?"

Iden turned a startled gaze on Captain Wellstood. He had evidently been saying something to him that his own thoughts had blotted out. "I beg your pardon," he responded. "I fear I was distracted."

"I was saying that I fear we might be having heavy weather ahead. There's a darkness on the horizon." The captain appeared understandably annoyed at Iden's sudden burst of dry laughter.

"I am sorry, Wellstood." Iden apologized hastily. "But there's more truth than you might imagine in those words." His eyes were not on the horizon but rather on his wife. In that moment, she had turned and looked at him, startled, no doubt, by his laughter. In her dark cloak, with her hood fallen back and her ebony locks caught by the wind, she looked like the very personification of a Fury!

Had Iden been able to follow her to her cabin, he would have thought the similarity to be heightened. After a fortnight at sea, her anger was naturally on the increase, especially when she contrasted this voyage with her journey to Greece! Given Iden's presence on board, the comparison was unavoidable. Then, though she had been burdened by Miss

Gore, she had been compensated by her increasing passion for Mr. Peverell, a fact which only served to heighten the irony of her situation. If she had been able to gaze into the future and know she would be wed to the man she had looked upon as a combination of Helios and Dionysus, divinely beautiful but with the earthiness of the wine god, she would have believed herself upon Mount Olympus. Instead, she might as well be located in the outer reaches of Eleusis, that spot said to be the mouth of Hades where she must needs remain for four more months or eight weeks or one hundred and twenty-two days!

She took off her cloak and hung it on a hook near the door. Not for the first or even the twentieth time, she wondered how Iden had procured it and the other gowns that lay on the chest. They had been carefully selected from her extensive wardrobe and were, for the most part, her newer and lighter garments, suitable for traveling in warmer climes. Their presence in that chest meant that Iden had had an accomplice among her servants.

In her mind's eye, she had staged a parade of them all, from the cook's helper to Rosie, and had exonerated them one by one. Subsequently, she had asked Minnie if she could shed any light on the mystery. Minnie had looked blank. Of course, given her obvious respect for "the master," she might have been lying, but Minnie, transparently honest by nature, was a poor liar at best. The only person who could enlighten her was, of course, Iden, and if she were to unbend and speak to him, she would *not* be discussing anything so trivial as her wardrobe! However, she had absolutely no intention of speaking to him. Her protracted silence was, she knew, extremely perplexing to him and, she was sure, equally annoying. Probably it was an entirely new experience for one who was used to having females swoon at his feet if he so much as cast an eye in their direction! His obvious confusion was balm to her lacerated soul! Indeed, it compensated in some degree for her own feelings of frustration and, on occasion, despair at the sudden disruption of her existence.

In London, her days had followed a definite pattern. Weather permitting, she rarely missed a morning ride in the Park with dearest Robert at her side. A wry little smile played about her lips. Lottie had protested that she ought to be chaperoned and she had replied that as a matron, she did not need to be. That had been one benefit deriving from her marriage that she had really appreciated.

She sighed as she envisioned herself on her spirited little thoroughbred, the lively and high-stepping Mercury. Robert, looking his best in the blue coat that was only a little lighter than his eyes, would be mounted on Horace, his gray. They would race and the one who lost would have to pay a forfeit, which in her case meant being briefly caught in his strong embrace. She must needs thrust that particular memory from her mind—and quickly!

She had also gone to the British Museum of a morning. Since Sir Arthur had been more than generous in his support of that institution, giving money as well as many of the artifacts he had found in Greece, the directors always welcomed her visits and Mr. Messinger, one of the chief curators, would regale her with stories of the days when he and her late father, just down from Cambridge, had gone on a walking tour along the Roman wall. That was another memory that, evoking her father as it did, must needs be hastily dismissed.

Her afternoons had been devoted to visiting friends. She had made quite a few since her return from Greece—though she still favored Carola. At night, there would have been the opera or dancing at Almack's on Wednesdays or the theater or—her mind skipped forward into the summer when, Iden's having consented to the annulment, she would have been wed to Robert. They had planned a July wedding. A small sob escaped her as she envisioned Robert's confusion and misery. No doubt, he was totally distracted. Furthermore, given the touch of melancholy that she had noted on occasion, she knew he must be entirely cast-down, as she was herself, but at least he could suffer in London and not where his every glance brought him only the unchanging vista of sea, sky, and ship!

"Oh, oh, oh," Ariadne moaned. "How could he have done such a thing? He has no heart! I hate him!" She grimaced. It did no good to utter these sentiments to herself. Her abductor ought to hear them. She wished he could—but that would be breaking her vow. It surprised her that she had managed to hold to it. Fortunately, she had not condemned herself to total silence. She did converse with Minnie and with Edward Quigley, whom she liked almost as much as his wife. She also spoke with Captain Wellstood and she exchanged greetings with the crew.

She did have one diversion: the ship's library. In common with the rest of what was, she realized, a most luxurious yacht, the library was a very pleasant place. It was well-stocked with books on a variety of subjects—not excluding works by Walter Scott, Mrs. Edgeworth, Mrs. James, and Miss Austen. There were also the poems of Byron, Milton, Wordsworth, Keats, Shelley, and Coleridge. Some of the volumes were autographed and Byron had scribbled part of a poem, which he had addressed to Iden! That did not surprise her. Judging from what she had heard about Byron and his heartless treatment of poor little Caroline Lamb, they were two of a kind! Of course Lottie Kingsmith had opined that Caroline Lamb had made a fool of herself over Byron. Carola held that same opinion, saying that she had followed him about like a dog. Perhaps Byron, in common with Sir Iden Peverell, having encouraged her, had ruthlessly deserted her, cutting her out of his life.

A sob escaped her and, at the same time, horrified her. For whom was she weeping? For Caroline Lamb, of course! Who would not feel some pity for poor, deserted, ignored Caroline Lamb—but at least *she* had had a husband who adored her.

Ariadne stamped her foot. She could not like the way her thoughts were tending. She picked up a volume which she had taken from the library that morning. It was entitled *Guy Mannering* and it was written by Sir Walter Scott. She had been very pleased to discover upon opening it that its endpapers bore no fulsome inscriptions, but only the bookplate of its owner. Settling down in a chair, she forthwith immersed herself in the trials and tribulations of its hero.

Chapter Four

The porthole of her cabin was dark and her candle was burning low. Having eaten her solitary meal and read several more chapters of *Guy Mannering*, Ariadne closed the book. She was weary of the miseries of Henry Bertram, its beleaguered hero. Actually, she ought to have been able to identify with him since he, too, had been kidnapped, though at a considerably earlier age. She did not identify with him, however. There were *several* people ready and willing to take up *his* cause, including Meg Merrilees, a kind-hearted gypsy. No one on board this vessel appeared to view her with a similar sympathy. They were, to a man, singularly devoted to Iden Peverell.

She could include Minnie among that number. While her ex-abigail admitted that she did not approve his method of bringing his wife on board *The Argonaut II*, she always looked extremely uncomfortable whenever Ariadne waxed too eloquent on the matter of his villainy. It was a subject which, if the truth were to be told, was also beginning to weary her, especially since she could add no new cruelties to her list of grievances. If she sometimes felt that Iden was watching her from afar, that did not constitute an invasion of her solitude. Conversely, she wished he would speak to her so that she could give him the cold stare that his actions warranted. Yet, she could not initiate such a happening and consequently must needs remain frustrated.

Slipping out of her gown, she took it to the chest, wondering once again how Iden had come by all her gowns. With a short sigh of frustration, she placed her gown in the chest, performed her ablutions, and, slipping into bed, resentfully closed her eyes. Though she often wished she could blame a series of sleepless nights and tormented dreams on him, she had experienced neither. Tonight was no different. As soon as her head touched her pillows, she fell asleep, lulled by the motion of the ship.

Ariadne awakened to a loud noise, which, at first, she could not identify. Then, her cabin was momentarily illuminated by a blinding brightness. There was movement, too. The bed, though firmly bolted to the floor, was rising and falling or, rather, the vessel was pitching and tossing, caught, Ariadne realized, in the grip of a storm or, rather, she decided as another mighty clap of thunder resounded in her ears, a tempest!

Slipping from her bed and clutching first the bedpost and then a chair, she staggered to the porthole. Just as she reached it, she was startled by another clap of thunder, even louder than that which must have awakened her. Clinging to the window frame, she was momentarily blinded by a second brilliant flash of lightning, quickly succeeded by darkness. It was a darkness, however, that was intermittently leavened as massive storm clouds parted to let the moon shine through and giving Ariadne a view of the pelting raindrops as they were swallowed by the moiling sea.

A few minutes later, she heard a heavy pounding at her door. "Are you all right?" someone shouted hoarsely.

Turning away from the porthole, Ariadne was reaching for the chair when a heave from the vessel threw her to the floor. Before she could clutch a chairleg, she was sliding toward the door which had been thrust open by a tall figure in dripping oilskins. He was carrying a ship's lantern.

"Are you hurt?" he demanded concernedly and in a voice she recognized.

"Not in the *slightest*," she emphasized coldly as she made a futile effort to rise.

"You need not be afraid," he continued moving further into the cabin and closing the door.

"I am not afraid," she assured him equably. "In fact, I find storms exciting."

"Exciting!" His laughter filled her ears. "I'd forgotten how very brave you are, little Ariadne."

"I am used to bad weather," she returned.

"And so you are. Well then, I will leave you, but first. . ." He hung the lantern on the doorknob and before she knew what he intended, he had lifted her and carried her to the bed. "There," he added, as he put her gently down. "You'd best hold onto that post until this squall blows itself out. I would guess, however, that the worst is over."

Before she could respond, he had taken the lantern and left the cabin.

Finding that her arms as well as the front of her gown were wet from contact with his dripping oilskins, Ariadne wiped off the water with the edge of the sheet and hoped that the covers would dry her shift. She glared at the door. Memories she did not want to entertain were flooding back into her mind which, given her present circumstances, were only natural. She did not want them to be natural, did not want to dwell on a past when she had given her heart to the man who had rejected that gift. He had lifted her so very easily, too, as if she were still adoring little Ariadne. But she was not, and she did not adore him. On the contrary, she disliked him heartily! The sound of his voice had lost its power to thrill her just as his touch carried with it no feeling of excitement. Indeed, she actively resented the casual way in which he had picked her up and deposited her on her bed. He should have, at the very most, helped her to walk back to her bed. He ought not to have been in her cabin at all! Furthermore, she should not have been here either. She ought to be in London. The bed tilted and, remembering his advice, she swiftly grabbed the bedpost, saving herself another journey to the floor.

"Better the floor," she hissed, and felt water on her cheeks which, she guessed, must have come from his oilskins. She refused to consider any other source as, defensively, she curled up and buried her head in the pillow, hoping that she could manage to sleep even while still clutching the post.

*   *   *

"Oh, milady, you do look a picture." Minnie, having placed a light straw bonnet on Ariadne's head, stepped back smilingly.

Looking into the small mirror attached to the wall, Ariadne frowned at her reflected image. She was wearing a yellow muslin gown and her bonnet, of a golden straw, *was* very fetching. She wished that the traitorous creature who had packed her garments had not included that particular bonnet, for she had to agree with Minnie that it was, indeed, most becoming. It had a high crown and a brim wide enough to shade her face from the sunlight, blindingly reflected from waters that might never have known the turbulence of the previous evening. She had *not* worn it for any other reason than to shade her face. She had chosen her gown because of its tiny puffed sleeves and low neck, perfect for so warm a day. Yet, *he* might imagine that she was deliberately trying to draw attention to herself. Minnie's exclamations of admiration had only served to strengthen that supposition.

She hoped that the exigencies of the previous evening might have wrought upon him to the point that he was still abed. And, if she had not promised herself that she would not mention his name, she would have asked Minnie if that were indeed the case. As it was, she would have to take her chances.

However, these cavils could not tie her to her cabin, not when it was so very hot! There would be a cool breeze on deck and she need not acknowledge *his* presence, even if he were there. That she had broken her vow last night could be blamed on the *unusual* circumstances. There would be none of these when she went aloft. Picking up her parasol, Ariadne took a deep breath and moved to the door.

The wind was stronger than she had expected. It tugged at her parasol as she went aloft, but it was delightfully fresh and cool. Without it, the sun, climbing toward its zenith, would have been warm indeed.

As usual, there was considerable activity on deck. There were men at the ropes and others mending sails. The decks had already been swabbed down and a few of the crew were fishing. As usual, the atmosphere was cheerful. Captain Wellstood was, Minnie had told her, one of those rare men who did not believe in treating the sailors as if they were little better than dogs. Her husband had described horrendous punishments meted out to crews aboard navy vessels and commercial and even private sailing ships. Men were flogged with the cat o'nine tails until the decks ran red with blood or they were made to wear "iron garters," which were shackles that tied them to iron bars. Even worse was the infamous practice of "keel-hauling," when a seaman who had broken one or another of the many rules on shipboard was dropped into the water underneath the keel of the ship and held there by ropes while the vessel continued on its course.

"There be none o' that 'ere," Minnie had informed Ariadne proudly. "That's why the men'd do anythin' for the captain, or the master, too."

Minnie's admiration for the "master" was like a wedge between them. Sometimes, it seemed to Ariadne that the girl had set herself up as a peacemaker and this morning had been no different. She had been full of glowing descriptions of his labors during the storm; he had been everywhere, helping with ropes and sails. "I 'alf expected to see 'im climbin' into the crow's nest, I did. 'E would if 'e were needed."

Evidently the exertions of the previous night had, as she hoped, wearied him to the point that he had remained in his cabin, for a swift glance had not netted a glimpse of him. She was extremely glad of that. It was a lovely morning and she appreciated the opportunity to stroll about the deck without the sense of being constantly observed by the man she still must needs call husband! Some of the crew looked at her admiringly, but they kept their distance. She had no trouble believing that they were fanatically loyal to Mr. Peverell. Minnie had been full of tales describing his derring-do.

"Once 'e leaped into the sea to rescue a green lad wot 'ad fallen overboard, 'n there's many times 'e's saved a man from bein' given extra duty on account of sleepin' on watch. 'E's took over for 'em 'isself." To hear Minnie tell it, Ariadne thought bitterly, she might have been married to a saint! It was extremely difficult to listen to a constant stream

of encomiums, and Minnie should have understood that—
especially when she greeted them with silence—but the girl
went on chattering anyhow. Only the fact that she did not
want to alienate her one real friend on board kept her from
giving Minnie a set-down. She could almost wish that Mr.
Peverell had strode the decks with whip in hand and cursing
like the pirate he really was!

Standing by the ropes on the starboard side of the vessel,
Ariadne looked out across the miles and miles of ocean. It
was an awesome sight to view a horizon that appeared to be
stretching into infinity. One could almost imagine that the
hungry sea had devoured all the continents of the world and
that they, in their tiny ship, were alone on this vast, watery
plain. Once more, she was filled with frustration. She ought
not to have been here. She ought to have been meeting
Robert and riding through the Park. She tossed her head and
then uttered a small shriek of dismay as her bonnet sailed into
the water! Her distress increased as she saw it bobbing on the
waves. Casting an anguished glance about her, she saw that
no one was near her. Even if they had been, she could hardly
ask them to attempt a rescue! With a long sigh, she watched
the waters inexorably bearing it away. She raised her parasol
but hastily lowered it against the pull of those threatening
gusts of wind which could easily turn it inside out. However,
they did feel delightfully cool against her skin. It was really
delightful to stand here with no one troubling her—if anything could be delightful, she amended, given her miserable
situation!

"Might I ask why you are out here without even a proper
head-covering? This is not the same sun that shines over
London, you know!"

Ariadne, lulled by the heat, had been half-dozing. Stiffen-
ing, she turned to find Iden scowling at her. "My bonnet . . .
it blew overboard," she said vaguely.

He bent and picked up her parasol, which must have fallen
without her noticing it. "Then, why did you not make use of
this? Surely it cannot help you down there."

"I expect it dropped," she replied, and was annoyed at the
inadvertently defensive note she heard in her voice. In stronger

and more belligerent tones she added, "I could not raise it. The wind was too strong."

"Then, why did you not go below and fetch another bonnet?"

"I do not have another!" she retorted. With a mixture of anger and curiosity, she continued, "I should very much like to know who it was removed my garments from my house!"

"That is hardly of moment now," he rasped. "How long have you been here?" Before she could reply, he continued, "No matter, you must go below immediately. Your skin is already pink and you are in danger of a bad sunburn."

"A sunburn?" she echoed. "It is shady here."

"It is not shady enough, not with the glare of the sun on the water. Your face and arms are not in the shade and neither is a good deal of your bosom. You must get below. I will send Minnie with unguents which, I hope, will serve to alleviate some of the discomfort you are bound to experience." He put his hand on her arm. "Now come, please. You must get out of this sun. 'Tis waxing brighter by the minute!"

She moved away from him quickly. "I am able to negotiate the distance from here to my cabin unaided, sir."

"As you choose." He shrugged. "But do not fail to go below. And I suggest that you rest. Good God!" he burst out. "Can you not remember how sunburned you were in Greece?"

Ariadne drew herself up to her full height. She said frostily, "I have done my very best to forget that I was ever in Greece, sir."

Much to her annoyance, the corners of his mouth twitched, as if rather than being annoyed at this thinly veiled insult, he was having difficulty suppressing a smile. However, his tone was suitably grave as he said, "That is possibly understandable, my dear, but it is also extremely unfortunate, given your present condition. You will have, I fear, some very uncomfortable days and nights, and I must advise that you do not attempt to brave the sunlight until you are better."

Ariadne, repeating that movement which had cost her her bonnet, retorted, "I do think you refine too much upon it, sir. I do not feel any the worse for this slight touch of sun."

"I hope you will believe me when I tell you that I am in hopes you will continue in that happy state."

"I have always been exceptionally healthy, sir."

"Health, my dear Ariadne, has nothing to do with sunburn."

More arguments crowded to Ariadne's lips but, she realized crossly, not only had she broken or rather *shattered* her vow of silence, he, manlike, was determined on having the last word and would have it, no matter what she said. Furthermore, her face was beginning to feel unpleasantly warm. With another toss of her head, she said, "I will go below and fetch my cloak. It has a hood and will protect me against your 'dangerous' sun."

"The sun can be very dangerous indeed to those unused to its rays. 'Tis a great pity you did not fetch your cloak an hour sooner."

Giving no sign of having heard him, Ariadne, head held high, walked to the hatchway. With an aggrieved sniff, she descended the steps.

"My chest . . . my chest and . . . and my forehead . . . hot . . . hot, they're so hot . . ." Ariadne moaned. "I'm burrrrrrning . . . burning . . . arms . . . arms . . ."

" 'Ere . . ." a man's voice murmured. "Gotta 'ave more grease on you."

"Where's Minnie? Who are you?" she muttered.

"Edward, milady. Minnie's 'usband. Now lie still, you'll only 'urt yerself, movin' around-like."

"Why does it burn and burn and burn . . . why does it not s-stop?"

"Got yerself a real burn, ye did, mum. Best not thrash about so, please."

"When will M-Minnie be back?"

"Anytime mum, she be restin'," Edward whispered.

"When will it stop, p-please t-tell me when?" she begged.

"Drink this 'ere . . . 'twill soothe ye, mum."

"It's been going on so long, so long . . . when will it be better?"

" 'Nother day or two, mum."

"B-but it's already been days and days and days . . ." she protested. "I . . . I feel as if I'm on fire."

"It's not been that long, mum, an' 'twill stop soon. Now drink this."

"What is it?"

"You'll sleep for a bit, mum, won't be long afore yer well, neither."

He held a bottle against her parched lips, but she shook her head. "What . . . what are you giving me?"

"Nothin' that'll 'urt, ye ma'am. Now drink."

"No . . . no . . . no." She turned her head away.

" 'Twill make you feel better, little Ariadne—ma'am. Now drink."

A hand was on her head, forcing it back, the bottle was at her mouth again, and liquid seeped in—trickling down her throat. She swallowed spasmodically and swallowed again. The taste was not unpleasant, but still the terrible burning sensation did not cease, had not ceased since the afternoon she had returned to her cabin at *his* orders. She groaned. "You must . . . must not tell him."

"Tell 'oo, mum?"

"Mr. P-Peverell. He will laugh."

"Oi don' think 'e'd do that, mum."

"He would . . . he . . . told me . . ." Her tongue felt heavy. She could no longer seem to articulate and a deeper darkness than the moon-shot blackness about her was descending. She vaguely remembered experiencing something similar before, but she did not know when . . . did not know . . . did not know . . . the darkness blotted out thought and pain as well.

"I wish I might have more of . . . of what your husband gave me, Minnie," Ariadne, her face half-muffled by her pillow, said beseechingly.

" 'Twas only for pain, milady," Minnie said firmly. "And the pain's been gone nigh on two weeks now. You ought to be up and about. 'Tis too warm by 'alf down 'ere 'n 'tis beautiful outside."

"The s-sun's outside," Ariadne shuddered. "Oh, God, I never want to see the sun again!"

"The master—"

"I beg you'll not mention him, either. I do not want to see him. He . . . he should have warned me."

" 'E says as 'ow 'e did."

" 'Twas too late," Ariadne moaned. "He purposely waited. 'Twas part of . . . of his revenge."

"His revenge, milady?"

"He wanted to make me ugly again."

"Oh, milady," Minnie said half in shock, half in pity. "You are not ugly. An' 'ow was 'e to know you'd gone 'n dropped yer bonnet overboard 'n was 'avin all that sun on yer arms 'n bosom?"

"He could have told me about the sun."

"You'd not speak to 'im, milady. If you 'ad, I am sure 'e'd 'ave said somethin. Wish I 'ad. It never occurred to me. 'E's been ever so concerned about you these past weeks. 'E—"

"I beg you will not keep mentioning him to me." Ariadne raised her head. "And sure you must have other things to do. You may go."

"I wish you'd change your mind an' come up on deck," Minnie said with a quite unfamiliar stubbornness. "The condition's not ugly, you know, milady. In fact, I think it's quite becomin'."

"Oh." Ariadne sat up and glared at her. "You do not need to lie to me, Minnie."

The abigail looked affronted. "I'm not lyin' to ye. I'm not in the 'abit o' lyin, milady. If you'd look in yer mirror again, you'd agree wi' me, you would."

"I never want to *see* another mirror, and please go. You are dismissed. I do not wish to hear any more of your false assurances, thank you!"

Minnie looked even more affronted as she replied, "Very well, milady, as you wish." Turning on her heel, she left the cabin, closing the door with the suggestion of a slam.

Left alone, Ariadne was immediately contrite. If she had not been so utterly, utterly miserable, she never would have spoken to Minnie in such a way. She was minded to call her back and apologize, but undoubtedly she had gone to report to the "master." Ariadne winced. She did not believe for a single moment that *he* was concerned. All he would feel was vindicated! He had chided her because she had exposed herself to the sun's harmful rays and he had been proved right. She had been just as miserable as he had hinted she might be. Indeed, she had never, never experienced such burning agony! Her sunburn in Greece was as nothing to this! And now she was ugly, ugly, ugly. Her face, her chest, her arms and hands were dark, almost as dark as those of the gypsies she and her father had been wont to see begging by the roadsides in Devonshire and Essex or seated by their tents at country fairs. If she were to hire herself out as a fortune teller, she was sure none would doubt her expertise!

"All I . . I need are gold rings in my ears," she sobbed, and sobbed again as she looked at her hand and arm. At first her skin had been a vivid red. Then, it had been pink and peeling. These conditions were unsightly enough, but who would have dreamed that her exposed flesh would have turned such a color!

She had not dared to look in a mirror, not since that first horrified glance ten days earlier. She would not soon recover from the effects of that shock. And, for the first time, she was glad Robert was not with her—Robert, who had so often praised the ivory hue of her skin, lovely, lovely words to fill the ears of one who remembered, only too well, the days of her spots.

Now, her complexion more resembled antique ivory, turned brown with age. She had reverted to the Ariadne that was, four years back. In those days, however, the disfiguring spots had gone away. If she were to come in contact with the horrid sun, she would only grow darker and darker, as dark as any of the sailors on board, as dark as Iden Peverell! Her cloak would not give her any protection, for her face would be exposed, and besides, it was too warm to wear so heavy a covering. It was far better to remain here in the cabin, no matter how stifling it became inside. More tears rolled down her cheeks.

Then she heard returning footsteps. Minnie was coming back, no doubt, and she ought to apologize—especially when she remembered the girl's devotion during her four days of

misery. She and her husband had taken turns at her bedside.
Young Edward had been there at various times during the
nights to relieve his wife. Minnie had said she hoped Ariadne
had not minded his being in the cabin. She had assured her
she had not. She had scarcely been aware of him or Minnie,
only of disembodied voices and of soothing ointments rubbed
on her face and the other afflicted spots. And there had been
the drink that had sent her to sleep. She wished she might
sleep for the rest of the voyage! However, she did feel a stab
of compunction. Minnie's patience had its limits and that was
as it should be. She was not a slave! The door opened and
closed.

"I . . . I'm sorry, Minnie," Ariadne said. She rasied her
head slightly from the pillow. "But . . . but it's so hard to
. . . to be ugly again."

The bed sagged under the abigail's weight and somewhat
to Ariadne's surprise, she felt Minnie's hand stroking her
tangled locks, but it was not Minnie who said gently, "Child,
you are not ugly. I have seen you and you are just as beautiful as ever. Why can you not understand that?"

Ariadne turned swiftly but yet kept her face averted as she
cried "Oh, go away, do. Or have you come to . . . to gloat
over my c-condition?"

Grasping her shoulders, he turned her around and a second
later, he had pried her shielding hands from her face, holding
them tightly. "My dear," he said insistently, "I beg you will
hear me out. I admit that I never should have carried you
aboard this ship. 'Twas unkind, cruel even. I acted on an
impulse, but I wish you'd believe that I had, or rather,
thought I had your best interests at heart. 'Tis not only that I
am your husband—I know I have no right to claim that title
and will not remind you of it again—but I feared you'd not be
as happy with Robert as you'd anticipated. However, if you
are determined on returning to him, we will be arriving at
Simon's Bay in South Africa in a fortnight and a little over. I
can make arrangements there for you to return to London.
And I will give you a paper with my agreement to the
annulment."

"How . . . how can I go back to him now?" she cried

woefully. "He . . . he'd not want me. No one ever will, again."

"Nonsense!" he exclaimed. "There's none that would not want you, my dear. As I have said, you are more beautiful than ever!"

"Beautiful, I . . . am as dark as any gypsy!" she moaned.

"Not quite, my dear, and the color's most becoming, particularly with your blue eyes." Rising he moved to the dressing table and, picking up a hand mirror, he sat down on the bed again. "Look at yourself, really look, as Minnie has said you'll not do. You'll see how kind the sun has been to you."

Ariadne shut her eyes. "Kind!" she exclaimed. "I was in agony!"

"I know," he said sympathetically. "You suffered even more than I had anticipated. I did not think you'd run so high a fever. But 'twill not happen again, you can take comfort in that."

"C-comfort," she moaned, "I wish I were dead."

"No, you do not, Ariadne," he said with touch of impatience. "Open your eyes. You cannot avoid the truth forever you know." He slipped his arm around her shoulders. "Come now, child. Look."

"Do go away!" she cried. "I do not want to look."

"I will not go away until you have," he said determinedly.

"You are c-cruel and . . . and heartless."

"You are stubborn and idiotic!" he retorted. "And I will stay here until you open your eyes and look—be it all the rest of the day and on into the night."

Since there was no other way of ridding herself of his odious presence, she opened her eyes and glared into the mirror he was holding some six inches from her face, her dusky face. Yet, it was not quite as dusky as she had thought and her eyes did look bluer. Her dark hair, however, did not appear quite so black. Robert had praised the contrast of her white skin and ebony locks, but, on staring into the mirror, she had to agree that it was not nearly as bad as she had anticipated. Still, she did not want to give this brute the satisfaction of agreeing with him. She did not actually agree with him, anyway. However, given time she expected she could become used to the change. After all, her features had not been distorted. Her nose was as straight as ever, her mouth as full, her eyes slightly tip-tilted under her slanting brows, giving her that almost oriental look Robert had also mentioned, though without praising it. In fact, he had actually asked if she had any, "er . . . exotic ancestors, my love." He had regarded her rather suspiciously even after she had assured him she had not.

"Well . . . ?" Iden asked. "Do you agree with me, little Ariadne?"

She raised her eyes to his face and found concern written large on it—concern and sympathy. She could not like his mode of address, "little Ariadne." It brought back memories of Naxos . . . and of something more recent—Edward's voice in the night saying, surprisingly, "You'll feel better soon, little Ariadne."

She had almost forgotten that. And, suddenly, she knew that it had not been Edward who had sat with her those four long nights, speaking to her so soothingly. "It was you!" she said positively.

He looked at her perplexedly. "I do not understand . . ."

"When I was ill," she said slowly. "It was you who sat with me in the night, not Edward."

He flushed. "Why would you think that?" he demanded diffidently.

"It was, it *was* you. Why?"

His flush deepened. He said defensively, "I could not trust another to care for one so . . . very precious to me."

Something hard had been lodged in her chest. She had hardly known it was there until it suddenly seemed to melt away. "Iden . . ." She swallowed and tears welled up in her eyes again. "Oh, Iden, my one incentive to go on deck was so I might thank Edward for his kindness to me in . . . in the night and all the time it was you. I . . . I think—I *know* I have wronged you. Will you forgive me?"

His own eyes were very bright. He said huskily, "You've not wronged me, Ariadne. I know I should not have acted in so arbitrary a fashion. 'Twas only . . ." He paused. "You see, my dear, I thought you far too good for Robert Heath. I am . . . I have always been fond of you. But I will say no more. I hope only that you will cease to regard me as your enemy.''

"I will . . . I have.'' She put out her hand.

He took it, holding it gently. "And, I did mean what I said about the annulment. There are ships at Simon's Bay . . .''

"I . . . I think that before I return to . . . England,'' she said hesitantly, "I think I should like to see India.''

"Are you sure, Ariadne?''

"Yes, I . . . I am sure.''

"And see it you will, my dear. On one condition.''

She stared at him in surprise. "And that is?'' she asked a little nervously, wondering now just what he might mean.

"I want you to end this forced and uncomfortable self-imprisonment and come on deck.''

She tensed, regarding him anxiously. "Are you really telling me the truth?''

"I think your mirror's already given you that truth, Ariadne, but if you must needs have further corroboration, I will gladly swear to it on the head of Dionysus.''

She found she could actually laugh, "Oh, then, I must come. If you will send Minnie to me, I will get dressed immediately.''

He rose and started for the door, then, coming back, stood at the bed. "I forgot something,'' he said.

"What?''

"This.'' Taking her hand, he kissed it and, bowing, strode to the door, leaving her confused by a sudden rush of sensations that were much akin to those she had experienced on the island. And, at the same time, she realized that, for all his obviously tender regard for her, Robert had never filled her with a tenth of the excitement she was currently experiencing.

An hour later, Ariadne came up on deck. She was wearing a white muslin chemise gown with a pale pink fischu. A lacy white shawl was draped around her shoulders. It was an ensemble which had always been one of her favorites. Rosie must have packed it. Had she been the one to participate in Iden's scheme? She shrugged the suspicion away as something that no longer had the power to trouble her.

She could not, however, shrug away her new fear of the sun. In spite of the protection afforded by her gown, her shawl, and her parasol, she viewed those fiery rays nervously. They seemed even brighter than they had three weeks ago—but still the coolness on deck was refreshing. She looked around for Iden but did not see him. However, several members of the crew paused in their tasks to smile and nod at her. There was a difference in the way they looked at her. They seemed much more cordial, as if, indeed, some manner of barrier had been lifted. Thinking about it, she realized that a barrier had indeed been lifted—one of her own making. Until this moment, she had, she realized, regarded the lot of them as enemies in the pay of the man who had heartlessly torn her from the arms of one she believed she had loved!

Struck by this realization, Ariadne came to a sudden stop. She did not love Robert! How could she love him when from the time she had been seventeen her heart had been in the possession of Iden Peverell? Beside his reality Robert's image dwindled like a spent candle. Staring at the ocean, she was reminded of another ocean with waves that broke upon the sandy shores of Naxos. It was an old vision, one she had, in the last years, tried to forget. But if, in her waking hours, she had sometimes succeeded in that attempt, she could not blot it from her dreams any more than she could blot out the image of Iden Peverell. Had those recurring dreams kept her from yielding to Robert's earlier and oft-repeated pleas that she sue for an annulment? Had she, unknowingly, continued to hope for Iden's return? The answer, of course, was yes. She had only relinquished that last thread of hope when three years had become four. And now her mind went back to the agonizing ordeal through which she had just passed and to the man who, in the untutored accents of "Edward" had patiently soothed and tended her during the long hours of the night.

"Ah, you are here, then."

Startled, she looked up into Iden's smiling face. "As you see," she said shyly.

"Come, then." He slipped his arm around her waist. "I have something to show you."

"And what would that be, sir?" she demanded breathlessly.

"Wait and be surprised." He led her to the railing and, producing a spy glass, pointed into the distance. "Take this and look. And never fear, I will hold your parasol."

"What will I see?" she asked confusedly as she stared into the watery distances.

"Nothing until you do as I asked."

Holding the spyglass to her eye, she gasped, seeing a distant mass of land. "Oh, what is it?"

" 'Tis Cape Ortegal."

"The coast of Spain!" she exclaimed excitedly.

"The same, and do you know what that means?"

"We have entered the torrid zone," she said glibly.

"You are well-informed, I must say." He looked at her in some surprise.

"I . . . I have had an interest in studying the routes to India, sir," she admitted diffidently.

"Oh, my dear Ariadne," he said regretfully. "What can I say in my own defense save that once you are in Hydrapore, you may understand why I was needed. I will tell you that I have some influence with Kitrachandra, the Maharajah. He is old, however, and gives ear to too many voices. He has two sons, both born of younger wives in his later years and after he had given up hope of ever having a son. He has three daughters. Five children, I might add, is a very small number for a maharajah—but to get back to his sons. They are as different in character as their mothers were different from each other. The mother of Rama, the eldest boy, was sweet and gentle while the mother of Narayan, the younger lad, was intensely ambitious. She wanted her son to inherit the kingdom. Narayan grew up with a large chip on his shoulder and, to complicate matters, Rama's mother died in childbed and the infant, another son, with her. From what I understand she was probably poisoned."

"Oh, how horrible!" Ariadne shuddered.

"Alas, 'tis not unusual in these situations. The Maharajah truly mourned her and he was very fond of Rama. According to palace gossip, he stayed away from Setu, who was Narayan's mother, and would have nothing more to do with her. He seldom sent for Narayan. And Setu, of course, poisoned her son's mind against his brother. In this, she was abetted by Arvind, who is the Maharajah's half-brother.'' He chuckled. ''I hope that you are keeping all of this straight?''

''I am, and it does not surprise me. I have read about these situations. They seem to arise very often in India.''

''True. I am glad you are so well-informed, my dear. Well, to continue, Rama was devastated by his mother's death. Though he was only five, he had adored her. However, he was fortunate in having a Scottish nurse, one Mrs. Martha MacDonald, who had been the wife of a British officer the Maharajah knew. He died and Kitrachandra who, in those days, was singularly far-seeing, hired her to teach his sons English. She was like a mother to Rama and she helped form his character. She was never fond of the other boy and Setu hated her. Setu tried to get the Maharajah to send Mrs. MacDonald away, but he refused. Consequently, Rama had the benefit of her good counsel as he grew up. I wish I had known her. She must have been a wonderful woman.''

''Did she go back to Scotland?'' Ariadne demanded, ''or,'' she added before he could reply, ''did she meet with some strange death?''

She received a surprised and respectful glance. ''You are very astute, my dear. She was bitten by a krait that had somehow gotten into her bed.''

''Ohhh,'' Ariadne shuddered.

''Her death did not go unavenged,'' Iden said with some satisfaction. ''Someone got to the Maharajah and explained the matter of Mrs. MacDonald's passing. He, rightly guessing the source, had Setu questioned. After persuasions the nature of which I prefer not to divulge, she admitted her complicity and died. Narayan, through no fault of his, was in disgrace and the only one who was kind to him in the palace was his Uncle Arvind. He became Narayan's mentor and completed the work begun by Setu. Narayan loathed Rama.

''Then, when the boys were respectively fifteen and eighteen, the Maharajah married Sita, aged twelve, who became the good friend of Rama after being mercilessly tormented by Narayan. He, of course, resented her for taking the place of his mother. He also feared the birth of another son which would widen the distance between himself and his father. Abetted by Arvind, he was always trying to blacken Sita's character and, in this, he was helped by Moti and Vimala, who being old and crochety, found Sita a handful and—"

"Wait," Ariadne interrupted. "Who are Moti and Vimala?"

He laughed, "I am sorry. I forgot them. They are Kitrachandra's first wives. Between them they had three daughters—all of whom are married and away from the palace."

"Poor Sita."

"Oh, you need not pity her. She emerged largely unscathed. She is even friends with them now. But, unfortunately, her greatest friend was Rama. They were very close, very affectionate with each other, though I doubt that they were in love.

"I was at the palace by then and I managed to keep them apart, but the Maharajah is old and more easily influenced these days, and shortly after my departure some manner of contretemps arose and Rama was banished. According to my sources, Narayan has been designated heir apparent. He hates the British and if he should rule, well, there are many, many pockets of resistance in India, and this one is far too close to Calcutta for our liking. We of the Company have chosen to cultivate a large garden of strange flowers that, at times, are prey to dangerous insects."

"I do understand. Is this Sita very beautiful?"

Iden smiled. "She is as beautiful as the fabled houris that live in the Mohammedan paradise, and adorable, too. She can be, however, incredibly headstrong and foolish, but she is a friend of the British and that is due to Rama's good counsel. She is in a most unfortunate position at this time and is much in need of my help, as is, of course, poor Rama. I am going back to see if I can mend matters. The Maharajah has listened to me in the past. I hope that he is not so angry with Rama that he cannot be swayed."

"Rama and Sita, they were the lovers of the Ramayan," Ariadne said.

"Yes, but again, I doubt that this Rama and Sita have

taken their cue from them. Rama is too astute for that, I think. However, as I have said, Sita is devoted to him and she is a very affectionate girl. A misunderstanding could easily arise, especially if Kitrachandra were in a mood to listen to Arvind's malicious gossip.''

''You have said that she is fabulously beautiful.'' Ariadne's clutch on the spyglass tightened. ''Does she resemble Radha, your bride? She was also from the Ramayan, was she not?''

''She was,'' he corroborated. ''You'll not be telling me that you have read much of that poem!''

''Not all of its hundred thousand lines, of course,'' she said, wishing devoutly that she had not mentioned the name she had once heard him mutter in his sleep. At least, he could not guess how much a younger Ariadne had resented that poor dead girl.

''Radha,'' he said musingly. ''Did I ever tell you about her?''

''A very little and you need not tell me any more now. I am sure that the memory must pain you.''

As if he had not heard her, he said thoughtfully, ''She was a dream, beautiful, graceful, poetry in motion, a princess from the Arabian Nights, a young man's fantasy stepped from the printed pages into reality. Whenever I think of her now, it seems to me that she is a dream from which, if she had lived, I might have early awakened.'' He frowned. ''You will believe me unfaithful to her memory, I fear, but 'tis not the case.

''When I met her, I had been away from home for a long time. Englishwomen were not in great supply in India.''

''I have heard that,'' Ariadne said. ''And are not our soldiers encouraged to wed Indian women?''

''Yes, that has been true—but I believe it is a custom that is dying out. However, some of these marriages have been very successful. Yet, one does tend to forget that there is a give and take in a relationship with one whose background is the same that is not the case when one weds a girl from a different culture, especially one who has been brought up to be subservient to her husband's every demand. In such a situation, a clash of beliefs is inevitable and not always desirable—I mean after the initial passion has spent itself. I do not know if my relationship with Radha would have continued as felicitously as it did in those first months of our marriage. She died too soon. I am sure that we must eventually have had our differences. I might have wearied of her submissiveness.'' His eyes rested on Ariadne. ''There are times when one prefers pepper to sugar, though a total diet of either must needs be injurious to the digestion. I hope you understand me. Do you?''

Ariadne's heart was beating in a vicinity that seemed very near her throat. She felt a strong kinship with the girl she had been four years earlier. At the same time, she was wary of this change of feeling, half-experienced already, but increasing in strength from moment to moment. It was less intimidating to dislike him but, of course, she had never *really* disliked him. She had only tried to shield herself from further agony. However, he had asked her a question and he was looking at her in a way that compelled an answer. She said, ''Of course, I understand.'' Impulsively, she stretched out her hand.

He grasped it with both his hands. ''I have always been fond of you, Ariadne. I was fond of you when we married, but I was not ready to bow to convention. My mind was still in a turmoil. I think you understood that.''

''I did,'' she nodded. ''But later . . .''

''Yes, later was too late, was it not? Yet, when I decided to return to England, I was ready to settle down. I was looking forward to seeing you and I hoped to make up to you for my long absence. Time in India seems as exotic as the country itself. The days have a way of melding one into the next, particularly in my position.

''Then, I received notice of the annulment. I was willing to accede to your demand. I felt I must atone for what you could only see as my neglect. I was regretful, however, and . . .'' his lips twisted into a mirthless smile, ''I . . . I admit that when I saw the changes time had wrought, I was even more regretful.'' He stared into her eyes. ''I do want you to understand that the change would have been nothing without the knowledge that the girl I had known was still there. Even if I could not reach her, I was sure she had not gone and I did not want her to be victimized by Robert Heath, not before I was positive that no lingering feeling for me existed. I hope you believe that."

"I . . . I do," she murmured.

"Yet," he added, "I meant it when I said I would send you home, and mean it still. I did not desire it, however, and desire it even less now."

"I have said that I want to see India, Iden. I . . . I meant, also, that I wanted to see it with you. As . . . as for the rest, I will need a little more time, I think."

He lifted her hand and brought it to his lips. Releasing it, he said, "That is enough for me, Ariadne. I will make no demands on you—until you are ready."

She was conscious of strange flutterings—butterflies, flitting through her body, odd stirring pulses, but she was wary of those feelings. "I think I will be . . . soon," she said nervously.

"I do understand, my dear, and I beg you'll not be intimidated by our most ambiguous situation. We cannot abolish the fact of our marriage, but we can, until further notice, call it a betrothal. I am sure you would find that more comfortable."

"Oh, yes, I . . . I should," she said gratefully. "I do thank you."

"You have nothing to thank me for," he said regretfully. "Let me thank you—for your generosity, my dear." He raised her hand to his lips again.

Chapter Five

A soft humming filled Ariadne's ears as she awoke from the afternoon nap necessary in these hot climes. It was a tune she did not recognize. Opening her eyes, she saw Minnie standing at a porthole turned gray in the wake of the setting sun. The abigail's figure seemed less slim. Yes, her waist was definitely thickening, and Ariadne was reminded of Carola. She remembered her friend's complaining that her mantua-maker had needed to fashion her some new gowns with wider waists. To Ariadne's teasing query, she had snapped, "No, 'tis not from overeating. I am increasing!"

Minnie, too, must be increasing, which was only natural. She and Edward had been married nearly four years. They had two other children, left in London with Edward's mother. And she, herself, had also been wed four years and might, by some mysterious process, have become the mother of two or three herself, but was not. She was still a maiden. She remembered her conversation with Iden. That had taken place four days ago and two of those succeeding days had been lovely. She could almost compare them to the time on the island, but not quite. There were moments when Iden's dark eyes were fixed on her with an intensity never visible four years back. It had sent little waves of excitement coursing through her, but if there were an intimacy in his gaze, it was missing from his speech and actions. To all intents and purposes they were a couple who might have been betrothed no longer than four days. His attitude was predicated on her own, she knew. He had promised to wait until she was ready, and as for herself, she could compare her sensations to those of a voyager come upon a fog-shrouded stretch of sea. Though she knew she must cross it to find a safe harbor, she was wary of what might await her were she to unfurl her sails to catch the breeze.

She smiled ironically. Her analogy was singularly apt. The sea breeze was eluding them, too. They had been becalmed since yesterday. That was odd, for on the morning they had crossed the Line, there had been wind a-plenty to swell the sails. It had been a beautiful day and toward seven in the evening, Edward, looking self-conscious and laughing over-much, had appeared on deck in a shiny green suit with scales painted on it. He had been carrying a battered wooden trident and wearing a crown of shells and seaweed. Bashfully, he had announced that he was Neptune, King of the Sea, and he had given a little speech to the assembled company, saying he welcomed them to his domains.

This ceremony, Iden had explained, took place every time a ship crossed the equator. Afterward they had drunk Neptune's health in mugs of grog and later that evening she had strolled on deck with Iden and he had shown her the Milky Way, looking brighter than she ever remembered seeing it, marked as it was by the famous Southern Cross. Last night, they had seen the Magellanic Clouds, two patches of stars attached to the Milky Way but so distant that they seemed to be only tiny points of light flickering like diamonds overlaid with a thick coating of black gauze.

Iden's arm had been around her waist and had remained in that position until he escorted her to her cabin door. She had expected he would take her in his arms, but instead he had merely kissed her hand and had punctiliously bade her good night. She had wanted him to remain but, out of shyness, she had not been able to speak the necessary words. Had she been shy, or fearful? She was not sure. And now, she feared she had discouraged him.

She had seen very little of him today. He had remained with Captain Wellstood until noon and when he emerged, he had seemed preoccupied and distant. She guessed that he was worried because he was anxious to get to India, but they would not be reaching their destination for another two months, particularly if they hit another calm. That, Captain Wellstood had told her, was very possible in this part of the ocean.

The sea had been amazingly still this morning. The vessel lay as "idle as a painted ship upon a painted ocean." Coleridge's poem *The Ancient Mariner* had been much in her mind, ever since yesterday afternoon when one of the sailors had pointed out a huge white bird which he had identified as an albatross. Another sailor had actually shot at it but missed and, aiming a second time, stopped, startled by her cry of protest.

Iden had laughed at her but he had ordered the man not to try to slay the creature. She wished she could forget the poem, but other stanzas were returning to her:

> All in a hot and copper sky,
> The bloody Sun, at noon,
> Right above the mast did stand,
> No bigger than the Moon.

And how long had the Mariner's vessel remained in that calm? A long, long time. She shuddered, remembering the heat of the decks this morning, with not even a fugitive breeze to cool them. Everyone had been short-tempered. The sailors had lain idle on the deck under a relentless and to her mind "small' sun. The fluttering of her fan could scarcely stir the heated air and the ship had been motionless on water that seemed like a sheet of gray-green glass.

"Ah!" Minnie exclaimed. Leaning forward, she stuck her hand out of the porthole.

"What is it, Minnie?" Ariadne inquired.

"Oh, milady, did I wake you?" the abigail asked anxiously.

"No, I have been awake . . . what is it?"

"There's a breeze comin' up, milady."

"Oh!" Ariadne slipped out of bed and felt the heave of the ship beneath her. "Finally! Iden will be pleased."

"Aye," Minnie agreed. " 'E be one who don't much care for idleness, 'specially now."

"Yes, I know he's anxious to reach India and Hydrapore."

" 'Ydrapore," Minnie murmured, giving her a penetrating look. "I expect 'e is." She paused, then added, "Oh, milady, do you not think . . ." She shook her head. "But 'tis not for me to say."

"What can you mean, Minnie?"

"Nothin', milady. Will you not go up on deck 'n look at the sky? 'Tis all red 'n gray . . . it do look pretty."

"That is not what you wanted to tell me," Ariadne pursued. "What can you not say?"

"I cannot remember," Minnie said firmly. "Will you be wantin' to dress now?"

"Yes, but I wish . . ." Looking at the girl's closed expression, Ariadne knew better than to pursue the matter any further. Yet, it was not difficult to guess the direction of her thoughts. She was thinking of Iden, of course, and their ambiguous situation which, now that they had become friends, must confuse her. She envied Minnie, who had found no barriers to knock down or surmount during Edward's brief courtship. They had seen and admired each other and they had come together as easily as a pair of doves, which was the way it ought to be—but again, Minnie had not had to contend with the persistent ghost of a dead girl or with four years of futile longing and waiting. Still, there was no reason to remember either now, Ariadne suddenly decided.

The fresh breeze issuing through the porthole was infinitely pleasant. Ariadne wanted to be out in it. She would wear her newest muslin, the blue one with the longer waist which her mantua-maker had praised as the precursor of an overdue change of style. Iden had not yet seen it. Undoubtedly, with the ship no longer becalmed, he would be in a better mood and that night they would stroll on deck under the stars. Later, when he escorted her to her cabin, she might have the courage to tell him . . . or perhaps, it would be better to say nothing. Instead, she would merely open the door and draw him inside. Envisioning his reaction, she flushed. Would he believe her too bold? She needed to devote more thought to her approach.

The storm had blown up out of nowhere. It had begun during dinner and now, some four hours later, it was at its height, with shrieking winds, battering rain, and a tumultuous sea. The ship either rocked from side to side or plunged down, down, down into veritable canyons of water. In

Ariadne's cabin, a table and both chairs had been shaken loose and slid back and forth across the floor, crashing into one wall and then into the other.

Where was Iden? That was the question that plagued her. She had not seen him when she had come on deck that afternoon and nor had he been at supper that night. Captain Wellstood had accompanied her back to her cabin when the gale sprang up.

In her mind's eye, she pictured Iden dashing into her cabin during that first bad squall. He had been in oilskins and he had lifted her in his arms, carrying her to the bed. She had been angry at his invasion. If he were to come now, he would not receive so chill a welcome—and where was he in this wild night? What if they rode out the storm and he drowned? If he were swept overboard tonight, there would be no saving his life, not in this tempest!

She did not know how long the shouts of the men and the violent battering of the winds and waves lasted, but finally the torrential rains were at an end and the wind turned to a breeze once more. At length, Ariadne relaxed her clutch on the bedpost. Her hands were shaking and she felt empty inside. However, her sensations were of little moment. Her main fears were for what must have taken place on deck during this fearful storm. What had happened to Iden? She could not sit here and wonder! She must *know*! She slid from the bed to a floor covered with a good six inches of water and groped her way toward the door. Just as she reached it, it shook under a frantic knocking.

"Ariadne . . . Ariadne . . . ." The voice was hoarse and rasping, but it was Iden! The relief that swept over her was well-nigh overwhelming. There was a pounding at her temples and the room seemed to whirl around her. She clutched the doorknob to steady herself.

"Ariadne! Are you in there?" Panic edged his tones.

Clumsily, she pulled at the door and, as it opened, blinked against the glow from the ship's lantern he was holding. As before, he was in dripping oilskins. "Iden . . . oh, Iden," she croaked.

"You . . . you're all right?" he demanded tensely.

She longed to throw her arms around him, she longed to cling to him and tell him how glad she was that he was alive and here, but instead she said foolishly, "Yes, but . . . but the floor is a bit watery."

"A bit watery!" He laughed weakly. "I thought it would be a great deal more watery. I feared we must go down. 'Twas a miracle we did not. I wanted to get to you sooner—I knew you must be frightened—but I was needed."

"Of course—I understand. And I was not frightened," she lied.

"Thank God," he said huskily. "To . . . to have brought you here, against your will like . . . like some damned pirate, and then to have you drown, oh God, Ariadne . . . my dearest." His voice broke.

Her heart went out to him. In the glow of the lantern, his face was pallid and he looked incredibly weary. His distress seemed almost tangible. "But, as you can plainly see, Iden dear, I did not drown and we did ride out the storm," she said gently.

"Oh, God, how can you be so brave and uncomplaining, when . . ." He swallowed and dashed a hand across his eyes.

"You are weary, my dearest," she said very gently. "Come." She caught his sleeve.

"Come where?" he muttered. "I must get back . . . hammock . . . rest there now I know you're safe."

Ariadne swallowed an obstruction in her throat. He had been sleeping in a hammock all this long voyage while she occupied his cabin, his bed. "Come with me," she repeated. She tightened her grasp on his sleeve, leading him toward the bed. He moved slowly, like a sleepwalker. Then he came to a stop. "You do not want . . ." He stared at the bed.

"Shhh." She took the lantern out of his hand and set it down near the bed. Then, she managed to take off his dripping oilskins. Beneath them, his garments were also soaked through. Gently, she slid his jacket off and unfastened his shirt.

He had stood passive under these ministrations, but now he protested, "You must not . . . not proper."

"Lie down." She pointed to the bed.

"But . . ." he protested. "Not right, must go . . ." He would have turned away, but she caught his hand.

"Why is it not right for a man to sleep in his wife's bed?"

"Ariadne," he whispered. "Do you . . . are you sure?"

"I am not sure how to undo your trousers, my love," she murmured. "I hope you are not too weary to help me."

"No." He fumbled at buttons and eventually eased them off, slipping quickly into the bed and pulling up the covers.

Ariadne hung his clothes over the chest and then, moving to the bed, she hesitated, staring down at him and finding, to her relief, that he had fallen fast asleep. She hesitated again, then going around the other side of the bed, lay down some distance away from him.

She did not believe she would be able to sleep. Her heart was pounding heavily and she felt . . . she was not sure what she felt, save that the sound of his breathing aroused a long-buried memory—the memory of a cave they had once shared. It had rained that night, too, she recalled, recalled also that he had muttered a name: Radha.

No such sound escaped him now. Had he quite recovered from Radha's passing, she wondered? She remembered his assurances of the other day. If he had not been entirely truthful, it hardly mattered. Radha was gone and he . . . and he . . . on thoughts that were becoming extremely convoluted, Ariadne, too, fell asleep.

"Ariadne . . ." Her name was uttered softly.

She opened her eyes to a cabin filled with morning light and with watery reflections that danced on the ceiling. She stirred and there was movement beside her. Turning, she looked into Iden's face. His dark eyes were fixed on her. She thought . . . she was not sure what. She tried to speak and, moving, felt the long length of his body pressed against her own. In the merest thread of a voice, she said, "Good morning, Iden, I . . . do hope you are feeling more the thing?"

His laughter, low and very tender, filled her ears. "Oh, much more the thing, my dearest. There were times during the storm that I thought my ship must founder and that nothing could save us. Then, to come here and have you welcome me . . . do you remember what you said to me last night?''

"I remember," she murmured.

"And did you mean it—in every sense of the word—when you called yourself my wife?''

A feeling of rightness filled her, of needing, and, at the same time, belonging. "I am your wife, Iden," she said, or rather whispered, her voice having suddenly refused to obey her.

"Oh, my dearest love," he murmured exultantly, "then I have been twice saved." Moving closer yet, he drew her against him.

If she had been asked to describe their first port of call, which was Simon's Bay on the southern coast of Africa, Ariadne would have been hard put to oblige.

Though she and Iden had strolled along the crooked streets of that tiny town and, later, put up at an inn in Cape Town, twenty-five miles away, and though she did admire the quaint, gabled houses built by Dutch settlers a hundred-odd years ago and also found the great flat-topped Table Mountain, looming over the town, awesome, her main concern was Iden. As an afterthought, she might have mentioned the masses of vivid rhododendrons that grew in the hedgerows, but once they were back on the ship, her memories of the ten days they had spent ashore were jumbled and minimized by the incredible excitement of her long-delayed union with the man she had always loved.

Even though she had loved him so deeply, there had been a distance between them. That was gone now, bridged by their mutual passion. Shy and timid at first, Ariadne found him a gentle instructor but one who led her step by step into realms of ecstasy she had never envisioned. Once they returned to the ship, her existence during the three weeks before they reached Madras was similarly dreamlike. There had been heavy seas and high winds after they left Simon's Bay, but these made scarcely any impression as, caught in Iden's passionate embrace, Ariadne heard little besides his words of love.

During the day as, arm and arm, they strolled on deck, he tried to prepare her for what she would see once she arrived in India. He had started by citing the heat, the masses of strangely clad natives and their equally strange customs, which seemed so odd and, often, so incredibly cruel to British eyes. He had found, however, that she had amassed quite a bit of knowledge by reading the accounts of various travelers who had visited the subcontinent. Hearing what she had to say, he had been, by turns, surprised at the amount of knowledge she had accumulated and yet regretful that he had not been her instructor.

"I agree that you are singularly well informed, my love," he said one morning as they neared the port of Madras, "but this James Forbes who wrote *Oriental Memoirs* . . . I do not mind telling you that I would like to call him out."

"Silly," she giggled. "He wrote mostly about flora and fauna . . . and besides, you ought to be pleased about my reading. You'll have quite enough to occupy you once we've arrived."

"Not enough to keep me from you, my angel. And the intelligent, informative Mr. Forbes notwithstanding, there'll be many sights that I fear must shock you. There is such a total disregard for human life in India."

"Suicide and suttee, I know." She shivered. " 'Tis terrible to think of marriages between mere children and men old enough to be their grandfathers—and then they die and the poor little wife must burn with them."

"Ah, but to glorious reincarnation or transmigration. They're all sure they'll live again, whether it be as a flea, a tiger, or even a maharajah. I am talking about the Hindu religion, of course. And you'll find just such a discrepancy between Kitrachandra and Sita."

She raised anxious eyes to his face. "You say he is in poor health?"

"Yes, he is definitely failing."

"Then . . ." She frowned. "Sita is in danger?" As he nodded, she said distressedly, "Can nothing be done?"

"Sita is very proud. I have a feeling she might deem it an honor to share her husband's pyre."

"But he is *half* a century older than she!" Ariadne protested.

"Their ways are not our ways." He shrugged.

She stopped midstep and stared up at him incredulously. "Iden, you'll not be telling me that you approve such a situation?"

"My love, of course I do not approve it," he assured her quickly. "I would very much like to stop this infamous practice of suttee—not just in Hydrapore but throughout India, but I, a lone individual, cannot challenge a custom that has been in existence for centuries. And I am not a missionary, my love, I am an employee of the Company and must necessarily watch my step in Hydrapore."

"What exactly do you do there?"

"I am by way of being an advisor to his Highness but, as I have said, my main or official occupation is representing the Company in what the Maharajah is pleased to call the Capital of Hydrapore."

"And what would you call it?" she asked curiously.

"Well," he answered smiling, "I would call it Bretforton, which, if you are not familiar with it, is a village in Worcestershire. It boasts a number of manor houses, a medieval church in reasonably good repair, and a castle which is definitely not. There is also a river. And, of course, there is a mayor.

"The Maharajah's domain is of comparable size. Though it is considerably more ornate, his palace is less well-laid-out than an English manor house. Then, there is the Old Palace, which fell into ruins a century or two ago, and there is the river. Yet, even though Hydrapore is not a large place, it has been and still may be a trouble spot, depending upon the Maharajah's relations with his two sons. Rama must be brought into his good graces again."

"And you will try and convince the old man of his error?"

"I will try," he agreed, a grim look in his eyes.

She guessed that he was anxious. "I am sure he will listen to you, the Maharajah," she said. "He has taken your advice before after all."

"He has also taken his brother's advice from time to time."

"I would imagine that is only when you are not there," she said staunchly.

He smiled down at her. "I hope I can justify your faith in me, my love."

"You have already," she said softly. "And when will we arrive . . . so that you can set matters straight?"

"That will depend on the weather and the transportation, which can be by land or river. If it is by land, we will take elephants."

"Oh, I should love that!" she said excitedly.

"You may have an opportunity. However, it's not always as enjoyable as you might think. Elephants have definite minds of their own."

"I have never read that they are dangerous."

"They are not usually dangerous, but they can be extremely determined."

"I think you are funning me," she accused.

"I swear I am not."

"How do they express this . . . determination?" she inquired suspiciously.

"With their trunks."

"Their trunks?" She gave him a skeptical glance. "How?"

"Well, I once saw a man, a sergeant in the Guards, strolling along in front of an elephant who happened to be in a hurry. Now these animals are very carefully trained and they, being intelligent, know that they are not to trample anyone who inadvertently gets in their way. The elephant trumpeted loudly but the sergeant, evidently believing that the elephant was the animal equivalent of a despised native, did not quicken his pace. Consequently, the elephant wrapped his trunk around our sergeant and, lifting him high in the air, gently deposited him by the side of the road. It was a long time before he stopped quaking in his boots."

"And did he not deserve it!" Ariadne clapped her hands. "I should love to see something like that. In fact, I shall love to see India!"

"And so you will, my darling." Iden pointed toward the horizon. "It is there in the distance awaiting us in all its dirt, its squalor, its decay, its roguery, its incredible beauty, and its magnificence!"

"And will I love it as much as you do?" she asked softly.

He gave her a quizzical look. "Did I say I loved it?" he inquired.

"Do you not?" she demanded.

"I . . . have," he said slowly, "but now . . . I am of two minds. And you possess one of them . . . and a good part of the other. I do not know if I have any space left for India."

Ariadne had read and read. She had listened closely to Iden's descriptions of Calcutta, Delhi, Bombay, Benares, Madras, of smaller cities, villages, mountains, hills, valleys, deep gorges, and fast-flowing rivers. She had seen pictures of the country, paintings of its myriads of people, of gods such as Vishnu, Krishna, Ganesha, the last being a four-armed, red-skinned individual with an elephant's head. They worshiped also Huneman, a monkey-god who had aided Rama, hero of the Ramayan, the epic poem of India. She knew that the Hindus believed the earth to be a circular plain, resembling a water-lily, its circumference 400,000,000 miles. It was borne on the back of eight huge elephants which in turn stood on the back of an enormous tortoise which stood on the coils of a thousand-headed serpent, and when the serpent became drowsy and nodded, an earthquake was the result. She knew that following an earthquake, Indian villagers thronged the streets beating drums and blowing horns to awaken the serpent and forestall another quake. But in spite of all that the printed page and the pictures had contained, as well as Iden's descriptions, Ariadne, standing at the side of *The Argonaut II*, anchored in the roads of Madras, realized that no one had really prepared her for the reality that was India.

She hardly knew where to look, the high white walls of the city were almost blinding under a hot and brilliant sun. The harbor was crowded with ships, among them were stately British warships, small Chinese junks, and vessels flying the flags of a world of nations. There were also native fishing boats and, incredibly, small dark men propelled across the waters by sails without boats and headed toward *The Argonaut*.

They were carrying various types of produce and, save for shiny caps on their heads, they were naked.

Pointing at them, Ariadne nudged Iden. "But can they walk on water?"

"No, no miracle workers, they!" he laughed. "They are on catamaran boats."

"I see only sails."

"They're standing on a sort of float made of logs. You can't see them because they're below the water. They'll be clambering up here like monkeys and trying to sell us the worst-tasting melons this side of paradise, or they'll offer us rotten mangoes and overripe plantains."

"Very well, I will try and remember the words you've taught me for 'no' and 'go away.' "

"Please," he said. "Alternate them."

"Sir?" Edward came up to them.

"Yes, Edward," Iden said. "Were you able to get us aboard one of the carriers?"

"Yes, sir. He's got room for all five of us."

"And how much is he charging you?"

"Twenty rupees, sir."

"Go back and tell the old pirate that there's someone here who knows that the fare to the docks is fifteen rupees. If he attempts to argue, refer him to me."

"Yes, sir." Edward grinned and turned away.

A few minutes later, they boarded a boat manned by six oarsmen and equipped with a bamboo enclosure which, Iden told Ariadne, was to shield the passengers from the sun and keep them cool. He grimaced. "Coolness, save for the snow that covers the Himalayas, is at a premium here in India."

The boat was not only not cool, its bamboo shelter was abominably close and the smell caused Minnie to cough and cringe.

" 'Twill not be a long voyage, this one," Iden comforted her. "We'll be on the quay very quickly."

"It's interesting . . . this boat," Ariadne said with determined cheerfulness.

"Is it?" He gave it an indifferent glance. "Possibly, to an outsider. I've had the misfortune to be in so many of them that I couple them only with India's lesser evils."

His term "outsider" was like a small, hard slap on the wrist. Inwardly, she winced, feeling gauche and even stupid. But in that same moment, he put his arm around her, giving her a loving little squeeze. "I do not mean to sound blasé, my love. 'Tis natural that you'd find everything new and strange—and that is as it should be."

She looked at him in some surprise. In the last weeks, she had found he could read her thoughts with an ease that seemed remarkable. She said shyly, "I thought I was entirely prepared for what I would see . . . but one cannot be prepared. I mean, 'tis so much more . . ."

"And will prove to be more and more and more. India is beautiful, but also it is terrible. You will be both enchanted and appalled. You will see sights that must repel you. If I could keep you from them I would—but very often they appear when you least expect them."

"I do know that," she emphasized. "I know about thugs and flying bugs and bats and bodies in the river and holy men—"

"And, I hope, those who are not in the least holy, but are merely out for the stray rupee." He laughed. "Many so-called fakirs are fakers. But enough, I'll let you supplement your reading for yourself. I only wish we could stay in Madras longer. We'll be on our way by the end of the week."

"I am looking forward to that journey," she said with a glowing smile. "Our wedding journey."

"Our wedding journey, true." His lips brushed her cheek. "And I promise you, we'll not remain very long in Hydrapore and nor will I need to return. Once we leave, I will show you all India, or at least as much as you want to see, and then we'll set sail for England and never return!"

"You'll not want to return after having spent so many years here?"

"Too many years, my beloved. This land was never made for Englishmen or women. They grow languid and dispirited here. They need the green fields, cloudy skies, cool rains, and country lanes. As for myself," there was a wistfulness to his tone she had never heard before, "I long to settle with you in the home I left when I was a wild and adventurous youth. 'Tis a place of mists and cold winds blowing down from the North, but they are fresh winds, and the moors in springtime . . . But enough, you'll see it for yourself, and in a not too distant future, I hope.''

"Sir," Edward said, turning around, "we've arrived."

"So we have." Iden looked up at the dock. "Come, Ariadne, they'll be lowering a chair to bring you ashore."

Taking his arm, Ariadne stood up carefully in the unsteady boat. It was with difficulty, however, that she kept herself from throwing her arms around him. His mention of settling down had struck a deep responsive chord. Though their lives had been lived separately, she, herself, had never really known a real home. Her father had traveled widely and she, ensconced in a school in Bath, had spent her summers following him over Roman roads or hunting for ancient British relics in Devon, Somerset, and Wales. Her life had differed little upon their return from Greece. She had rarely visited her house in the country. However, now was no time to wish they were in England, not when all India beckoned!

Ariadne's first impression of Madras was one of heat that was almost tangible. It progressed from stifling to unbearable once they came into the customs house. In addition, the place was extremely crowded. Ariadne, clinging tightly to Iden's arm, was both amazed and thankful at the progress he, Captain Wellstood, and Edward made through masses of people all seemingly going in different directions. Order appeared unknown to the Indian population. Those British travelers who had come on their boat and others like it were pushed every which way. The air was filled with angry voices speaking in a hundred different dialects.

Minnie, moving closer to Ariadne, added her voice to the babble. Judging from her expression and her accompanying gestures, she was trying to be reassuring, but Ariadne could not hear anything she was saying. After what seemed hours but was probably no more than forty minutes, they emerged onto a street that was equally noisy, equally hot, and just as crowded. The combination of strange odors, unrelenting heat, and the shrill high speech that filled her ears was daunting. Equally daunting were the sights about her—especially the strange costumes of the women! She had seen pictures of the sari, but only a few splashes of color had been used to depict the bangles, ankle bracelets, earrings, and nose-rings they wore, and naturally, these did not approach the reality. Everywhere she looked, Ariadne saw gold and silver bangles studded with precious and semiprecious stones encasing slender brown wrists and arms all the way up to the elbow. Many women wore three or four massive necklaces. Some of their nose ornaments were merely studs, but there were nose-rings quite as large as bracelets and covering half the face!

In spite of being so heavily encumbered, they moved very gracefully in their thin, vivid pink, purple, green, or multicolored saris. Many of the younger Indian women were quite beautiful and, Ariadne noted, they often visited admiring looks on Iden.

Inadvertently, she thought of Radha. Was she as lovely as some of the girls she had just seen? Undoubtedly, she was even lovelier, Ariadne guessed, and unwillingly remembered Iden sleeping in the island cave and calling out "Radha, Radha . . ." In the past four years, had there been no doe-eyed, lithe-bodied replacement for her? Iden was a passionate man. The name Sita flashed across her consciousness—Sita, the beautiful eighteen-year-old Maharani wed to a man fifty years her senior!

"My love." Iden turned to her. "I will take you to the guest house and then I must go to the Government House and speak to the Company representative. Possibly there will be further word from Hydrapore. Meanwhile, I want you to rest. And in the late afternoon, we will go to the bazaars. You must have a scarf to replace that cape, else you will suffer heat prostration."

"Oh, that would be lovely," she said gratefully. She added wistfully, "I wish I might dress like the Indian ladies. They do look cool—if anyone could be cool here."

His eyes gleamed. "I should like that, I think. I will buy you a few saris, if you like—but for my eyes only."

"Gracious!" she said teasingly. "Have I married an Othello, then? 'O beware, my lord, of jealousy!' "

"How can I not be jealous when I see the glances lavished

upon you by every man that passes? I am more than half inclined to buy you a veil such as the Muslim women wear!''

"You are teasing me," she chided. "I do think that is too bad of you.''

She was surprised by the intensity of his dark gaze as he replied in tones that bordered on the solemn, ''No, I am not, and I must tell you, my dearest, that the idea of the duties awaiting me has become much more irksome. If I had my way, I would spend my entire time in India—with you.''

"Did you really say that?" she breathed. "I think I must be living in a dream!''

"No, my dearest love, you are not. I am." Unmindful of the crowds, he bent and kissed her full on the mouth.

Chapter Six

Standing by a window in the main room of the small bungalow which served as their guest house, Ariadne peered out into the darkness. Iden should have returned ages ago! He had promised that his business at the Government House would take no longer than an hour, but she had heard the clock in a nearby church chime four, then five, then six, and now she was counting again and, of course, it was seven!

The night was full of unfamiliar sounds—chirping, buzzing, sharp little barks that did not quite sound doglike—maybe it was jackals. There was also the high twitter of bats. Futilely, she wondered where Minnie and Edward were. She had asked Iden to let them go off by themselves. Consequently, she had no one to tell her whether such long delays were usual. She had a feeling they might be, given the all-pervasive heat that made every movement a chore.

Her increasing anxiety was abruptly terminated by a familiar whistle—to which, as usual, her eager mind supplied the words:

> How happy could I be with either,
> Were t'other dear charmer away!

Footsteps ascended the three stairs to the veranda, the door was unlocked, and Iden hurried in. He was carrying a bundle and he looked considerably relieved. "I was detained. I feared you might venture out to look for me."

"Where were you?" she demanded. "I was so worried!"

He put down his bundle and slipped an arm around her waist. "I knew you would be, my dear. I was at Government House and I could not get away." He added regretfully,

"What's more, I have bad news for you. We have to leave Madras immediately."

"Tonight?" she asked.

"No, but first thing tomorrow morning. We'll sail to Calcutta, which, as you probably know, is on the Hooghly River. I'll have a brief meeting with my superiors at Company headquarters and then we'll be going upriver to Hydrapore. I've already alerted Edward and Minnie as to the change in plans."

"Why must we go so soon?"

"The Maharajah is said to be gravely ill. However, these reports have circulated before and he's recovered. In spite of years of indulgence, he has a surprisingly strong constitution. I hope that the gravity of his situation is exaggerated—for Rama's sake." He regarded her concernedly. "I have half a mind to leave you here in Madras. Because if it's true—"

"No!" she cried. "I forbid you to even think of such a thing!"

"My love, if the Maharajah is indeed ill, the conditions in Hydrapore might worsen and—"

"If there is trouble, Iden, I want to be with you." She lifted her chin. "I am no cringing violet."

"Shrinking, my love." He laughed and kissed her. "And of course I would not want to leave you. But before you make a final decision, I must tell you that we'll need to travel fast. And Hydrapore is not directly on the Hooghly. It is three or four hours through the jungle. The roads, if you can dignify them by so civilized a term, are rough and we'll be fording streams—all this without elephants, I fear, since the first leg of our journey must be aboard *The Argonaut II*, which is not equipped for elephants."

"Iden," she said indignantly, "do you imagine I could rest a single night knowing you were making your way through that jungle without me?"

"And do you think," he countered, "that I could rest a single night knowing you were in Madras and I unable to see you?"

"Oh, you!" Clenching her fists, Ariadne pounded him lightly on the chest. "Have you been teasing me, foul varlet?"

Seizing her hands, he brought first one and then the other to his lips. "Know, oh heavenly one, bringer of all earthly delights, and my heart's guardian, that I could never leave you behind—you being a part of me now. But I am sorry that we cannot remain in port for another day. I had wanted to show you the city and take you through the bazaars." Moving away from her, he brought the bundle back. "But this is for you, oh shining one." Pressing his palms together, he touched his forehead and bowed.

Ariadne giggled. "I hear you, lord of forty elephants and their complement in goats." Breaking the string of the package, she carefully unwrapped it. "Oh!" she exclaimed delightedly as she saw a length of white cotton and beneath it, turquoise gauze gleaming with golden threads and also a folded square of scarlet silk. "But this must be a sari!" she said excitedly, touching the turquoise gauze.

"It is. The cotton cloth must be wound into a turban and the red silk is the scarf I promised you. I thought one could find anything in the bazaars, but I did not come across a straw bonnet. You must have a head covering of some sort my dear."

"Indeed I must, and I do like this much better than a mere bonnet. You must show me how it is wound."

"The turban or the sari?" he inquired.

"Both, my lord," she dared to respond. "And . . . oh, what are these?" She looked down at the bundle again, finding a pile of gold and silver bangles, several set with turquoise, malachite, and carnelian, "Ohhh, how beautiful!"

"Come," he demurred. "These are paltry trifles! When we leave Hydrapore, I will pile the treasures of the East into your lap." He kissed her on the forehead and then on both cheeks. "But," he added with a worried frown. "I still wonder if I ought to take you there. If there's strife . . ."

"I do not believe there will be strife," she said positively. "The gods are smiling on us now. And to further ensure our safety, I will pray to Ganesha."

"Why Ganesha?" He laughed.

"Because he has an elephant's head and you told me elephants are to be respected."

"And do you know why Ganesha has an elephant's head?" he inquired.

"No, but I expect it must be for some complicated religious reason,"

" 'Tis not as complicated as you might think. Ganesha is the son of Shiva, and when he was born, he was so radiantly beautiful that his mother, Parvati, asked Saturn to look at him. In her pride, she had forgotten the force of the planet's power. Saturn obeyed and the child's head was immediately burned to ashes! Shiva was terrified and hastily searched for a new head to put on his son's shoulders. The first head he saw belonged to an elephant."

"Oh, dear," Ariadne sighed. "That must have caused considerable complications when he was nursing." As he broke into laughter, she added, "Iden, dear, we must think of Minnie. You're not having her come with us to Hydrapore, or Edward? I believe she's breeding, even though she's not mentioned it to me. She really ought to stay here in Madras and rest as much as possible."

He surprised her with a quick embrace. "And here I was wondering how I might tell you that I, too, thought she must remain behind," he said gaily. "I was about to ask you if you'd be willing to take a native servant with us. There's a young woman, Kamala by name, who was employed by a British family now returned home. She speaks a fair amount of English and I understand she's eager for a similar position."

"Good!" Ariadne exclaimed. "We must hire her, and I do think that since Minnie and Edward will be staying behind, we ought to see they're made as comfortable as possible. Perhaps they could have this bungalow?"

"Of course, that's a splendid idea." He added fondly, "I must congratulate you, my dear. I know of few memsahibs who would be so agreeable to change."

She smiled up at him. "I have come to appreciate . . . changes, my dearest."

From the deck of *The Argonaut*, Calcutta presented a surprising amalgam of East and West. Many of the buildings that rose on the banks of the mighty Hooghly River could have been transported directly from London on the back of some genie.

In addition to Fort William, with its massive structures, including a huge Gothic cathedral, the whole surrounded by a wide expanse of park, there was also the Government House, which was relatively new, having been finished in 1802, and a replica of Kedlestone Hall in Derbyshire. These and other British-accented buildings had given Calcutta the nickname City of Palaces. Again, as in Madras, the panorama before her seemed to waver in the heated distances and now that the vessel had dropped anchor, the heat enveloped them like an invisible blanket.

Ariadne shot an envious look at little Kamala, calm and cool in her cotton sari. She had worn her own turquoise sari in the privacy of their cabin and she wished she might have donned it at the moment. She chuckled, thinking of the horror with which the wives of Company officials would have regarded her, particularly if she, in common with Kamala, were to wear all the jingling bangles and bracelets Iden had given her.

"When in Rome do as the Romans do." The phrase flitted through her mind but, of course, they were in India, where the British were determined to set a good example for the poor heathens. Impossible not to wonder how her countrymen would have reacted had their island been invaded by foreigners determined on abolishing their beliefs and customs. She glanced at Iden, deep in conversation with Captain Wellstood. She had criticized this cultural invasion and he had agreed with her. They were in accord on a great many things, so many that they were like two halves come together to form a whole. Thinking suddenly of Robert, she winced. If she had married him, she would always have known something was missing. How foolish she had been, imagining that she could so easily exorcise Iden Peverell from her mind and heart. Now, she felt wholly possessed by him. Yet, though she had not admitted it to him that last night in Madras, she, too, wished they might have returned to England rather than going on to Hydrapore.

She grimaced. She did not want to go to Hydrapore where

Iden had once loved and wed a girl called Radha! It was ridiculous and also it was unworthy of her to be afraid of the dead, but the ghost of a lost love could be potent. She had had evidence of that in her own family. After her young mother had died, her father had never looked at another woman! Iden, however, had finally looked at her.

Yet, supposing he had not been forced to marry her? Despite all his protestations of love, was he yet trying to convince himself that he was really in love with her? He was so very affectionate, forever caressing her and lavishing kisses on her during the day and deeply passionate at night. Much as she welcomed and luxuriated in his embraces, she was surprised by them. Was he not being overdemonstrative? She knew Carola would have thought so. Her friend had confided that her husband rarely saw her during the day. He was generally at Boodles, gambling, or attending mills or going off to Newmarket for the races. And that, she knew, was the rule rather than the exception for fashionable couples in London and in the country, as well. Perhaps when she and Iden returned to England, they, too . . .

"Well, my dear, and what do you think of Calcutta?"

Startled, Ariadne glanced up at Iden, who, without her hearing his approach, now stood next to her. As usual, he slipped his arm around her waist, giving her a tender little squeeze. Her qualms vanished and she bit down a sigh, regretting her uncertainty as well as the unreasonable jealousy that yet afflicted her. She said, "Naturally, I am overwhelmed by the original of all the paintings I have seen!"

"One is," he agreed. "Have I told you that you look like Sheherezade in that turban?"

"Are you sure you're not telling me a tale?" she giggled.

"Entirely sure. Or would you prefer to be Gulnare of the Sea? That might not be quite appropriate, since we are about to disembark. Are you prepared to leave this vessel? Or have you left anything behind in the cabin?"

Much to her interior dismay, her earlier reluctance returned. However, since there was but one answer to his question, she said, "Nothing. I hear and obey, master of all masters."

"Come, then, my sapphire-eyed houri."

"Some sapphires are pink, I have heard." She forced a smile.

"And others are yellow, but I recognize no stone but that which is the blue of your glorious eyes."

Was he being too effusive? Was he not trying to hide his real feelings beneath this banter? They were not many leagues distant from their ultimate destination! With an effort, she forced herself to reply in kind. "Thou art besotted, O Prince!"

By that peculiar osmosis that enables ambitious hostesses to know when someone of particular importance has arrived in a city, numerous invitations from the wives of generals, colonels, and high officials in the East India Company awaited Ariadne and Iden in the small bungalow they were to occupy during their two days ashore.

Iden, counting them, pronounced himself amazed. "In the past, I have been able to come and go without remark," he told her. "I expect 'tis the report of your beauty, my love."

"I am of the opinion 'twas the official in Madras, announcing *your* arrival," she contradicted.

" 'Tis a long time since I have been welcomed by my fellow countrymen," he remarked dryly. "We are here for only a brief time and I would prefer to employ that in showing you the wonders of the city. That is, if you have no objection. I fear we are living like gypsies—always on the road."

"I have no objections at all!" she assured him enthusiastically. "Furthermore, I might mention that I've always envied the life of a gypsy. The freedom from convention and from paying courtesy calls is definitely beguiling."

"May you never have to experience a gypsy's freedom, my love. To those bound by society's demands, it does seem marvelously unhampered, but tribal laws are strict and gypsies are often cold and hungry, sleeping in fields, stealing poultry, risking imprisonment and cruel punishments that flay the soul as well as the body. There are gypsies in India, you know. And I have had occasion to converse with them—as well as some in England."

He had spoken as if he had more than conversed with

them, as if, in fact, he might have shared some of their hardships. She had not tried to probe deeper, but she had been left with the feeling of depths unexplored in Iden. Would she ever know him through and through? She was doubtful, and the fear that had invaded her that morning, still remained. She continued to dread their arrival in Hydrapore and the memories that the place could not help but invoke in him. At the same time, she regretted her fear. It bespoke a lack of trust in him and also in her own power to hold him. Too often, she harkened back to those years when she was short, plump, and spotty. Did butterflies, once they had emerged from their cocoons, ever reflect on the days when they had been furry little worms gnawing on leaves? Whether they did or not, the memories of Greece returned at odd moments during their stay in Calcutta. Fortunately, there was also a great deal about the city to divert her thoughts.

As she and Iden walked along the city streets, their progress was often impeded by wandering animals and by beggars, some horribly and, Iden had told her, purposely mutilated so that they might excite the pity of strangers. To her surprise, he seemed largely indifferent to these horrid sights.

"One becomes hardened," he explained in answer to her indignant accusation. "I could scatter a few rupees about, but systematic charity is what is needed here. And the Indians do not think that way. Many of these beggars are Untouchables or pariahs, as they are called. For a member of a higher caste to offer assistance would be for the so-called Good Samaritan to lose caste and be ostracized forever."

"Can nothing be done to instruct them?"

"They'd not accept the instruction."

"Oh, Iden." She came to a stop. "Does it not gall you to accept these conventions?"

"What can I do about it, my love? We've had this conversation before. You, with your well-developed sense of right and wrong, must needs recognize the fact that a different sense exists here in India."

"India, I begin to believe, is a place of no sense!" she muttered.

"Ah, hah!" He laughed. "And this is the memsahib who

frowned on the British habit of meddling with established traditions!''

She laughed too. '' 'Tis a strange country. Maybe we oughtn't to be here at all. I do not mean *us*, in particular, but the British in general. Some of the ladies I have seen looked so yellow, so languid and weary.''

"The climate is debilitating. We are in the temperate season now and you can see how hot it is. And unfortunately, most British will not change either their eating or their drinking habits to conform with this location. A great many Indians exist on a strictly vegetarian diet, one that we shall continue to follow, if you do not mind, my love.''

Since she had hardly been aware of what she had been eating, save that there had been more vegetables than meat, she was able to say, "I do not mind. I feel so well.''

"And look so beautiful. I am glad that Kitrachandra is so old, else he might want to add you to his collection of wives.''

"His collection," she repeated. "Oh, dear, there are those others, Moti and . . . and . . .''

"Vimala.''

"How old are they?''

"Moti is forty-nine and Vimala is fifty-seven, I believe.''

"And Sita is only eighteen. They must feel very bitter.''

"I doubt it. They've nothing to feel bitter about. None of them are sharing the Maharajah's affections and they, at least, have borne children. Sita remains a virgin.''

"And may go to her death as such . . . and they with her?''

He said gravely, "I do not see how it can be avoided, given custom and the temper of the people. 'Tis expected, you see.''

"Oh, King, live forever," Ariadne said fervently.

"For many reasons, let us say amen to that," he agreed.

They embarked for Hydrapore as scheduled. The crew of the boat was augmented by Edward's replacement, David Palmer, a charming young man whose uncle was connected with the Company. His knowledge of boats came from acting in a number of capacities aboard his father's yacht, which was generally anchored off Brighton. Aside from Mr. Palmer, there were eight native bearers who would carry such luggage and supplies as they needed during their stay in Hydrapore—and the palanquin which Iden had insisted Ariadne must use.

In answer to her protest that she was well able to walk in the jungle, he had said stubbornly, "Though there is a road from the river to Hydrapore, it is difficult to traverse for someone unused to jungle travel. You could be tripped by hanging vines and there are snakes among the grasses."

At the mention of snakes, Ariadne had abandoned her arguments. Now, standing at the side of the vessel as it sailed slowly upriver, the breeze not being strong that morning, Ariadne shifted her gaze from the small boats along the side of them to the heavily wooded shore. As she did, she heard Mr. Palmer's cheerful whistle and smiled. She had liked him immediately and, talking about Brighton, she had found they had some friends in common. He had come to India, he had told her, on a whim. His real destination had been China, where he would be picking up some vases and ivories for his father, Sir Gladwin Palmer.

"My dear papa is a friend of the Regent's and he has been infected by what I called the China craze—you will know what I mean if you have ever been inside the Pavillion." He had grimaced.

Ariadne, who had found the Pavillion's fantasies very heavy-footed could agree. She had also agreed with Mr. Palmer's observations on India, which he found not to his liking. "I'd rather spend my time in a place where the sea wind blows fresh and you do not see dead bodies lying on the river mud nor burning ghats along the shore. You are not plagued by mosquitoes nor threatened by crocodiles should you stray too near the riverbank or plagued by monkeys leaping at you from the nearest branch. And nor are you sickened by beggars who look as if they'd been born in a dung heap!" He had sighed. "And their religion, or rather religions—human life's not worth a groat here. Either they're sticking pins or knives into some part of their anatomy in the name of their gods or they are rushing off to Juggernaut to cast themselves under that idol they drag out on its cart seemingly for the sole purpose of crushing the faithful to death . . . but why go on? I loathe fanaticism."

She looked toward him now and found that he was staring at her. She flushed, unwillingly reminded of someone she would prefer to forget.

Robert.

Mr. Palmer bore a singular resemblance to Robert. Not only was he tall, blond, and blue-eyed, but he had the same slight curve to his nose and his hair was wavy. Iden had agreed with her on that resemblance, saying lightly that he hoped that their characters, at least, differed. She had not replied. There were times when she could not help feeling guilty about Robert. Occasionally, she had had dreams about meeting him on the docks once they disembarked in England and going into a long explanation as to why they could not go ahead with the annulment. Obviously, some manner of explanation would eventually need to be proffered to Robert.

"And is not yon wooded bank beautiful?"

Ariadne started and, looking up, she flushed again, finding Mr. Palmer at her side. Struck anew by his startling resemblance to Robert, it was a moment before she could reply, "It is certainly beautiful, all those different trees of the sort never seen in England. Those must be mangoes over there." She pointed.

"Yes, they are and there are coconut palms and peepul trees and there are probably fig trees and banana palms. 'Tis a veritable Garden of Paradise, all that it needs is an houri—but she is on shipboard." He smiled down at her. "However, I think I am straying into Moslem territory."

Ariadne could not conceal a smile, but she said pointedly, "Rather, I should say *forbidden* territory, sir."

He flung back his head and laughed merrily. "A stand well taken, but are not all such gardens forbidden—and guarded with sword-bearing angels and such? I fear I have wandered into one by mistake and I know that I must apologize but, my dear Lady Peverell, surely you cannot blame me for finding you beautiful!"

He was really audacious and he deserved a sharp set-down,

but Ariadne, with the shade of Robert hovering at the back of her mind, could not bring herself to say more than, "Do not be silly, sir," Turning away, she leaned over the railing, adding, "Look at that bird. I do think it's a parrot of some kind."

"I would think 'twas a bird of paradise, but I pray you'll take care, Lady Peverell!" He caught her around the waist, pulling her back against him but releasing her immediately. "You must not lean over the railing so far. You could fall into the water and scare the . . . crocodiles."

It was Ariadne's turn to laugh. "I would certainly not want to do *that*."

"No, you would not. A scared crocodile is a hungry crocodile. And you are a most delicate and delectable morsel."

She stared up at him and was momentarily confused by the intensity of his gaze. However, he was flirting with her and she ought not to be allowing it. "I think, sir . . ." she began.

"Mr. Palmer," Iden said, "did you not hear Captain Wellstood call you?"

"Oh!" Ariadne, finding Iden directly behind them, said confusedly, "I did not know you were here."

He eyed her coldly. "I am sure you did not." He glanced at Mr. Palmer. "And you, sir, would be advised to keep your mind on your work."

Mr. Palmer reddened. "Yes, sir. I am sorry, sir." He moved away.

"He deserved that," Ariadne murmured.

"Oh?" Iden questioned. "You surprise me, my dear. I was under the impression that you would fly to his defense."

Ariadne stared up at him in some surprise. "And why should I, if he were malingering?"

"Or . . . merely lingering?" Iden questioned.

"And what is that supposed to mean?" she demanded, not liking the sarcasm she heard in his tone or the way he was looking at her.

"David Palmer, I might remind you, my dear, is, despite his connections and references, a member of the crew."

Ariadne's eyes widened. "I am quite aware of that."

"Indeed? I had the distinct impression that you thought you were in some London drawing room."

"Iden!" she scanned his face, looking for some hint that he was teasing her, but found none, On the contrary, he was looking at her very coldly. Obviously, he was angry and more specifically, he suspected that she . . . that David Palmer . . . but he could not imagine . . . She too was beginning to be angry. "Again, it seems I must probe for meanings," she said.

"Is it so difficult for you to understand that my wife should not be encouraging young Palmer?"

"Encouraging him, sir?" she snapped.

"What else were you doing?"

"I was under the impression that I was being extremely discouraging to him."

"It did not look that way to me . . . letting him put his hands on you . . ."

Ariadne backed away, staring at him incredulously. "Letting him put . . . For your information, he thought I might fall in the water. Or would you have preferred it if I had? Then, at least, no one would have suspected that I was attempting to entice . . . are you possibly hinting that I meant to seduce him?"

"You were in no danger of falling into the water. The railing would have prevented it."

"Then, 'twas his mistake not mine!"

"Oh? Did you consider it a mistake?" Iden demanded sarcastically. "You were smiling at him so cordially . . . and I might add that you and Mr. Palmer were not alone on the deck. You were in a position to be observed by most of the crew."

"I do hope they were tolerably well entertained," she said freezingly. "Obviously, you were, sir."

"Damn it, have you no sense of propriety!" He glared at her.

Her bosom swelled. She lifted her chin, "How dare you speak to me in such a manner, sir? No doubt, you are confusing me with some one of your Indian doxies." She saw fury leap into his eyes and discretion being the better part of valor, she whirled away from him and crossed to the larboard side of the boat. She half expected him to follow her, but evidently he was as angry as herself—and with no reason, none at all. "How dared he . . ." She glared down at the water. Her heart was beating faster and it was pounding in her throat as well. Intermingled with her righteous anger was amazement that Iden could have been unjust. To accuse her of encouraging David Palmer, when all she had done was talk to him! Had he expected her to ignore him. . . . would he expect her to ignore every personable man who spoke to her? Obviously, he had lived far too long in India, where women of her rank were shut up in purdah. Is that what he had in mind for her? She gave a little gasp. Something that she had taken to be a floating log had suddenly opened wide a mouth filled with two rows of sharp, white, gleaming teeth—a crocodile. It reminded her of Iden!

A rough and twisting road but yet a road and not merely a crooked path, stretched from the banks of the Hooghly to the palace of the Maharajah of Hydrapore.

Ariadne, ensconced at last in the palanquin, had been roused from her bitter thoughts by her amazement at the complexity of its interior. In her reading, she had found pictures of native bearers with such conveyances on their shoulders, but all had concentrated on the *outside*. None of the texts had mentioned drawers and shelves front and back, one shelf with a net drawn across it to keep foodstuffs from tumbling out. There was a place for books and there were hooks on which to hang outer garments. Under the mattress were all manner of flat objects, including a small Hindustani dictionary and a drawing pad. Venetian blinds that could be raised or lowered hung on either side and there were lamps for reading at night.

The palanquin had one long pole before it and a similar one behind. Though there were eight bearers, only four carried it at a time, changing with the other four every half mile and muttering and groaning as they did—as if the burden were so heavy they were bowed beneath its weight. The texts had not mentioned that either, and nor had they described the lack of space. The interior, she was sure, had been designed for a pygmy! By the time the bearers had covered what might amount to half a mile, she was feeling as uncomfortable as they seemed. She was also regretting the fact that she had acquired her additional inches. Undoubtedly, Aladdin's love, the Princess Badr-al-Badur was tiny, probably about four feet two. But palanquins were used by men, also. Probably they, too, were small.

As for herself, she could not really sit up; she had to lie against the backrest, and the lack of space made it impossible to change her position. She had to sit with her legs partially drawn up and her hands close to her sides. Furthermore, the bearers had a most unfortunate habit of shifting the pole from one shoulder to the other, a maneuver accompanied by exhausted grunts. Kamala, walking beside them, was smiling broadly, Ariadne noted. She wished that she, too, were walking and would have liked to say as much to Iden—but since he had coldly overseen her being deposited in the palanquin, he had not come near it! He was walking ahead with Captain Wellstood. She drew a deep annoyed breath. From the few glimpses she had had of his back, he was holding himself stiffly, presenting the very image of an outraged husband! And how dare he? One would have thought from his ridiculous attitude that he had discovered her locked in a long embrace with Mr. Palmer! However, coupled with her own anger was a hollow feeling. She had never seen Iden in this mood. She wondered if his anger would smoulder for the entire day and into the next and the next . . . she would not put it past him, flaring up over so slight an incident.

He was being idiotic!

Did he expect that she would apologize to him—possibly creeping to his feet to humbly kiss them? Is that what Indian ladies did? She ought to ask him—he was the expert on that particular subject! He had been wed to Radha, the beautiful, the perfect . . . Perhaps he had thought she meant his lost bride when she had referred to "Indian doxies." She swallowed a burgeoning lump in her throat. That would have been unforgivable and she had not meant that. She had meant . . . The dense trees with their curtains of vines were suddenly haloed by a nimbus of tears. She blinked them away furiously. In another moment, *she* would begging *his* pardon—

when it ought to be the other way around! She glared at a bright green parrot, one of the many that flew from bough to bough, their raucous voices much at variance with their plumage. It was a bird that had gotten her into trouble. If she had not leaned forward and Mr. Palmer had not grabbed her—grabbed her, not embraced her . . . she would not think about that. She fixed her eyes on the passing scenery.

Vividly beautiful flowers were to be glimpsed through the foliage. She had seen clumps of jungle grass that grew to an astonishing five or six feet in height. She could imagine that tigers lurked in some of those sequestered glades but, if they were present, they were also silent. Once she thought she saw a green snake descending down a tree trunk but a second look revealed leaves sprouting from its belly and her heart dropped from her mouth to its proper spot in her bosom. The vines were so thick here, it was a marvel they did not choke the trees. In fact, they had become trees themselves. She started as, at a sharp command from Iden, her bearers halted and deposited the palanquin on the ground.

"What is it?" Ariadne asked nervously. "What has happened?"

"Nothing has happened." Iden strode to her side. "I wanted to show you this . . . it marks the boundaries of Hydrapore. If you are finding your mode of transportation difficult, it will soon be at an end." He reached down, adding, "Come, let me help you out."

She could hear traces of hauteur in his tone. She regarded him coolly. "I am capable of getting to my own feet, sir." Avoiding his outstretched hands, she crawled out of the palanquin. Unfortunately, when she tried to get up, her knees buckled and she might have fallen had he not put an arm around her, holding her up. Her legs were numb.

"You will naturally feel stiff," he explained. "And you'd best hold on to me until your circulation returns or better yet . . ." He picked her up and carried her to a clump of jungle grass. Setting her down, he added, "Hold onto my arm, please."

"That is not necessary. My legs feel better now." She took an experimental step and nearly fell again, would have, in fact, fallen, had he not grabbed her.

"Very well, Ariadne," he said rather grandly, "since I do not want you to injure yourself, I apologize."

She felt an immense surge of relief, but she said merely, "You were completely wrong, you know."

His lips twitched. "I have said I am sorry."

"I . . . I expect I'm sorry for the way I spoke to you," muttered Ariadne, her gaze fixed on the ground.

"Very well, my dear, we are both sorry, are we not?"

She raised her eyes to find him smiling. "I . . . expect we are," she admitted gruffly.

His laughter rang out, startling several parrots who flew from a nearby branch in a marked manner. "And we will never have another misunderstanding . . ."

She laughed, too. "Oh, never, never again . . . until the next time."

"Until the next time." He grinned. "Can you stand?" he added.

She moved away from him. "Yes, thank you. The pins and needles are gone."

"Good. Now look!" Pulling several handfuls of grass back, he revealed the sculpture of a warrier seated upon an elephant.

"Oh!" she exclaimed in surprise. "But it is marvelously sculpted. What is it doing way out here, hidden in the grass and all by itself?"

"One of India's many mysteries," he said. "It's very, very old."

"I see that it is. Much of the detail has been worn away. Who is it?"

"It is believed to be one of their gods. But the features being largely obliterated, it is doubtful if anyone knows which of the three hundred and thirty million it is."

"Three hundred and thirty *million* gods!" she marveled. "I remember reading that and finding it difficult to believe, even though I know some are the same god in different incarnations. I might tell you 'tis not so difficult anymore. India is truly amazing and, if you do not mind my saying so, rather frightening."

Iden said gravely, "Yes, it is frightening. I hope you never find out how very frightening it can be. But come, we must be on our way." He let the grasses spring back. "And," a gleam of amusement glittered in his eyes, "I beg you'll not let your bearers intimidate you with their grunts and groans. They could as easily carry a horse in that palanquin—but complaining is a way of life with them and also a bid to get more rupees."

"Very well, I'll not waste any more sorrow on them." She laughed.

She laughed again, but silently, as with an even louder chorus of groans, her bearers hoisted the palanquin to their shoulders. Though she was still determined not to acknowledge any wrongdoing on her part, it was pleasant to have Iden in a good mood once more. And—her thoughts were suddenly dispersed by the sound of hooves, a horse galloping swiftly along the path.

Her bearers came to another jerking halt as a youth on a fleet white horse approached. He was wearing a gold and black turban and he was clad in rich silks. She caught the sparkle of gems as he galloped past, but his pace was so fast that she was unable to see his face. Then, turning around, he uttered a wild cry and rode back. Her startled bearers set her on the ground so hastily that her teeth came down hurtfully against her tongue. At the same time, she saw the youth leap from his horse and, advancing on Iden, throw his arms around her husband's neck, crying in a high voice and in English, "You are returned, Iden. Ah, I could not believe it until I saw you for myself. Can you imagine that I have ridden over this road nearly every day since your message arrived—and every day I have been disappointed. I did not believe you would really come again, but you are here—a thousand welcomes, my dear!"

Confounded by that exuberant, even loving greeting, Ariadne was further amazed to see Iden embrace the youth warmly. "Ah, 'tis good to see you again. And how did you manage to get away?"

"Oh . . . ." The youth shrugged and laughed. "I can get away whenever I choose—if, of course, I choose the right time."

"That is more to the point, I should think," Iden said severely. "You will always take unnecessary risks. But you must come and meet my wife."

"Your wife? You have brought your woman to Hydrapore?" The young man spoke, Ariadne thought indignantly, as if she were a concubine! Furthermore, his voice had been tinged with incredulity and, she guessed, he must be remembering Radha. And who was he? He appeared to be too youthful to be either Rama or Narayan. Yet, judging from his rich attire, he must be a member of the Maharajah's immediate family. An adopted son perhaps? She knew that maharajahs often chose their heirs from the children of sisters, aunts, or uncles when they had none to succeed them, but Kitrachandra did have a successor—the evil Narayan.

The youth was still standing very close to Iden, she noted. And did Indians, in common with the French, embrace each other? She waited rather tensely as Iden and his companion approached the palanquin. Then, as they came closer, her eyes widened. The boy was a girl! Indeed, she was an incredibly beautiful girl with a pale brown complexion and huge dark eyes under slanting brows. Her mouth was full and red and the wisp of hair that emerged from her turban was, amazingly, auburn. She heard a gasp and a side glance showed her that Kamala was staring at the newcomer wonderingly.

"Your Highness, may I present my wife?" Iden said. He added, "Ariadne, my dear, this is the Maharani Sita of Hydrapore."

"But she is beautiful, Iden!" the girl exclaimed before Ariadne had a chance to acknowledge the introduction. "And dark, too. I could not bear it if you were a yellow-haired, milk-white English maiden with the so-pale blue eyes. Your eyes, they are also blue, but 'tis the blue of the deepening sky, just as the sun sets. Or perhaps it is the blue of the storm-tossed waves. Are you really British?"

"Yes, your Highness, I am," Ariadne said coolly.

"I do not like the British," the Maharani stated, her eyes on Iden. "Only you, Iden, my heart, but I expect I will come to like your woman once we are better acquainted." She smiled coldly at Ariandne and before she could reply, added, "But I will go now that I have assured myself you are here at last and may give aid to my poor Rama!" She ran back to her horse and, flinging herself on its back with an ease that startled Ariadne, she administered a sharp slap to its rump and galloped away.

"Well!" Iden exclaimed. "You have now met the youngest Maharani of Hydrapore. It remains for you to see his Highness and the palace, which is not far away." He had spoken lightly, but there was a frown between his eyes. "She takes too many chances, does the little Sita."

"She is very beautiful," Ariadne commented.

"All the more reason why she ought not to take chances— riding in the woods alone, not to mention sneaking out of the palace! She has always been too daring for her own good, and also she is overindulged by her husband. And what he does not give her, she takes. I am referring to freedom, of course. She is impatient of restrictions, and has been from a child—quarreling with her ayah, wanting to dress herself."

"That is not surprising, surely. The winding of a sari is not very difficult."

"That is not the point." He laughed. "Dressing is a ceremony here. From the time of their birth, the children of the rajahas are waited on hand and foot. They are massaged and bathed. They do not know how to put on so much as a slipper. It is all done for them. Rama has told me that as a babe, he was not allowed to touch the ground until he was two—before that he was always carried in the arms of servants. Narayan, I understand, was four before his mother would allow him to be 'defiled' by putting a foot on a marble floor or a silken carpet."

"No wonder he was spoiled," Ariadne said. "And Sita, also."

"Sita is not really spoiled," Iden said. "I think you will like her when you get to know her. But, come, we must be on our way."

He addressed the bearers in sharp staccato phrases and, predictably groaning in unison, they rose slowly to their feet and lifted the palanquin to their shoulders.

As Iden rejoined Captain Wellstood, Ariadne felt singularly complacent. Other wives might have resented the way Sita had thrown her arms around Iden, an embrace he had not scrupled to return. However, she had said nothing. She did hope that Iden had noticed the forebearance with which she had accepted that greeting. If it had been Mr. Palmer and herself, Iden would undoubtedly have sent forth another volley of accusations—and why was Sita so very friendly with him and so cold to herself? She refused to speculate on these questions. She, at least, did not have a jealous nature!

Chapter Seven

Iden had said they were near the end of their journey, but Ariadne, faced with the green vastness of the jungle, had not really believed him. Then, without warning, it fell away and so quickly, so unexpectedly that it seemed to her that a genie escaped from one of King Solomon's copper vessels had preceded them, clearing away the foliage and replacing it with a double row of stately acacia, Bo, and neem trees bordering a broad road leading up to high sandstone walls. These were a dusky rose in hue and notched at the top. They were bisected by a wrought iron gate through which Ariadne glimpsed a courtyard and a flight of stairs fronting a massive building. Gazing upward, she saw a high domed roof of red sandstone glittering under the afternoon sun.

On either side of the gate stood a guard in a plain blue tunic, narrow white trousers, and a black turban. Both men were tall and husky with heavy mustaches and eyebrows that stretched across their brown faces in unbroken bars. There was something forbidding in their dark gaze, she thought. Yet, as Iden and Captain Wellstood approached, the guards suddenly smiled broadly and bowed, obsequiously pressing their hands together and touching their foreheads.

Iden smiled back and spoke to each man causing them to break into laughter. Opening the gates, the guards waved them through and Ariadne, encountering interested stares, smiled shyly and waved. She received appreciative stares and wide grins as they bowed again.

The courtyard proved to be covered with slabs of sandstone and the palace, set back and built on a rise of ground, proved to have what appeared to be hundreds of windows—most of them arched. Ariadne, remembering that Iden had told her the palace could not be compared with those in Nepal and Oudh, was still amazed at the vast stretch of pavillions, gateways, pools, fountains, and towers.

She could hardly wait until her bearers had set down the palanquin and immediately she started to crawl out.

"Wait, my love." Iden, hurrying to her side, extended his hand. "You might experience more discomfort. Best let me help you up."

"I do not believe . . ." she began as she let him pull her to her feet. "Oh, goodness, they are asleep again." Again, it took a few minutes before she could move about freely. She laughed. "This is the last time that I will avail myself of a palanquin. You really should have warned me."

His laughter echoed her own. "There are some experiences one cannot describe."

"When we leave Hydrapore, I will walk," she said decisively. "I have always enjoyed walking. And . . ." she glanced away from him and immediately forgot what she had been about to say as she saw a large pavillion at the far end of the courtyard. It was covered with a square stone canopy, set on four pillars carved with images representing various gods. The capitol of each pillar was in the shape of a coiled serpent, its fanged jaws depicted with a disturbing realism. She was reminded of the krait that had dispatched the nurse of little Rama. It gave her an unpleasant thrill, reminding her that behind the massive facade of this palace, evil, like a coiled serpent, could strike when least expected. She turned back to Iden. "What is that pavillion over there used for?"

"Nothing now. But some years ago, it sheltered a fakir who, with the tenacity of his kind, sat cross-legged upon it night and day in all weathers for fifty-three years. The Maharajah told me that when he died, they could not uncross his legs and so burned him in that same position."

"Ugh!" Ariadne shuddered. "I am beginning to find . . ." She paused as she discovered that she no longer held her husband's attention. Iden and Captain Wellstood were staring at the arched entrance to the palace which, in common with the gateway, was flanked by armed guards. At the moment, they, Kamala, and the bearers carrying the luggage were bowing obsequiously to a slender young man, clad in gold brocade with a matching turban, who had just emerged.

Ariadne stiffened. Undoubtedly, here was the evil Narayan. Her supposition was confirmed as Captain Wellstood, frowning, said sharply, "Good God, isn't that . . . ?"

"It is," Iden snapped.

As the usurper drew nearer, Ariadne's incipient anxiety was replaced by a startled appreciation of features which might have graced one of the handsome heroes of the Arabian Nights. His face, a slender oval, was lighted by huge dark eyes under heavy but well-shaped brows. His cheekbones were high, his nose straight, and his mouth, topped by a thin mustache, was full-lipped but firm. He was not above medium height, but he was very well proportioned. His shoulders were broad and the cut of his long coat did not disguise his narrow waist. He moved gracefully and, amazingly, he had a most cordial smile for Iden and for the captain, too.

Neither man returned his smile. Inadvertently, Ariadne glanced at the snake-crested pillars of the pavillion. Evil, she thought angrily, ought to have the equivalent of claws and fangs, but possibly young Narayan was the more dangerous because he was so very attractive.

"Iden and Captain Wellstood," the young man said in English. He had a slight accent, but it was not Indian. As she tried to place it, he continued, "How very good to see you both again." He seemed honestly pleased, which also surprised Ariadne. And now, he addressed Iden again. "I hear that you have brought your bride with you, a most beautiful bride, I see. Will you not present her to me?"

"Of course, Rama, this is Lady Peverell. My love, this is Rama . . ." He broke off, adding, "Am I to tell my bride that you are still the heir apparent to the throne of Hydrapore?"

Rama grinned. "You may tell her that, Iden—and also I will say that I bid her welcome to Hydrapore in the name of the Maharajah Kitrachandra, who is my father, and in my name as well. I cannot speak for my brother Narayan, since he is banished."

"Banished!" Captain Wellstood exclaimed.

"Did not my stepmother explain? She has told me that she met you in the jungle."

"She explained nothing," Iden said shortly. "Then, 'twas a tempest in a teapot."

Rama threw back his head and laughed. "Ah, you remind me of the good Mrs. MacDonald. That was one of her sayings, too."

"And here's another, Rama. Have I come clear across the world on a wild goose chase?"

Ariadne had traced the young prince's accent. He had, she realized, a slight Scottish burr, which must stem from the late lady he had just mentioned and was very evident now as he said, "It would have to be a saying, Iden, since I cannot think there would be any sport in chasing geese, not even in England. But," he continued, "you will find that while I am no longer in peril, your presence is most desirable. My father will want to see you after you have rested from the rigors of your journey, of course. You have set this time aside for us, yes?"

"I have set aside the time," Iden acknowledged.

"And you have hastened here on my account, for which I am deeply grateful . . ." he looked at Iden quizzically, "though I do not understand why my stepmother did not explain about Narayan."

"Nor do I," Iden agreed.

Rama turned toward Ariadne again. "But we are being rude. We talk of this and that and ignore your most beautiful wife. It is your first journey to India, Lady Peverell?"

"Yes, your Highness, it is."

"And how do you find my country?"

His direct question brought a slight flush to her face, but she said diplomatically, "I find it unlike any other, your Highness." She hoped that he would not ask her to clarify her statement. She was in no mood to manufacture false and fulsome encomiums about India in general, not when she was as surprised and annoyed as no doubt Iden was himself. Though she was pleased that this handsome young man no longer needed to fear his brother's machinations, she could well understand Iden's surprise and anger at being hurried here for nothing more than what promised to be a pleasant visit. And why had Sita not given him some inkling of the situation rather than deliberately lying, which is what she had done when she had mentioned "giving aid to my poor Rama." Probably, she *had* come to meet him with the news of Narayan's banishment, and, for some reason, had changed her mind.

A vision of Sita's exuberant greeting arose in Ariadne's mind and with it a most unwelcome notion. Could she have withheld that information to punish him for not having arrived alone?

Rama's voice broke into her speculations. " 'Tis passing warm here in the courtyard and you must be excessively weary from your journey, Lady Peverell. Would you care to rest?" He looked at Iden. "And you also, my friend?"

Iden shook his head, "My wife, I am sure, would welcome a rest, but I hope to pay my respects to your father."

"He will be pleased to see you, extremely pleased, I can assure you, but he is sleeping." There was anxiety in Rama's eyes as he continued, "I am worried about his health, Iden. As you know, it has been declining for some time now. The problems created by Narayan have wrought upon him in mind and body."

"Indeed? I am sorry to hear that." Iden frowned.

"I thank you. And as I have said, there is much to discuss. But first let me have you and Captain Wellstood, here, shown to your quarters." He turned to Ariadne. "And perhaps, since her ladyship must be very warm, she could go to the Zanana where old Preeta can bathe her. Your servant, of course, may accompany you."

"The Zanana?" Ariadne questioned. "That would be the women's quarters?"

"Yes, my love," Iden corroborated. "Would you like that? You'll find Preeta's ministrations most refreshing."

A pool, filled with flowers, had been one of the illustrations in a book she had read. With her dusty clothes, sweat-drenched and clinging to her body, the prospect was singularly enticing. "Yes, thank you, your Highness, I think I would."

As soon as she had voiced her agreement, she remembered that the Maharajah's women lived apart from their lords. Did that mean that once she entered the Zanana she would be lodged there for the remainder of her stay in Hydrapore?

Her anxiety was quickly abolished as Rama said, "Good. And afterward, you will be shown to the suite of rooms you will share with your husband, Lady Peverell." He turned to Iden, "And when you are rested, my friend, we will talk further. May I repeat that I am *very* glad that you are here, *especially now*. You and Captain Wellstood, also."

Iden's eyes narrowed. "In that case, Rama, let me say that I am glad that I have come."

"And I, too, your Highness," the captain said.

A young woman in a dark blue sari, who gazed at Ariadne with shy amazement and admiration, conducted her and Kamala to the Zanana. By the time they reached it, Ariadne's head was awhirl with the sheer richness of a palace which, she must needs remember, could not vie in luxury with those located in the large Indian states.

She had seen rich silken carpets and walls patterned with stylized flowers and birds done in the most intricate mosaic. There were mosaic-covered floors, as well. The red sandstone walls of one chamber were intricately carved with vines and flowers and, amazingly, the material had been fashioned into an open grillwork of a most complicated design. Passing through it, she had come to a stop, too overwhelmed by the sheer beauty of the conception to move. Kamala and their guide seemed surprised by her reaction. On the other hand, however, they had been fascinated by her simple muslin gown. In another room, she was once more amazed by the geometrical shapes painted on its walls. The floors everywhere were either marble or inlaid wood.

The Zanana, located in a wing that was almost a palace in itself, was a series of large rooms with latticed stone screens facing the jungle and obviously designed to give its sequestered inmates a view of the world they were never allowed to visit. Some of the windows overlooked a sunny courtyard in which grew mango trees and banana palms as well as flowering trees for which she had no name. The courtyard was paved with marble and in a series of square and octagonal beds grew pink, gold, red, and white roses. The whole was centered by a square pool reflecting the red towers of the palace as well as the surrounding trees. Kamala, following quietly after Ariadne, seemed more intrigued by the Zanana than she had been by the rest of the palace.

"I have been told of these," she remarked at one point. "But it has never been given me to view the quarters of a Maharani."

"Would you like to live in all this splendor?" Ariadne inquired.

Kamala shook her head vigorously. "I would rather die," she said in a low voice. "To be secluded seeing naught but one's husband or son or possibly a cousin or two and to hear only the chatter of women is not for me. I am not rich, but I come and go as I please, and because I earn rupees, I am no man's slave."

"You are right," Ariadne said softly, warming to the girl. "And I agree with you. The rooms here are exquisite—but to see them day after day for years and years and years must certainly pall on one." If the truth were to be told, the beauty was already palling on her. She thought of the broken pillars of Greece, white and sun-bleached. They were more to her liking than the intricate Hindu art with its minute intertwining flowers and plants, its geometric variations repeated on the walls.

She had a sudden longing for Greece and, more specifically, for Naxos, where she had been so briefly happy with Iden.

It was ridiculous to conjure up the past! It was equally ridiculous to feel so depressed and intimidated by all this magnificence. Or did her feelings spring less from her surroundings than from one who dwelt therein—Sita. Sita, who was beautiful and restless, predatory as a tigress and spoiled by her ancient husband? Did she long for fulfillment with Iden? Had they . . . Ariadne loosed a short impatient sigh. She was basing her suspicions on that exuberant greeting in the jungle. She was, in fact, being just as ridiculous as Iden

when he had angrily accused her of dallying with Mr. Palmer!
She was sure that his feelings were partially based on Mr.
Palmer's resemblance to Robert, and her anger over Sita was
similarly based on her possible resemblance to Radha. However, *she* had spent very little time in Mr. Palmer's company,
while Iden had been in Hydrapore for four long years and in
Sita's company. No, not with her alone—but with Rama,
with Kitrachandra, and with others whom he, as a Company
representative, must needs deal. That was the only sensible
way to regard the situation.

As they moved through the halls of the Zanana, Ariadne
was aware of whispers and movement. Though she saw no
one, she was sure that she and Kamala were being closely
observed from behind velvet curtains and intricately carved
wooden screens. She was glad when they finally reached the
bathing room, a large square chamber with unadorned walls
and windows, covered by venetian blinds. In the center was a
marble tub and nearby, an old woman in a plain cotton sari
stood smiling and nodding.

Her face was dark brown and heavily scored by time. Her
hair, gathered into a knot at the base of her neck, was snow
white and she looked very frail. However, when Ariadne's
guide addressed a few words to her, she nodded and smiled at
Ariadne. The guide smiled, too, and hurried out of the room.

"This is Preeta, who will bathe you," Kamala explained.
"I will disrobe you."

"Thank you," Ariadne said. She would relish a long bath,
she thought gratefully.

A few moments later, sitting in the tub, she heard the old
woman clap her hands and issue a string of instructions in the
direction of the doorway. Ariadne expected that she was
signaling the servants to bring in the cans of water. Consequently, she was surprised to see a bevy of young girls in
bright saris bring in three silver bowls and four tall copper
vases, which they set down near the tub. They lingered
briefly, staring wide-eyed at Ariadne, until the old woman
clapped her hands again and uttered more words in a scolding
tone of voice, at which they all giggled and hurried out.

During the ensuing hour, Ariadne was extremely grateful

for the presence of Kamala, who could explain the various steps of what proved to be a singular bath. Rather than pouring water over her and rubbing her with soap and a sponge as Minnie and Rosie did, Preeta turned her attention to Ariadne's hair, rubbing it with a green substance which Kamala called "thali paste," made, she explained, from freshly plucked leaves. Subsequently, her hair was washed with water from one of the copper vessels and covered with coconut oil. It was dried with a thin, porous material which Kamala called "*tortu.*"

Subsequently, Preeta piled Ariadne's hair on top of her head, securing it with a tortoise shell comb. She grinned approvingly at her and said something.

"What did she say?" Ariadne asked Kamala.

The girl smiled. "She says she likes your hair because though it is curly, it is not yellow or orange like that of a *ferangi* woman."

"Oh." Ariadne remembered Sita's remark. At least she had that in common with Radha, she thought to herself, and wished she had not remembered her at this precise moment. Had Radha looked anything like Sita? If so, she must have been even more beautiful than she had imagined. "Oh!" she exclaimed as warm, scented water gushed over her shoulders. "That's a pleasant odor. What is it?"

"Some sort of herb," Kamala said.

"And what is this?" Ariadne demanded a moment later as Preeta rubbed her with a rough sponge which made her skin tingle and which also left a thin coating of powder on her body.

"It is very good for the skin," Kamala explained.

"Gracious!" Ariadne exclaimed nervously as Preeta, picking up another copper vessel, suddenly deluged her with more warm water, bright red in hue. "I hope that's not a dye!"

"No, no." Kamala laughed. "It is called Nalpamaravellam water, which also is very good for the skin. It is made from boiling the barks of forty different trees!"

The operation completed, the old woman turned to Kamala and uttered another string of words.

"You must lie down on the tile and Preeta will massage you," Kamala explained.

The massage was wonderfuly relaxing. Relaxing, too, was the drying of Ariadne's hair, which took place over fragrant smoke issuing from what Kamala called a *karandi,* and which had proved to be an iron pot filled with hot coals and aromatic herbs.

After her bath, Ariadne was given a silken sari, which Kamala draped around her. Her guide returned and led her to the room she would share with Iden. It was furnished with a wide, low divan covered with silken sheets. Ariadne was aware of Kamala muttering something to her, but she hardly heard her. Lying back on what proved to be an incredibly soft mattress, she fell deeply asleep the moment her head touched the pillows.

She was running, running, running from a pursuer—Robert, in a golden mask, she was sure it was Robert, but it had been Iden who had worn the mask. Then, there was a woman, incredibly lovely, dark, much darker than herself. She was wearing a white turban and she was standing with Iden in the garden that had suddenly sprung up in the middle of a dance floor. Nearby was the statue of the warrior on an elephant and as she stared at it, the elephant trumpeted and threw his trunk around her, lifting her high, high, high into the air and Sita was laughing—no, it was not Sita, but Radha, standing close, close, close to Iden and as Ariadne, loosed from the confining trunk, approached, Radha stood in front of him, arms outstretched guarding him. She was reminded of St. Michael with his flaming sword, standing at the gates of Paradise. The woman was signaling her to go back, telling her that she was Iden's own true love.

"No," Ariadne moaned, and in that moment felt herself clutched by a shadowy something she could not see—the elephant? "Put me down," she muttered. As the pressure grew stronger, she tried to scream and a hand was held gently against her mouth.

"Hush, my love," came a whisper in her ears. "You are dreaming."

Ariadne opened her eyes to a room bathed in moonlight, its

soft glow full on the beloved features of the man who lay beside her, cradling her in his arms. "Iden," she whispered. "Oh, I had such a strange dream."

"I know, you were moaning. I did not want to awaken you, but it seemed to me that you were frightened."

"I was." She moved closer to him, luxuriating in his nearness.

"Why?" he asked, dropping a kiss on her cheek.

"I saw a crocodile coming after me," she improvised. It would never do to tell him the truth, to remind him, if indeed he needed reminding, of Radha. "You know, I did see a crocodile on the river and thought it was a floating log—until it opened its mouth!"

"One can make that mistake." He laughed softly. "But you are not on the river now, beautiful. Do you feel better now that you've had your bath and a sleep?"

"I feel ever so much better. I must have slept a very long time. 'Twas sunny when I went to bed."

"Yes, you've slept for hours, and no wonder—given that journey through the jungle. Are you hungry? I brought you some fruit and cakes. I did not think you would want me to rouse you for a long and courtly dinner."

"Oh, I am very glad you did not. I could not have eaten it. I am not hungry now. I just want to stay where I am."

"Oddly enough, my dearest Lady Peverell, I am in total agreement," he murmured.

As his arms tightened about her, she had the strange feeling that she was still dreaming, little Ariadne Caswell-Drake in her seaside cave, dreaming of Mr. Peverell. Then, under the pressure of his seeking mouth, she knew that she was gloriously awake!

On an afternoon three days after their arrival at the palace, Ariadne, awakening from an afternoon siesta that had lasted no more than half an hour, felt uncomfortably warm. She stared through the open door into a walled garden. She could go out there and sit by the fountain, but she disliked those high walls. She felt caged in—and the flowers and the trees were also caged in their marble bordered plots. She longed to see an English garden with grassy paths and trees, grown a little shaggy because the gardener might not have trimmed them. At home, the lake washed muddy shores because it was natural, not water captured in a marble basin!

They had been away from England for nearly six months. It was the fall now and the trees would be turning. In another month they would be red or gold and the chivvying winds would be sending showers of them to the ground, while others would still cling tightly to their branches. Of course, she was thinking of her own home in Sussex. When they returned, they would be living in Iden's house. She had seen it only once, shortly after her return from Greece. She and her father had, out of curiosity, taken the long journey to Northumberland. They had stayed overnight in York and then they had gone on to Craster Village and beyond to the estate, then in the hands of a caretaker, since Sir Marcus had gone to Rome.

Somewhat to her surprise, it had proved to be a Georgian mansion, rather than the castle she had expected, knowing that the Peverell family had lived in Northumberland since the time of Henry II. Her father had explained that the castle had been pulled down in Cromwell's time, the Peverell's having fought for Charles I. They had fled to Brussels and, their fortunes depleted, they had not received their lands again until late in the reign of Charles II. Until then, they had lived frugally in a small cottage in the village that had once been part of their estate. Fortunately, Iden's great-great-grandfather had not fallen in with the schemes of a deposed James II and nor had he been moved by the plight of Bonnie Prince Charlie. He had fought for King and country and been amply reward by William and Mary and later by Queen Anne. The mansion had been built by his son during the reign of George I.

Ariadne remembered having found it much to her liking and there had been a beautiful park surrounding it—as well as extensive farmlands. She had pictured herself riding over them with Iden and now, she thought with a surge of happiness, she could conjure up such an image without fear of disappointment.

She remembered that it had been a changeable day when she had finally arrived at Peverell Manor. Clouds had been drifting over a pale yellow sun and there had been a smell of rain in the air. There did not seem to be any clouds in India, but that, of course, was because rain was not expected for another three months. She longed for clouds and for the wildflowers that grew in the deep grass of an English meadow. She could find no buttercups or daisies here, but she could see trees from the windows on a higher floor, the strange trees that grew in the tangled jungles adjacent to the palace. They must needs suffice until she and Iden could return home—and when would that be?

In the last two days, she had scarcely seen him. He came to bed late and arose early, and he was extremely preoccupied. He had reason to be. The Maharajah was gravely ill; he might be near death, and Rama needed advice. She had not received that information from her husband. Captain Wellstood had proffered it today during a midday meal at which neither Iden nor Rama had been present. She had not seen Sita, either, not since the day when she had so fondly greeted Iden. She was probably at the bedside of her husband, and if he died—what then? Ariadne shivered. Would that beautiful young woman be forced to share his burning pyre? She did not want to dwell on that. She wanted . . . trees. Slipping out of bed, she wrapped herself in a sari and went into the hall.

As she moved toward the stairway to the upper floor, Ariadne was aware of an unusual silence. Generally, the halls were filled with masses of chattering flunkeys, hangers-on, astrologers, relatives of the Maharajah, court officials, merchants, servants. Today, she did not see anyone, not even when she started up the curving flight of stairs leading to the next floor. She had been there only once, when Iden had showed her that part of the palace that was not closed off, but she remembered that there was a window not far from the head of the stairs. It had provided them with a panoramic view of the grounds and the encroaching jungle which, Iden had said, might engulf the palace one day.

He had mentioned other defunct city-states where towns were deserted and ancient palaces stood empty, inhabited only by jackals, bats, monkeys, and other wild creatures. She did not believe that such a fate would overtake Hydrapore. From the little she had seen of Rama, he appeared forward-looking and energetic. Now that he was free of his half-brother's menace and open to suggestions from the Company, he would probably enjoy a long and prosperous reign.

She chuckled, remembering that at first she had not approved of Company influence and had privately believed that the British had no right in India. At present, she was not so sure. There was so much that needed changing: the caste system, for instance, with its impregnable barriers. Then, there were the benighted zealots who tortured their bodies to prove their devotion to their cruel gods, and the total subjugation of women, which included selling mere babies to old men, and the elderly, willingly drowning themselves in the waters of the Holy Ganges. She shivered, struck suddenly by a feeling of menace which she might blame on her thoughts, or possibly on the unnatural silence that was currently prevailing in the palace.

She had reached the top of the stairs and there was the window, wide open. She went toward it and, leaning on the sill, she stared into the sunny courtyard and beyond to the jungle. In the distance, she could see the river, blindingly bright in the relentless afternoon sunshine. The Hooghly, she recalled, was a tributary of the Ganges and consequently semi-sacred, as were many of India's rivers. One could commit suicide in the Hooghly, too, and why was she so preoccupied with thoughts of death? Probably, because of the Maharajah.

She stared down at the jungle—at the trees with their strangely shaped leaves, their brilliant flowers, many caught in the strangling tendrils of the vines. And there were the parrots and monkeys as well, their screams and chattering diminished by distance. Her eyes widened and she leaned forward, staring at the man who had just come into view. Iden! It was Iden. She raised her hand to wave and let it fall, laughing at her foolishness. Even if he looked in her direction, he would never see her, he would see only the red sandstone facade of the palace with its many, many windows.

She watched him. He was walking slowly, his head down. He was staring at the ground, a habit of his when deep in thought, but what was he doing out in the jungle? Had he gone there to get away from the moribund atmosphere of the palace? Perhaps he was sharing her thoughts about England, finding the greenery an oasis in this sun-baked land. More and more they seemed to know what the other was thinking. He had laughed about it the other day, saying such transferences were common among couples. She wished that he had an even deeper insight into her thinking this afternoon. Then he might have asked her to come walking with him. Perhaps he had come to their room and found her deeply asleep?

He had stopped and was looking around—looking for what? Then she gasped, seeing a man moving through the jungle, moving from tree to tree, stealthily, as if he were hiding from someone or, perhaps, stalking an enemy, *Iden*? Her hand crept to her mouth. Was her husband being followed by this man, who might do him an injury? He must be warned! She turned toward the stairs and then turned back. She could never reach him in time and nor could she shriek out a warning. She was too far away and meanwhile Iden, all unaware, stood there.

Her heart was pounding heavily in her throat. Tears came into her eyes. Iden was in danger, she was sure of it! And she could do nothing, nothing, nothing! She leaned forward, directing her thoughts at him, willing him to turn and look in her direction. She would lean from the window and wave at him with both hands, but he would not understand and meanwhile, his enemy was moving closer, closer, and Iden, alerted at last, turned swiftly!

The man rushed toward him, hands outstretched menacingly. No, not menacingly, *not* menacingly at all! He threw his arms around Iden, clinging to him, and Iden, *Iden* was holding him tightly and patting his shoulder, and now there was no mistaking that slender figure in the bright silks and the white turban—it was Sita, of course! Sita, who was now being held close, close, close in the arms of *her* husband!

Turning away from the window, Ariadne went slowly across to the stairs. Coming into the chamber she shared with this man who, after all, had only pretended to love her, she sank down on the bed. Her earlier, all-but-forgotten fears had returned to torment her. Her suspicions had been founded on fact. He had not turned from Radha to herself, he had turned to the beautiful Sita; she was the beacon light that had brought him across the world!

Why, then, had he been so eager to claim her, Ariadne, again? She had an answer for that: her fortune. He had not wanted to relinquish it. He had received her dowry, but her dowry was not enough. She stared at the door. Eventually, he would return and what could she say to this man, this man who had pretended to love her, had pretended to be jealous of her, and who had possessed her body, mind, and spirit? Until that moment at the window she had been his completely, so very completely that he had come to dominate her every waking thought, and now . . . now what?

If they had been in England, she could have fled from him, fled to her old home in Sussex. She would have ordered her servants to bar the door against him—but she was here and there was nowhere she could run, not in this miserable, hot, inhospitable country. Ironically, her only recourse was to depend on Iden, her betrayer! She must needs pretend that nothing untoward had happened. What made her go to that window? Fate! The Indians believed in fate and so must she. but the scene she had witnessed from there must be pushed into the back of her mind until they were out of India and back in England. Then, she would tell him the truth and go home—home to loneliness and misery and the knowledge that once she had given him his freedom, Iden would return to India to spend his days with Sita!

Her head throbbed, not surprisingly, given the circumstances. She lay down and when the tears came, she angrily blinked them back. She would not grieve over Iden's perfidy! She . . . she blinked as the door was pushed open and Iden strode in.

"My love," he said in a low voice, "I am glad you are here and awake." Closing the door softly behind him, he hurried to the window and closed it too.

Ariadne sat up, staring at him incredulously. His jungle

tryst with Sita had not lasted long. And how dare he address her as "my love," as if nothing had happened. However, she must not display any anger at this cruelly-false greeting, not when she was totally dependent on him and, as far as he knew, nothing had happened. She said, "I have been wondering where you were. 'Tis so very quiet in the palace."

"The Maharajah is dying," he said gravely. "And we, my own, must leave within the hour. We will have received a message from Calcutta requiring our presence there. 'Tis all arranged, and Kamala has agreed."

"K-Kamala?" she said confusedly. "I do not understand you," she added with a touch of the anger she had vowed to conceal from him.

"Oh, my dearest love . . ." He regarded her regretfully. "I am putting the cart before the horse, am I not? How would you understand? Listen to me, we are to take Sita with us, disguised as your maid."

"Sita!" Her amazement grew and her anger exceeded it. His temerity shocked her. He was proposing to take the woman he loved with them. But, of course, he was unaware that they had been observed! And she must needs make sure that he remained in ignorance of that observation. As calmly as she could, given her chaotic state of mind, she said, "And why would you want to take Sita with us?"

"Hear me, my own." Sitting down on the edge of the bed, he continued, " 'Tis a wild scheme, but 'tis the only way to save her life."

"Her life?" she repeated, and knew what he meant. "From death on the pyre?"

"Yes," he acknowledged grimly. "Rama is beside himself with misery. I was unaware of this, but he and Sita have adored each other since they were children. That was the wedge that Narayan and Arvind used to separate him from his father. They produced witnesses who swore that they had seen the pair making love in a sequestered part of the palace grounds. Of course, it was untrue. They have never been overt about their mutual passion. Both were all too aware of the consequences—but they have met in the jungle from time to time and 'twas Narayan, they think, who saw them.

"Fortunately, Sita was able to convince that Maharajah that there was no truth to Arvind's allegations."

"How could she do that?" Ariadne inquired.

"She produced her own witnesses—her fellow Maharanis—who backed up her statements that she was with them at the time that Arvind's supposed witnesses saw them. Since the old man adores Rama, he forgave him, and you know the rest. Unfortunately, that has placed Rama in a difficult position. As the heir, he might be able to intercede for Sita and keep her from the pyre, but that is exactly what Narayan and Arvind want. They would hint at an unlawful liason and to quell the gossip, Rama would be forced to let her go to her death. That is why he has arranged her escape."

"And will she never see him again?" Ariadne asked.

Iden smiled. "Once the period of mourning for his father is at an end, Rama will be forced to marry. He intends to send for Sita's twin sister."

"Ah, she has a twin?"

"She *had* a twin; it is not generally known, but two years ago, Sita's entire family was wiped out by the cholera."

"But . . ." Ariadne began and stopped. "You mean that Sita . . ."

"Exactly," he said. "She will return as her twin. However, it remains for us to get her out of the palace. I have just seen her. She is wild with terror, but she has agreed to the disguise. We have but to get her to the yacht. We must go, and soon, before the Maharajah breathes his last. According to his doctors, he will be dead before morning. All in the palace are awaiting that. Rama will explain that Sita has fled."

He broke off, staring down at her. "My love, why are you weeping? Are you afraid of what we must do?"

"No, no, no," Ariadne sobbed. "I . . . I feel so ashamed."

"Why?"

"I . . . I cannot tell you."

"Tell me." He pulled her into his arms.

"Because . . ." She explained her baseless suspicions and wept until he stopped her tears with his kisses. Moments later, he released her, saying regretfully, "We will have to leave very soon, my angel. And . . . I do not believe we will be in danger, but there is a chance . . ."

"I am not afraid," she said staunchly. "I will be with you. And—" She would have said more had he not kissed her again.

Chapter Eight

Once more Ariadne, seated in her palanquin, was traveling through the jungle. They had left the palace with a speed that startled her; it occurred to her that their journey had been in the planning stage even before they had arrived. Possibly that was why Iden had spent so much time closeted with Rama. Naturally, with the Maharajah's approaching death, his son would have left little to chance. Once they were back on shipboard, she would ask Iden about that. She leaned out of the palanquin trying to catch sight of him, but he had been walking fast—a good deal faster than her bearers who, as usual, were groaning at every other step. She glanced nervously about her at the dense foliage. As before, she had the feeling they were being observed. That had proved to be her imagination before, and probably she was imagining more terrors that did not exist.

There had been nothing remarkable about their departure, nothing to arouse suspicion among those who were concentrating solely upon the imminent death of the old Maharajah. Rama and three elderly members of his council saw them off. They were tense, and Ariadne had the feeling that they were only too eager to speed parting guests for whom they had no particular affection. Rama, too, had looked very grave. He had spoken in English, and though he had voiced his regret at the message summoning Iden back to Calcutta, his attitude was similar to that of his companions.

He had not visited so much as a glance at the girl standing beside Ariadne, Sita, become a humble servant in a plain cotton sari, the end of which covered her hair and face. She wore Kamala's cheap bangles and earrings. Her feet were bare. None of the officials had appeared to notice her, but Ariadne, painfully aware of her "servant's" identity, had felt that at any moment someone must cry out or, if not that, rip up the mattress of the palanquin to expose the fortune in rubies, sapphires, emeralds, and pearls that lay beneath it.

"Only to the ship . . . only to the ship . . . we need only reach the ship . . ." The words ran through her mind. There they would be safe, or rather, nearly safe. They would need to sail downriver to the house of one Bertram Sahib, a wealthy merchant, half Indian, half English, and Rama's trusted ally. He would shelter Sita until such time as it was possible for her to assume the identity of Sundari, her twin. Sundari, Iden had told her, meant "beautiful." And would his people believe that Rama had wed Sundari rather than Sita? Hopefully, they would. The only difference between the two young women was said to be their hair. Sita's locks were dark red, an inheritance from the Irish woman who, amazingly enough, had been one of the wives of her great-grandfather. Sundari's hair was raven black, and the girl striding beside Ariadne's palanquin was also dark-haired from a concoction rubbed in her locks by old Preeta.

How had Sita managed to escape the vigilance of the Zanana guards? And were the other two wives as complacent as they pretended? She had questioned Iden on this count and been told that they looked on her more as a daughter than another wife. As for her servants and the guards, they would never betray her. They loved her.

Evidently, this proud and, to her mind, rather disagreeable young woman had an affectionate side to her nature which she, Ariadne, had not been able to discern. Possibly, her impression arose from her own prejudices. Even before meeting Sita, she had feared and resented her—but it was useless to dwell on what could, unfortunately, be termed unreasonable jealousy. Certainly, she was glad that they were able to "snatch a brand from the burning," as the old Scottish preachers used to say, for quite different reasons. The thought of what Sita was escaping sent shudders through her not only for the girl but for all the hapless widows who perished so needlessly.

Yet, Iden had told her that some of them considered their dread fate an honor, while others preferred it to the life they would lead after their husbands' demise. Those who were not burned, were sent home to be no more than servants in the houses of parents or relatives. Hindu law did not permit them to marry again. Yet, even given this ignominious life, would it not be preferable to being burned alive? A startled grunt from one of her bearers roused her from her thoughts. She glanced around her and, as before, saw only the tangled vines and overhanging trees of the jungle.

She strained her ears, wondering if she could hear the rushing of the river, but she heard only the groaning of her bearers, the screams of the parrots, and the chattering of the monkeys. Neither Iden nor Captain Wellstood spoke and to Ariadne, their tenseness seemed almost palpable.

How much time had passed since they had left the palace? Two hours? Two and a half hours? They ought to be reaching the river soon. How long had it taken them to arrive at the palace? No more than three hours and a little over. Again, she stared at the trees rising on either side of the path. Impossible not to think or rather fear that behind them lurked those who believed that a maharani, no matter how young or how beautiful, ought to be burned to ashes with her aged husband and were abiding their time until . . . But in the palanquin were guns and ammunition. If worse came to worst, they could defend Sita and themselves—but against how many? She leaned back against the pillow and closed her eyes.

She opened them a short time later to find that it was growing darker. She was glad of that. It would be better when the sun descended. Indian nights came down like black curtains; there was no more than a scant half hour of twilight. However, they would have no difficulty in keeping to the path. Word, she remembered, had been carried to the ship by one of Rama's trusted messengers. The men would be waiting to help them aboard; they would set sail immediately. There was nothing to worry about, nothing.

Ariadne swallowed nervously and kept her eyes fixed on her husband's back. Iden was striding ahead purposefully.

Captain Wellstood was now on the other side of the palanquin. She threw a glance at him and saw that he was looking very grim. And "Kamala," too, appeared tense, even though she held her head high and her back was straight. Soon, soon they would be at the river. Yes, very soon, now—for through the trees she could see the glimmer of water. She exhaled a long quavering breath and leaned back in her seat. She could hear the sounds of the river and other sounds for which she had no name—the sounds of the jungle, the cries of birds. The river, the river . . . there it was, pale silver in the declining light. And suddenly the bearers halted, setting the palanquin down quickly.

Ariadne, jolted by his maneuver but not surprised, guessed that they were about to change with the other men, but then the murmur of voices reached her, male voices. She glanced at Sita and saw that she had come to a stop, too. And now Iden spoke sharply in Hindi and was answered by sneering laughter—laughter from many throats.

Captain Wellstood, edging close to the palanquin, stooped and grabbed a pistol, shoving it into his belt. Ariadne experienced a hollow feeling in her chest and her heart was pounding so heavily that she wondered that she could not hear its thumping. The voices were coming closer and they were growing louder. Iden was talking again and someone was answering him, one voice out of the crowd she could not yet glimpse, a gutteral voice which, though she did not understand the language, sounded insulting and menacing—and now she did see them, a group of men, twenty or thirty of them, she guessed, and two others moving ahead of them, their leaders. One was tall and thin, the other shorter and plump. Both were richly dressed.

Then, Iden spoke again and in English. "You are mad, Narayan. There is none here of that description and we have a safe conduct pass from the Maharajah."

"From the Maharajah, indeed, Iden Peverell!" It was the plump man who was speaking, his tone soft and sibilant. "The Maharajah has gone to his death and his passing spirit craves Sita, his bride."

"He must seek her at the palace, then. We are on our way

to Calcutta—we have business with the Company. I charge you, let us pass.''

"Not yet, Iden Peverell, friend to my damned brother. You have business with us, first. I claim my father's woman and, when this ruse becomes known, more than one will burn! I speak of my wily brother Rama, who loves Sita so much that he is willing to commit this great sin and bring upon himself and his subjects the wrath of the gods!''

"Do you see your father's bride here, Narayan? And you, Arvind, do you see her?''

"You will speak Hindi to my uncle. He does not understand English. He understands, however, what he sees. He understands the sin that is being committed by my virtuous brother and those who abet him in this sacrilege!''

The voices were louder and Ariadne saw that many of the men were carrying cudgels. She shrank back against her pillow. Her worst fears had been realized—and why would they not be? Someone in the palace had betrayed them. There was always someone. And though Rama was well liked, Narayan would have spies and followers, men who hoped to feather their own nests by their support of him. He had been in power once and could be again, given the volatile nature of the Indians. Iden had called him a tyrant, but again, they were used to tyranny—to centuries upon centuries of tyranny!

The history of that embattled land had been written in blood and terror. One great king after another had waged war, had triumphed only to go to his doom, often at the hands of a close relative. Fathers had slain sons, sons had slain fathers, and brothers were equally virulent as were wives, as witness Narayan's mother, who had instructed her son well in the art of duplicity. Life among the natives was similarly cheap, and death a grim specter at every bend in the road. One could say that the Indians lived so that they might die and live again.

She wished she might share so comforting a belief, but she could not. She wanted to live—to live with Iden—but it was more likely that she would die with him, and for Sita! Still, she no longer believed that he cared for the girl. He, in common with Rama and possibly because of Rama, his longtime friend, could not bear the idea of her fiery agony, and so with this quixotic resolve, he had brought doom to them all! He was looking toward her and she read agony in his eyes. Impulsively, she slid from the palanquin and stood there a moment while the numbness left her limbs—then she hurried to his side.

"Ariadne," he groaned, "why are you here?"

"I am here because you are here," she said softly. "Did you imagine they did not see me? I want to spend my last moments with you." She moved closer to him, staring at Narayan and Arvind. Their characters were etched deep into their countenances.

Arvind was old, thin, and short. His face was narrow, his forehead low, and his expression bestial. Narayan bore a definite resemblance to Rama—but it was as though his face were reflected in a stone-troubled pool. The features were subtly distorted, his body, plump and soft.

"Oh, God, my own darling," Iden groaned.

Narayan laughed, his eyes on Ariadne. "I must congratulate you, Iden, on your excellent taste in women. First, there was the beautiful Radha, whom you stole from me. And now this *ferangi* woman, who has her own beauties, the which I shall soon enjoy, but first, where is my stepmother?"

"At the Zanana—where she should be," Iden said coldly.

"Liar!" Narayan moved forward and caught Ariadne's arm, twisting it savagely. Taken by surprise, she could not restrain a cry of pain.

With a growl of pure fury, Iden launched himself at Narayan, his fists clenched, only to be caught and held by two of the men.

Narayan, his grasp still hard on Ariadne's arm, growled, "Where is my stepmother?"

There was a sudden howl from the crowd as Sita sped toward the river, throwing herself into it. In a trice, Arvind, with a roar of triumph, ran after her, flinging himself into the water. A split second later, he shouted again or rather screamed in agony.

Narayan had loosed his grip on Ariadne's arm. There was another scream from the river and a great moan from the men as they crowded to the riverbank. Narayan, joining them, was shouting and gesticulating.

"What happened?" Ariadne cried. She looked toward the river but could see nothing, for the men were lined along the shore.

"You must not look," Iden said hoarsely. Arvind's cries were continuing and suddenly a shot rang out and, a second later, another. "Thank God," Iden groaned. "I pray it put him out of his misery, and the beast with him."

There was a loud gabbling among the crowd. Iden, clutching Ariadne's arm, moved ahead. The men, massing behind him, surged forward, pushing Iden and Ariadne before them. Iden, taller than most of them, kept his eyes over their heads and on the river.

"What do you see?" Ariadne cried.

"I am looking for Wellstood. 'Twas he who shot Arvind. Let us hope—"

"He *shot* Arvind?" she questioned, and then remembered what Iden had said about the beast. A vision of what she had once imagined to be a floating log, opening teeth-lined jaws, came to her and she shuddered, guessing now the source of Arvind's agony. And had Sita suffered that same fate?

Another cry arose from the crowd, followed by a long scream, a woman! Again the men around them surged forward and if Iden's arm had not been tight about her waist, she would have fallen and been trampled. And where was Narayan? And what would happen to them, and when? As these frenzied questions rose in her mind, Iden suddenly moved forward, pushing through the crowds and dragging her with him, down to the riverbank. And then, Ariadne saw Narayan. He was at the edge of the river and Sita, half-naked, was trying to break free of him. Iden muttered, "Stay close to me!" and then yelled out something in Hindi and, loosening his hold on Ariadne, he reached the water's edge and, coming to Sita's side, threw an arm around her, speaking even louder than before—as with a yell of rage, Narayan drew his dagger. But in that same moment, several men came forward and, to Ariadne's amazement, caught Narayan, wresting the weapon from him and pinioning his arms behind his back. They held him there while another of their number placed a hand over his mouth, stifling his yells. Someone cried out to Iden, who went on talking. There was much muttering, but it subsided and Iden still continued to speak.

Finally, he finished whatever he was saying. There was more muttering among the men and then someone called out and another followed suit and fell on his knees. To a man, they followed his example, while Narayan, breaking free from his captors, screamed at them in an hysterical fury until one of them struck him down.

Iden divested himself of his jacket and put it over Sita's shoulders. Taking her hand, he came back to Ariadne and seized her hand also. "Come," he urged.

To Ariadne's amazement, he did not run, he walked up the shore and then, a short distance away, she saw *The Argonaut* crew with Wellstood and David Palmer striding ahead of them. All the men carried rifles. The ship, she saw, was anchored a little further down the river.

"Come, my love," Iden repeated.

Ariadne, looking back over her shoulder, saw that the crowd on the bank were still kneeling. They appeared to be praying. She did not understand what had happened, but she did understand Sita's joyful expression and she understood the fact that they were not being pursued. She would hear the explanation later, later when they were on board *The Argonaut* and really safe.

The first hint of how Iden had managed their release and, at the same time, accomplished what appeared to be the total defeat of Narayan, came as they reached the deck of *The Argonaut* and were surrounded by the crew, who, with Captain Wellstood, were smiling and patting Iden on the back. It was impossible to catch what they were saying, for they were all speaking at once. However, she had the impression that he had performed what everyone appeared to consider a miracle.

Then, Captain Wellstood, clearing his throat and blinking actual tears out of his eyes, said shakily, "To my mind, *'twas* a miracle, Iden. I pray you'll not deny it. I thought we must be dead men."

"Yes," Sita, still pale, agreed. "And it could have been me rather than Arvind who was seized by that crocodile."

Her guess corroborated, Ariadne shuddered. She moved closer to Iden. "But what did you say to them?" she demanded.

It was Sita who responded. "He attributed my escape to the River Gods, saying that 'twas they who bore me downstream. He said they had signaled their forgiveness by this action and deemed that I was not to die by fire—since I had been saved by water. Oh, Iden, I do believe you were inspired. How may I thank you?"

"No need to thank me, my dear Sita," he said gently. "But I must tell you, I think you will not need to remain with Bertram Sahib for long—and nor will you need to disguise yourself as Sundari."

"I . . . I do not understand." She regarded him uncertainly.

He smiled at her. "My dear Sita, your future subjects can only welcome a maharani who has been saved from peril by divine intervention."

To Ariadne's amazement, Sita burst into tears and knelt at Iden's feet. "Oh, how . . . how can I ever thank you?" she cried.

He raised her gently. "Thank the River Gods, my dear, and be a good wife to Rama, who is my friend."

Later, lying with him in their cabin, Ariadne whispered, "I think it was a miracle, myself."

He held her against him. "The miracle was you, my love. If you had not been there, I might not have been so inspired. Oh, God, Ariadne—I never dreamed that this contretemps would arise. I had been assured that Arvind and his nephew had been sent far, far away—but of course Rama, who is ambitious only for the State, underestimated his brother's hunger for power. I should not have let him convince me that there was no danger in our undertaking. Will you ever forgive me for having placed you in such jeopardy? How can I ever make it up to you, my own?"

She stroked his cheek. "Could we go home, do you think?"

"As fast as the winds will take us, my angel," he promised.

Chapter Nine

The post chaise, a bright new one, dark green in hue and with a golden crest on its paneled door, rolled up in front of Ariadne's house. Lottie Kingsmith, who had been standing at the drawing room window for over an hour, did not wait for the coachman to bring it to a stop. She dashed down the stairs to the front door and was at the gate just as the footman opened the door of the equipage.

With a wary glance to her left and another to her right, Miss Kingsmith thrust open the gate and was on the sidewalk by the time a tall dark man lifted a laughing and protesting young woman out of the carriage and started toward the gate.

"Iden!" Ariadne protested. "Do put me down! I am quite able to walk!" Her bright glance fell on Miss Kingsmith. "Dearest Lottie," she caroled, "there you are at last."

Miss Kingsmith, who had been holding herself rather stiffly, relaxed. "Ariadne, my dearest girl," she said emotionally. "And Sir Iden. Oh, I cannot tell you how very delightful it is to have you back after so very long a time!"

" 'Tis equally delightful to see you, dear Lottie, and pray tell my husband that I can still go into the house on my own two feet!"

"He will tell you, Miss Kingsmith," Iden's arms tightened about his fair burden, "that he has never had the opportunity to carry his bride over the threshold, and he must needs do it."

"Liar!" Ariadne shook a finger at him. "You have carried me over the thresholds of three separate inns and you will have the opportunity to carry me over the threshold of your family domicile outside of Craster Village, which is the only threshold you ought to carry me over. And truly, my love, I am feeling wonderously well—and the physician you induced me to visit in Gravesend is in total agreement with me.''

"Have you been ill, then?" Miss Kingsmith demanded anxiously. "You said nothing about it in your letter.''

"Because there was nothing to say." Ariadne wriggled in her husband's strong grip. "Now, love, do put me down. I can see that all the servants are in the hall to greet me. Most have been with me since Papa's day and they will worry if I do not walk in, and will hover over me during the rest of our stay here—and I cannot abide that when I am in the very pink of condition!''

"Very well," Iden said reluctantly. "But I want you to lie down, directly we are inside. It has been a long journey and the road rough in places and—''

"And," interrupted his wife, "The post chaise wonderfully well-sprung and you to hold me and cushion me against all the jolts and bumps." She kissed him on the cheek.

As Iden set Ariadne down, the reason for his concern became immediately apparent to Miss Kingsmith. Her eyes widened and a look of alarm crossed her countenance. She glanced about her once more and put a trembling hand to her spare bosom. "Oh, my dearest," she said shakily, "you are . . .''

"Increasing, Lottie," Ariadne corroborated. "And," she glanced lovingly up at her husband, "Iden seems to believe that I am fashioned from blown glass and must be set on a high shelf until the event occurs, which will not be for another three months.''

"Her mother . . ." Iden began.

"I am not my mother," Ariadne said soothingly. "Papa always said I took after his side of the family—and I am already a year older than poor Mama was when she died. Furthermore, I have absolutely no intention of dying—and if you do not mind my being a mite indelicate, Lottie, I intend to have several children. 'Tis no fun at all to be an only child, as Iden and I can both tell you. The physician in Gravesend, I might add, agreed. He also said that I should have no trouble bearing children, because I have a wide pelvis. Poor Mama was a veritable sylph!'' She glanced up at her husband. ''You will see her portrait, my angel. It is at the turn of the stairs.''

Miss Kingsmith found her voice. ''My love, I am delighted for you—for you both.'' She shivered and drew her shawl tighter about her thin shoulders. ''It is passing cool. Do let us go inside.''

''Lottie!'' Ariadne said challengingly. ''I will not allow you to hover, either. I love the coolness.'' She glanced upward. ''And the *clouds,* are they not beautiful clouds, Iden? So billowy and white—with a touch of gray. April clouds!''

''There is the smell of rain in the air.'' Miss Kingsmith frowned. '' 'Twould not do if you were to get a chill.''

''I should welcome a chill.''

''Still, you have been used to much warmer weather.'' Miss Kingsmith moved back toward the gate.

''Indeed, yes,'' Ariadne grimaced. ''And I beg you'll not remind me of it. 'Tis wonderful, wonderful, wonderful to be in England again, is it not, Iden?''

''Wonderful,'' he agreed softly, adoring her with his eyes.

''And,'' Ariadne continued, ''I shall welcome the rain, too. I would like to walk in it.''

''But you will not,'' her husband said with a touch of sternness to his tone. ''Now come in!'' Scooping her up in his arms and ignoring her squeal of protest, he pushed open the gate and bore her up the pathway to the front door. .

The greetings and the congratulations being over at last and Ariadne, having yielded to Iden's persuasions, resting in her room, Miss Kingsmith was once more at the drawing room window, her thin body tense. Iden, coming into the room, gave her a narrow look and then cleared his throat. As he had half-anticipated, she turned swiftly, her eyes full of alarm, which faded as soon as she saw him.

''Did I startle you, then?'' he asked.

''You did, rather,'' she said. ''I am unused to gentlemen being in this house.''

''There's the butler and the footmen and . . .''

''Of course, but . . .''

''Well, no matter.'' He came to her side. ''I have not

thanked you for a certain piece of advice you gave me some time back—and for which I am most grateful, since it is responsible for my present joy.''

"I am very glad to have been of help, sir," she said softly. " 'Tis a great pleasure to see you both so happy."

"I owe it all to you, and I hope you will accept this as a very small expression of my gratitude.'' He proffered a small box.

"Oh, sir," she protested. "I did not expect. Please . . ." Miss Kingsmith flushed.

"Come, you must take it, and if you are not fond of the color, I will give you something that is more to your taste." Taking her hand, he pressed the box into it. "I insist, Miss Kingsmith—as does my wife."

"She . . . she knows," Miss Kingsmith whispered.

"We have no secrets from each other, Miss Kingsmith. She has seen and approved this gift, save that she thinks you must have more. And I promise you—you will."

Miss Kingsmith's eyes were very bright. "I . . . I am glad she knows. I was fearful—"

"Do not be," he interrupted.

Her hands were trembling slightly as she opened the box. Staring down at it, she whispered, "Oh, but . . . but I cannot accept this! It is . . . must be an emerald!"

"And, my wife says 'tis the exact color of your eyes, Miss Kingsmith. Now, please slip it on your finger and hold it to your cheek that I may see if I agree with her."

"But, sir . . ."

"Please, I have laid a bet upon it and must win money if your eyes are either darker or lighter than the stone."

She slipped the large square-cut emerald on her finger and obediently held it to her cheek. "There . . ." she said tremulously. "Have you won?"

"Alas, my wife has won," he said, smiling.

"Oh, sir . . ." She stared at her hand. "It is so beautiful, but it must also be so costly!"

"You must remember that it comes from India, where they hang emerald necklaces around the necks of elephants.' '' He gave her a mischievous smile. "I hope I have not spoiled your pleasure by telling you such a thing."

"You have not. Oh, sir, I do thank you!"

"And I thank you, a million times, my dear, my very dear Miss Kingsmith." There was a grave look in his eyes, however, as he added. "And now I pray you will tell me what is amiss?"

She stiffened. "I . . . beg your pardon, sir?"

"You are uncommon edgy, Miss Kingsmith. I noticed that when we first came out of the carriage. Now, you must please explain to me what the matter can be?"

She sighed. "I have not wanted to spoil your first day here, sir. And . . . it might be that I am unnecessarily concerned. But, Sir Robert . . . I do wish you'd not written to him explaining what happened at the Opera House that night."

He frowned. "I thought it only fair. Is he still angry, and after all this time? Surely, by now, he must have found another heiress!"

"Oh, sir, he . . . he took the incident in very bad part and insists that you have broken his heart and blighted his life!"

"As he would have blighted mine," Iden said sarcastically.

"Yes, sir, but he believed and may still believe that you took her against her will. He is, I fear, determined to have her back and also to exact his revenge. And he has come here quite often."

"He cannot know that you were my informant!" Iden frowned. "Or does he?"

"Oh, no, sir, she assured him. "He believes that you had him watched and followed. And he has sworn that he will watch and follow until you are back and then . . ."

"I see. So you are afraid that he will suddenly come bursting in here, but he cannot do that, Miss Kingsmith, until someone lets him in. I shall give orders to the servants that they not admit him."

"He may linger in the street, sir. I have seen him pass by and he looks a little mad. I never dreamed that he would persevere, but I do wish you could go away—far away, where he could not follow. I am sure he means to challenge you to a duel."

"But you must calm yourself, Miss Kingsmith." Iden

smiled. "Robert's not a menace to anyone. And I am a pretty fair shot." Meeting her troubled glance, he continued, "Of course, if he issues a challenge, I could play the poltroon and refuse to meet him. I am within my rights. To all intents and purposes, I should challenge *him*—since he was pursuing my wife."

"He frightens me," said Miss Kingsmith. "You have been away a year and a little over—and still he watches. One would think—"

"I hope *you* will think no more of this, Miss Kingsmith," Iden interrupted. "Sir Robert Heath might frighten women—I hope you'll not be offended at my saying so—but I cannot think of him as frightening to me. Now I beg you will put him out of your mind and I pray you, say nothing to my wife."

"Oh, I would not, sir, particularly at a time like this. But I do wish you would leave London and go to your estate at an earlier date."

He smiled. "You have, I fear, set me an impossible task. I do not think I could pry Ariadne away from London yet, not until she has seen Carola and the mantua-makers. Besides, April is a most uncertain month in the North—its chills and winds and rains and frosts would be even more virulent than Robert."

She still regarded him concernedly. "I wish . . ." she began.

"If wishes were horses, Miss Kingsmith, beggars would ride," he said lightly and, bowing, kissed her hand. "I pray you will excuse me. I must tell Ariadne that she has won her bet and that I am in her debt." He went whistling out of the room.

"But you cannot come with me to Carola's *also*," Ariadne, cloaked and carrying her reticule, said much more plaintively than was her wont when talking to her husband.

Iden said lightly, "Why not? Am I no longer welcome at Lady Brynston's?"

"Oh, Iden." Ariadne gave him an exasperated stare. "Of course, you are welcome, but you would find our conversation so dreadfully *dull*."

"Will you not give me a chance to decide for myself?"

Ariadne sighed. "Iden, my dearest love, may I again remind you that I am not fashioned from either glass or spun sugar. I will take no harm at Carola's, and I will not stay long, and I shall come right home."

He visited a quizzical look on her upturned face. "I accuse you of wanting to talk . . . secrets."

Ariadne loosed another sigh. "Not secrets, just talk which would be of no possible interest to you, my darling, but Lottie is coming with me, so if I should swoon, which has not happened yet, she will see that I am carried home immediately!"

He looked relieved. "Ah, if Miss Kingsmith is going with you, that is all right and tight, but I beg you'll not stay too long. 'Tis a blustery day."

She glanced out the window. "It is not. There is a wind, but it could never be termed blustery, not in the least. I vow, I have never known you like this, not even when we were in deadly peril in India! And as I have warned you, I intend that we shall have a decent-sized family. I pray you will not be on edge every time."

He kissed her lingeringly. "I promise I will not. It is only that I love you so much."

"And I love you and I have loved you a good deal longer than you have loved me," she said softly. "You did not love me on the boat to Greece nor when we were cast away on the island—nor when we were married either, so there!"

"I hope that I have properly atoned for my blindness."

"You have." She caressed his cheek and then ruffled the white streak in his hair. "I hope that by the time I return, no more than two hours from now, the rest of your hair will not be of this shade."

"Do not remain any longer or it might be," he threatened.

"Silly." She kissed him again and went to fetch Lottie.

"My dear, they are all alike." Carola turned wise green eyes on Ariadne. "But they do calm down by the second lying-in. I can tell you that from my own experience. You will recall my first Season . . . when you went to Greece?

Willie would not let me return to town for the entire nine months. I was incarcerated in his miserable castle, which is draughty and isolated—miles from anywhere! I cried, I pleaded, but nothing I could say had any effect on him. It was much better with the second, and now that we have three he is perfectly content to let me do as I choose. Of course, I have a disgustingly easy time of it. Are you listening to me, Ariadne?''

"Oh yes, dear, of course," Ariadne replied, forcing herself to smile. She had been listening but with only half an ear. Carola's conversation was not particularly interesting and also she knew Iden would worry about her until she returned. He was uncommonly nervous these days and she really did not like to cause him concern. She said apologetically, "I do think I ought to go home.''

Miss Kingsmith, who had been sipping tea, put her cup down at once. "Perhaps you should, dear.''

Carola stared at Ariadne in amazement. "But you've been here less than a hour!''

"I know, but—''

"But you are concerned about your husband," Carola finished. "And I tell you, 'tis not wise to humor them.''

"I promise I will stay longer the next time, but I am really feeling rather uncomfortable," Ariadne lied. "I beg that you will forgive me, Carola dear.''

Carola put her hands on hips that had grown considerably wider since the last time Ariadne had seen her. She had also developed a ponderous manner and an annoying habit of making what she considered "wise" pronouncements. She appeared to be on the verge of delivering one of these now.

"My dear, you are spoiling him. You must not let him think that you are living in his pocket. The more you are concerned over *him*, the less he will be concerned over you. The last time I was breeding, Willie spent most of his days at Brooks!''

"But did you not just tell me that you preferred it that way?" Ariadne asked.

"I prefer a happy medium," Carola replied with the suggestion of a pout. "Come, have another dish of tea.''

"I do feel rather queasy," Ariadne insisted.

"Very well," Carola said disapprovingly. "But you wait. . ." She had other warnings which she voiced all the way to the door.

"I do hope his hair will not have turned white by the time I return!" Ariadne giggled as she and Miss Kingsmith took their seats in the post chaise. "And I cannot think 'twill hurt to spoil him a little."

"Nor I," Miss Kingsmith agreed. "I would not, if I were you, pay too much attention to Lady Brynston's advice. She does not seem very happy and all too often, misery loves company."

"If the truth were to be told, I did not really want to call on her," Ariadne confided. "But Iden has been so concerned over me of late and it cannot be good for him. He ought not to spend all his time with me. I know for a fact that many of his old friends have left their cards and he ought to see them. We will be leaving for the country in another fortnight."

"I am sure that he does not regret his friends, my dear. He is so very much in love. It is really delightful to see."

"Oh, it is, is it not?" Ariadne agreed softly. "Years ago, if anyone would ever have told me . . . and to think I almost married Robert Heath. Do you know, I have been half afraid he would try to do Iden an injury. He must have been very angry."

"I expect he was," Miss Kingsmith murmured. "Ah, here we are," she added with some relief as the post chaise drew to a stop.

"And we have a visitor!" Ariadne exclaimed. "That is a beautiful animal—a thoroughbred."

"Indeed, yes," Miss Kingsmith agreed, as she leaned forward to look out the window.

The postboy brought the steps but Ariadne, remaining in her corner, said with a laugh, "Iden did not mention that he was expecting a friend. Perhaps I should go back to Carola."

"I think you must go inside," Miss Kingsmith said firmly.

"I expect I must." Ariadne let the postboy help her down the steps.

A grave-faced butler met them at the door. "Milady . . . er, Miss Kingsmith . . ."

Reading concern in his eyes, Miss Kingsmith said quickly, "What is it?"

"It's 'im," the butler muttered.

"Oh! Why ever did you admit him?" Miss Kingsmith gasped.

"I 'adn't no choice. The master come across the 'all at that time 'n said as 'ow 'e'd see 'im. They're in the library."

"How long has he been here?"

"A bit over 'alf an hour, Miss Kingsmith."

Miss Kingsmith's hand crept to her throat. "He must have seen us leave," she said.

Ariadne, who had listened to this hasty exchange in growing confusion and concern, said, "What are you talking about?"

" 'Tis Sir Robert 'Eath, milady," the butler said.

"Sir Robert?" Ariadne looked at Miss Kingsmith and, reading anxiety in her eyes, she said, "Something is the matter. You are afraid of Robert, are you not? Why? Never mind, I must see him."

"No, my dear, I beg that you will not." Miss Kingsmith caught her arm. "Sir Robert is . . . is not at his best. Let your husband deal with him."

"What more do you know that you've not told me?" Ariadne cried. "No, never mind, I cannot hear it now. He might call Iden out. I will not have it, I tell you." She ran up the stairs.

"Ariadne!" Miss Kingsmith ran after her.

Unheeding, Ariadne sped down the hall and had reached the library door when Miss Kingsmith caught up with her. "Ariadne," she panted. "You do not understand. Sir Robert is . . . is, I think, ill. Oh, I have been expecting this. I warned Sir Iden, but I did not think— No, do not go in!" Miss Kingsmith made a futile effort to catch Ariadne's arm and pull her back, but it was too late, she had opened the door.

Going inside, Ariadne froze on the threshold, staring incredulously at Sir Robert, who was holding a small pistol trained on Iden, who sat at the desk, writing. He looked up as Ariadne entered and paled.

"Go back, for God's sake!" he cried.

Robert half turned. "Ariadne!" he exclaimed.

"Robert," she whispered, caught between fear and incredulity. He had grown so very gaunt. His eyes looked huge in his wasted face and his clothes hung on him. Furthermore, he who had always been the epitome of neatness was wearing a badly soiled and disordered cravat. There was a stubble of beard on his chin.

"My love," he said in a trembling voice. "At . . . at last you . . . you have come . . . but 'tis too early . . . I wanted to . . . to be rid of this rogue before . . . before you arrived . . . I mean to kill him . . . for what he has done to you . . . to us . . . oh, my God, I have been in . . . in torment these past months." He turned toward the desk, glaring at Iden, who had stopped writing. "Go on, damn you, write, write, write! He is writing his confession, Ariadne . . ." He waved the pistol at Iden. "Write," he repeated, "write down your perfidy so all the world will know you deserved to die!"

"Robert!" Ariadne found her voice. "You . . . you are mad." She started forward.

"Go back, go back," Iden yelled. "For God's sake, get out of here."

"Yes, let him finish what he is doing so I may kill him and we can go. You do want him dead, must want him dead, my poor Ariadne, my poor love, he must die . . ."

"No!" she shrieked. Hardly aware of what she was doing, she rushed across the room and around the desk to stand in front of Iden. "Kill me!" she cried. "Kill me, Robert, for without Iden, I do not want to live!"

"Ariadne!" Iden groaned, trying to push her away.

"Damn you, you doxy, would you protect him," Robert snarled, "who took from me everything! I beggared myself to win you. You must wed me, they are after me . . . I promised them I would pay, and you promised we would wed . . . damn you, damn you, 'twill be the Marshalsea for me." He fell to his knees sobbing. "I will be in prison, in prison . . . they are looking for me." The gun dropped from his hand as he began to sob wildly.

Miss Kingsmith dashed across the room and, grabbing the

fallen pistol, leaned over the desk, thrusting it at Iden. Taking it, he pointed it at Robert and then put it down as the butler, accompanied by two stalwart young footmen, entered the room. One of the footmen strode forward and stood over the weeping man, his fists clenched.

"Wot'll I do wi' 'im, sir?" he growled.

"Take him to the cellar," Iden commanded. "I will send for a physician I know. The man's in need of care and food, I think. He looks half-starved."

"You cannot let him be sent to the Marshalsea!" Ariadne cried, looking at Robert with a mixture of regret and pity. "We must see that he has money."

"Yes, that can be arranged," Iden assured her. He stared down at Robert who, oblivious of them all, was still weeping. "I'll see to it in due course. Meanwhile," he looked at the butler, "do as I asked. I do not think he's in any condition to escape—but lock him in."

"We'll see to it, sir," the butler replied.

"Please be gentle with him," Ariadne added. "Oh!" she exclaimed as Iden, coming to her side, suddenly lifted her and, skirting the footman and the fallen Robert, carried her out of the room and up the stairs to their bedchamber, depositing her gently on the bed.

She stared up at him, still shaken by what she had witnessed. "He . . . must be half-mad and . . . oh, you were right about him . . . he . . . he . . . wanted an heiress . . . that's all."

"No, I do not believe that was all he wanted, my love. He loved you. That was very evident and, indeed, how could he help it, but Robert has always spent more than he has and he has always lived in the expectation of his uncle dying or . . . But never mind him." He frowned at her. "Let us talk about you. I begin to think that you, too, must be mad. What possessed you to do such a thing?"

"To do . . . what?" she asked confusedly.

"Did you imagine I could not handle him?" he demanded angrily. "I was biding my time until his attention would be diverted, as I knew it must be. And for you to . . . to have exposed yourself to such danger to run in front of me. Oh,

Ariadne," his voice trembled, "do you imagine I . . . I could live if anything were to happen to you?"

"Oh, my darling." She reached up and pulled him down beside her. "I would not want to live without you, either." She stroked his hair. "But we are both going to live forever and ever, do you not agree?"

"Forever and ever . . ." he said softly. "But I am going to take you where it is safe."

"And where is that?"

"To the Manor, our home in the country, tomorrow morning. And . . ." he gave her a stern look, "I will hear no arguments from you, either. My mind is made up."

"And so is mine!" She laughed. "You will hear no arguments from me. I will be ready to start at dawn and . . ." But she could say no more, for the pressure of his lips had silenced her.

About the Author

Ellen Fitzgerald is a pseudonym for a well-known romance writer. A graduate of the University of Southern California with a B.A. in English and M.A. in Drama, Ms. Fitzgerald has also attended Yale University and has had numerous plays produced throughout the country. In her spare time, she designs and sells jewelry. Ms. Fitzgerald lives in New York City.